THE FLORENTINE'S SECRET

The Agency of the Ancient Lost & Found 3

JANE THORNLEY

PROLOGUE

Florence, Italy, 1497

The workroom was dark when Gabriela entered late that afternoon. After hanging up her cloak, she stepped into the long room, noting that the curtains were drawn along the courtyard-facing windows. Her father usually kept their workers sewing until the very last bit of sun had leeched from the sky, straining their eyes in the half-light to finish a seam or sew a hem or needle a few remaining pearls onto an embroidered bodice for some important client. They were far too busy to waste a single moment and yet today their workshop lay empty.

She tried to remember if Father had mentioned an appointment with an important client or some other explanation that would draw him away. By necessity, he arranged such meetings in secrecy now. Even if he had such an assignation, the workers would have remained under Jacobo's watchful eye until darkness fell. Once important visitors like the Medici would be whisked away into one of the private anterooms or met inside their homes but not now, never now.

As a very young girl she had attended the city's noblewomen in the privacy of their quarters. Women who had preferred a female to fit them were happy that her father could afford that service but now their clients were more reluctant to have her visit under any circumstances. Clarice de'

Medici had once used her services exclusively but that was long ago before that lady had died and the great Medici had fallen. Fallen, yes, but not forsaken, at least not by her. Gabriela would enact the instructions of the late Lorenzo the Magnificent no matter how long it took or what the cost.

She had passed by the Medici palazzo that very afternoon, keeping her head low and her hood up so as not to attract attention in streets that did not welcome unattended women. Something was afoot in the city that day, she could feel it. Men gathered, talking excitedly. Friars called to any passerby to relinquish their luxuries and some seething energy seemed to boil up from the very dirt beneath her feet.

She shook herself from her reverie. Enough time wasted. Father would explain all once he returned, and in the meantime she could not squander this opportunity.

Gabriela scanned the massive tables where lengths of silk and velvet were spread in jewel-colored sweeps awaiting the first cut or the continuation of some fine detail upon the rich fabric. These were her paints, her tools, and she resisted the urge to stroke them in passing lest she snag a pin or worse.

Lighting a lantern, she carried it past the tables, averting her eyes from the dress forms that stood around the room in various states of undress. They always seemed to watch her reproachfully and, in the twilight, cast distorted shadows that had once frightened her as a child. Perhaps even still...

But she was no longer a child, she reminded herself. In the Florentine Republic few knew the truth: that she, Gabriela di Domenico, a mere woman, was in fact the designer of the most fabulous gowns for which her father's house had become famous. Her—not her father, not their assistant, Jacobo—but her, a woman daring to take the work of God into her own hands to create exquisite designs for the Florence nobility, designs that had gathered such fame that wealthy houses as far away as Rome had requested their artistry. Yet, in these days when such luxury was viewed as sinful, her involvement would only draw further wrath upon their heads and must remain secret, as must another, much darker confidence.

If Florence knew the truth, her father would be ruined, the great Medici might be further sullied, and Gabriela herself sent to a convent or much, much worse. She could not bear to imagine what cruel humiliation might be inflicted upon her should the secret be exposed.

Women were put on earth for but one role. How many times had she heard that? She was to bear children and to serve men and God, at times the two seeming one and the same: marry, bear children, obey, obey. But Gabriela was not born to obey but to create. Why else would she have been given this gift—to transform a bolt of cloth into something extraordinary, something that served as a tribute to God since all the glorious details were crafted in His name?

She delighted most in imagining God's creatures—the birds, the flowers, the insects, and bringing them alive on a sleeve or a hem. The craftspeople breathed life into her sketches, a great design became reality, and beauty sang its song in her art. How could this be sinful?

She strode down the long room toward the secret door, driven by her determination to see this thing through. Time was running out. The great Lorenzo de' Medici had made but one request of her before he died, a simple one on the surface, but one she knew bore unknown repercussions for all involved. He knew it might take years to bring into fruition but implored her to wait, if necessary, and wait she had. Now could not be a worse time to put his request into action. Nevertheless, a promise made must be honored, especially to the dead.

Fingering the key in her purse at her waist, she imagined the small flat object slipping into the seam in such a way as to be unnoticeable amid the velvets and silks. It would be transported as requested along with the corresponding message and her reward duly accepted, a reward she was only too eager to receive considering that there was no other way she could ever obtain the largesse otherwise. Though her father had been successful and his coffers had swelled accordingly, they would never be permitted to wear the clothes they crafted even if they could afford them, *especially* if they could afford them. The sumptuary laws made that clear: beautiful clothes were for noble citizens only and then for special occasions with the details carefully regulated—that is, before the friar Savonarola preached that all such luxuries were sin incarnate. But Gabriela would enact more than one defiance before this game was over.

The edges of the door blended seamlessly with the end wall, expertly camouflaged by the playful drawing Fili had sketched of the Florentine citizens garbed in Domenico finery. She followed the line of a full-skirted gamurra with her finger until she heard the mechanism spring loose.

Stepping into the darkened room, she latched the door behind her and set the lantern on the table. Her eyes were drawn immediately to the center of the floor. There, glowing in the lamplight stood the dress on its form just as she had left it, a vision in solitary glory on a mannequin crafted exactly to her size—and originally Clarice and Lorenzo de' Medici's eldest daughter, Lucrezia, by happenstance and ingenuity. That noble lady would never wear this piece now. If Savonarola had his way, no one would.

Here was her art, a multilayered column of the finest gold-threaded lemon-colored embroidered velvet overlaying a soft silk camicia the color of molten pearls. How her heart sang when she had first touched that fabric, enchanted by the way in which the colors changed every time she lifted the lengths this way and that—from lemon to deepest gold, a trick of the weaver's art where two colors of silk were napped to fool the light. When worn, the piece would shimmer and glow as if touched by a nymph or some other marvelous mythological creature who altered matter with a sweep of her hand.

Let Fili and Sandro work their magic on flat surfaces with their paint but her alchemy moved with the body, blew with the wind, danced in the nuances of light and shadow. Living art, she had teased them. "Can you make your creations move?" she called out to her betrothed one afternoon as he stood painting in his studio.

"I cannot, my love!" he had laughed over his shoulder, his brush held aloft, but in truth Fillipino, like Sandro, were such masters of their art that it was as though his figures breathed from the wood they were painted upon. His work caused her breath to still and her heart to flutter. Or maybe that was his doing...

Gabriela smiled at the memory as she untied her brown work dress and let it drop to the floor. Carefully lifting the lemon-gold gamurra from the mannequin, she dropped it over her head and allowed it to flow down over her cotton chemise. As always, it fit perfectly, causing her to sigh as her hands smoothed over the raised velvet pattern.

Her father would scold her if he were to catch her doing this again. To wear this gown even for a moment was like tempting the fates, he claimed. It didn't matter if she was the one to fashion it into existence. To all eyes

THE FLORENTINE'S SECRET

they were supposedly made for another one gone, but even Father would agree that this garment was special. This one she prayed might even become her own wedding gown.

Gently, she picked up one of the sleeves from the pair lying on the table and slipped her left arm inside, holding it to her shoulder by the ribbon ties. Here was her true masterpiece, every motif crafted to her and the Magnificent's specifications before he had drawn his last breath. Every image told a story—her story as well as the secret the Medici requested embedded amid the creatures of garden and field. The great Lorenzo had caught the meaning when he had first studied Sandro's sketch years before but had only nodded and smiled. He had so enjoyed her little puzzles as he had told her often enough.

As long as she fulfilled her obligations, the dress and all else would be hers. Whether she would risk wearing it was another story and one not destined to be told within the walls of the Republic. Their deal had been sealed years ago though it would take much longer for her to enact now that the Medici power had bled from the streets of Florence. Yet she prayed that there were those still able to help.

Holding the ribbon, her gaze swung toward the secret compartment where the sketch lay hidden. Sandro's promise of that painting for their wedding gift had thrilled Fili, too, even though Sandro warned that the portrait might take years to complete given his current work schedule. All that was needed was patience, apparently, patience and great care that they could play this game of intrigue in a city fraught with dangerous secrets. She could only hope that she was up to the challenge.

A sharp sound shattered her reverie. Swinging around, she stared at the front wall. It was all that she could do to keep from crying out. Was that Father? She slipped off the sleeve and picked up the lantern, holding it high as she tiptoed toward the door, keeping the gamurra raised in one hand.

She thought only to open the door a crack and check the workroom but something cautioned her to freeze. Voices calling out. Someone stifling a sharp cry while another shouted her name—her father! What was happening? And then she knew: they had been found out, their secret discovered.

She swung away, torn between helping her father and escaping with what she alone could salvage but, in truth, there was no choice to be made. All had been agreed in advance: if ever the day came and their secret exposed, she was to run, run as far as she could, escape Florence forever. She had promised, more a pact than a decision, and one to which she was bound.

Her heart galloping, she swiftly stepped out of the gamurra and bundled up every precious piece of the fabric into an old cloth before donning her own clothes. The banging shook the walls. She did not have the time to cover the dress properly. With her head bare and her identity revealed to all who would look closely, she slipped across the room to another secret door that would take her down a set of stairs to a back lane, her parcel held like a limp body in her arms. At the last minute, she snatched a scrap of fabric from the floor and threw it over her head.

As her feet scuffed down the stone steps, she could not believe what she was doing, could not believe that she might never see her father again, that she would escape her beloved city that very night. Though the price of her failure was great, the price of her success was equally so.

In the dark lane between the buildings, she gripped her bundle like a huge swaddled child before stepping into a main road. Startled, she was immediately swept into a stream of moving bodies heading in the direction of the city center. With their torches and lanterns held aloft, it was as if a seething human tide pushed her forward without a care to her distress.

They all carried something, she realized—parcels, paintings, even fistfuls of jewelry—and they were not peasants but noblemen. She struggled to break free, to turn and run towards the Porta al Prato as planned, but no, the crowd held her tight. Men, they were all men.

"What is that you carry, woman?" called the man to her right. "Do you bring a trifle of luxury to feed the flames?"

"Flames?" she cried. "I know nothing of flames! I desire only to deliver this dress to my mistress. She awaits!"

But already the man had been swallowed up by other bodies surging in from neighboring streets as the crowd pushed their heaving force into the Piazza della Signoria.

Even from a distance, she could feel the heat and smell the smoke but Gabriela was not prepared for the sight that awaited. A massive bonfire burned like the jaws of hell in the center of the piazza sending boiling smoke and licks of flame far into the night. Citizens could be seen throwing objects into the fire—paintings, dresses, books!

Somebody shoved her forward. A friar in dark robes stepped towards her. "Feed the flames in the name of God!" he cried, pointing to her bundle. She looked down, aghast. A single sleeve had loosened from her arms and hung gleaming naked in the firelight.

I

I sat studying my computer screen, a position I'd inhabited so often lately that I often felt fused to the chair. In a mythological world, I'd probably be a chairtaur—half chair, half human. Once entranced with something, it's like it owned me body and soul so that I couldn't pull away until I dove deep into its mysteries.

The object that possessed me this time was a photo my colleague in Rome had sent by email that morning. Among all of the treasures our agency had retrieved from my criminal brother's hoard years ago, this one remained among those yet to be repatriated. I had studied it before, of course, but it had just become even more intriguing.

A sketch which looked to be worked in metalpoint and white gouache on paper, it's as if the piece had invited me to enter its world. I gazed from the image on my screen to a letter I'd received from my brother the day before. As usual, Toby wrote in brief banalities—descriptions of prison food, mention of a television show he'd watched with other inmates—and as always enlivened his descriptions with humorous drawings in the margins. I recognized the octopi and other comic characters that had once inhabited the video games he'd created years ago. But in this letter, the drawings had changed. Now I was seeing things like a little bomb attached to what looked to be a partially unfolded scroll, a baffling geometric sketch that looked nothing like his usual doodles.

Nicolina: *Are you still there?*

Nicolina and I had been bouncing texts back and forth for the last hour —the photo on my desktop screen, the texts on my phone.

Me: *Yes, sorry. You say you originally found it rolled up in a tube with part of Toby's hoard?*

Nicolina: *Yes, in a crate between two eighteenth-century landscapes.*

Me: *Would it have looked like a scroll?*

Nicolina: *Yes, I suppose.*

I peered at the screen. At first glance, the picture appeared to be of a Florentine noblewoman circa 1450-80. A profile portrait, it could have been quickly but deftly executed and perhaps served as a preliminary sketch for a painting. As far as we knew, no such painting existed, not that that was surprising. The artist may have only been studying a subject with no intention of exploring further, or if there had been a painting, it had been lost long ago.

The woman sat upright in profile in the Renaissance Florentine style, the drawing encompassing her full torso down to the hands folded in her lap. Her hair was pulled back in a simple topknot but not bejeweled, and her face, though pleasant, was not beautiful. A plain linen kerchief partially covered her hair. A real woman, then, and either this real woman or her menfolk had been intent on displaying only one aspect of her dress at the expense of all else.

Nicolina: *Still there?*

Me: *Yes. That sleeve is extraordinary.*

Nicolina: *Yes. Still.*

As a textile expert, that was the thing I had noticed first. Though an art historian by training, my expertise was textiles and my interest recently focused primarily on the Renaissance. That sleeve was fabulous in an age when fabulousness in apparel was the norm for the wealthy at the same time that such displays were closely regulated, even illegal.

Real fashion police roamed the streets of Florence during the fourteenth and fifteenth centuries apprehending citizens who broke the sumptuary laws, regardless of their station. Strict rules existed as to when and who could wear what and any infringement that might be considered excesses of fashion.

Whether this particular woman was permitted to wear that particular sleeve was another matter but it seemed as though she wore it proudly. It had several curious attributes and details that I longed to study more carefully but had never taken the opportunity until now.

Nicolina: *Are you still there?*

Me: *Still here. It's definitely from the mid-century Renaissance Florentine period.*

Nicolina: *I know it is important.*

Me: *I need to see it in person.*

I couldn't mention Toby's letter on the phone or in our texts. These days, I expected constant surveillance so took special care with when and how I communicated. Actually, that little bomb icon in the margins had to mean Toby was also employing caution. I recognized a warning when I saw one.

Nicolina: *I agree. Come to Rome and we will go to Florence and to the Uffizi. I have a friend there who might help us confirm attribution. Besides, it has been too long since we have been together.*

Florence. A brief image of that museum of treasures flashed through my mind at the exact moment that my lower back delivered such a vicious twinge that it forced me to my feet. I bent down into a curve before stretching up, arms over my head the way my physiotherapist had shown. Ah, there. If I didn't start moving more regularly, I probably would fuse to the chair.

Nicolina: *Still there?*

Me: *Sorry. Back problems. Let me see if I can pull an excursion together for Peaches and me. A dose of Italy is desperately needed. Plenty of wine and pasta, too, please. I'll text you with the details.*

Nicolina: *Wine and pasta, it is! I am excited to see you! Rupert called yesterday from Orvieto and plans a jaunt to Capri next.*

I straightened. I knew Rupert was in Italy, of course. Evan was somewhere there, too. I hadn't seen either of them for weeks but remained in touch through email and text.

Nicolina: *Evan is still in Venice visiting his son.*

I swear sometimes she read my mind. So Evan was still in Venice? I would have known had I asked him. The man was more than willing to keep me appraised of his movements. It was I who held back. I was not ready to cross the relationship threshold any time soon but we at least stayed connected.

Me: *I'll be in touch. Ciao!*

Pocketing my phone, I stretched again before seeking out Peaches. In August, the lab was quiet. Max had taken our manager, Serena, for a holiday like the rest of the city, it seemed. The moment Londoners had received their final Covid vaccinations and lockdown had lifted, anyone who could bolted for freedom about the same time that tourists began flocking to British shores. We joked that the city was running on a skeleton crew.

At our storefront, Baker and Mermaid, the ethnographic gallery was now closed to drop-in clients and we managed sales either by website or appointment. Most of the real work continued behind the scenes in the Agency of the Ancient Lost and Found's new basement facility where we still had unclaimed artifacts waiting to be repatriated. Considering all that had happened in the world lately, that bust of the Artemis staring at me from the top shelf could wait awhile longer.

I found Peaches downstairs in our showroom with her feet on Serena's desk reading on her iPad, probably devouring one of her man-chest romances, her preferred reading material when not delving into engineering tomes. She looked up as I descended the stairs. "Have you been talking to Evan lately? He's taking his son on a road trip."

My mistake: she was reading her emails.

"I know," I remarked. "Look, something's—"

"What's his ex-wife like, anyway?" She sat up and dropped her feet to the floor. "I always wondered. I asked him once and he was very complimentary about her but otherwise evasive. She sounded like a paragon of virtue."

I sighed. "Yes, she's very pleasant and gorgeous and why are you asking?"

"Just curious. He said they broke up because she wanted to live in her hometown in Venice but he was traveling all over the world. It was too much of a long-distance relationship to work out. That must have been back in his MI6 days. He said that they divorced long ago and still he never remarried. Bet you never asked him that."

"I didn't."

"Why not? Aren't you curious? And what if he finds someone else while you're keeping him at arm's length?"

I heaved an exaggerated sigh as I arrived beside her. "I'm not here to discuss my love life. I—"

"That's because you don't have a love life."

"Neither do you," I pointed out.

She grinned down at me. "Yeah, but I'm open for business, just waiting for the perfect guy to come knocking on my door and realize that I am his goddess, his queen bee in the main squeeze department. You, on the other hand, may as well have 'closed until further notice' tattooed on your forehead."

Time for a major distraction. "Want to go to Italy?" I inserted quickly.

She pulled back in mock shock. "Are you kidding me? May as well ask if I want to keep eating and breathing. Do we finally have another case?"

"Yes and no." I pulled up the sketch on my phone. "We're going to Italy to meet Nicolina and see if we can find out anything more about this. No one has reported it missing. There's nothing fitting this description in the databases, either, yet I'm certain that's the scroll-like thing Toby drew in his letter."

"The one attached to the bomb?"

"That one."

"Why would Toby even refer to any of the stolen loot? He's been in prison for years and never has before."

"That's what I wonder. Something's happening; things are on the move. I just don't know how or what. We've only been exchanging letters for a couple of months but his other illustrations were similar to his comic characters. This one's different. He's using what we used to call as kids 'doodle code' to warn me of something."

Peaches continued to stare at the picture. "Doodle code, huh? If one of our two brothers stole this, it has to be worth something—a lot, is my guess."

"It may even be from one of Noel's heists." My ex had an appetite for stealing priceless art, too, and actually leaned more toward the Renaissance variety. "Actually, Noel had the real eye for priceless art."

"Then it has to be valuable. Our thieving brothers and your ex had standards. Actually, they had no standards. Forget I said that."

"Speaking of thieving brothers, I'll be talking to Toby at 11:30 this morning," I said, glancing at my phone. "In ten minutes, in fact." My gut twisted.

"So, you managed to arrange a live call at last?"

"Yes. I don't know what finally convinced him that letters weren't enough. Maybe he relented when I said how I needed to hear his voice. Maybe now that he's been detoxed and has had time to process things, we can finally talk about all that went down in our past. I thought we could do that in letters but he never responds to anything I write."

"Won't the call be monitored by prison staff?"

"Probably but I want to discuss relationship stuff, nothing sensitive. If staff want to listen in on that, let them. Toby knows I'm affiliated with Interpol. He wouldn't say anything damning. He's using doodle code for that."

"Okay, so are you nervous?"

"I may lose my breakfast but otherwise I'm completely calm. I've been waiting for this moment a long time."

"Need me to stay around?"

"No, thanks. Some things need to be done alone and a reckoning with one's brother is one of them."

"Got you. I'll just take off down the high street to buy a toothbrush. I never travel anywhere without a new one. Going for the electric variety this time. It could give me a bit of buzz. Text if you need support."

"What about *your* brother?" I called out as she headed for the door.

"Once a slimeball, always a slimeball," she said over her shoulder. "When I saw Mom and Dad last month, they told me that he'd found Jesus. Skeptic that I am, I figure it's more likely that he's found a ticket to early release. See you later."

The door shut behind her, leaving me alone in the capacious showroom where our priceless carpets hung in lonely splendor. I had time for my traditional once-around to greet every carpet in our collection before Toby called. He'd be ringing the gallery phone collect so I couldn't stray far from Serena's desk.

The Elgin-Middlesex Detention Center outside of London, Ontario, had been my brother's home for the past two years, ever since I helped incarcerate him and Peaches's brother for stealing a fortune in art and artifacts. In all that time, we'd exchanged letters only recently but hadn't spoken once.

Then came the email: *Be at the office tomorrow at 11:30 London time. Tobias McCabe to call collect from prison.* No signature and only an email address that seemed to be from some kind of automated scheduling program.

I waited, pacing the room in circles. I'd been warned that prison changes people, hardens them, turns them into something scarred and steely. Then I reminded myself that the drugs had changed him long before that. His letters had given little away. In fact, they had been so stilted that I was afraid he'd changed irrevocably. Only the little doodles hinted that the old jovial Toby might still be lurking somewhere.

When the call came, I nearly I pounced on the desk phone, accepting the collect charges while repeating: "Toby, are you there? Toby, are you there?"

For a moment nothing but silence swallowed up the distance between us along with sounds of people talking far in the background. Finally: "Hello, Phoebe." A voice both familiar and faraway almost brought me to tears. We had been close once. So much had happened since.

My words tumbled out in a rush. "Toby, I'm sorry. I love you. I did what was necessary to save your life and preserve art when I put you in prison. Surely you understand that? You were in such bad shape in Jamaica. I thought for sure you'd overdose and die but a day hasn't passed where I haven't thought of you. How are you doing? Tell me you're all right." I started to cry like an idiot. It was as if the sound of his voice had pressed some kind of sob button.

Again silence and then came: "How do you think I'm doing, Phoeb? I'm stuck in a wheelchair serving time in prison."

It was as if he'd slapped me. I swallowed hard, thinking how grueling, how humiliating, and how dangerous his life had to be. And that it was all my fault. I put him there, put my own *brother* in prison. Everything was all my fault. "Toby, I'm sorry—"

"Stop. You're not sorry. You'd do it all over again if I was standing between you and some priceless piece of art. You've become some kind of art warrior hotshot. Think I haven't seen the news? 'Phoebe McCabe of the Agency of the Ancient Lost and Found throws priceless Spanish artifact into the sea.' You work with Interpol. What happened to my little sister?"

"What's happened...to your...?" The question almost stuck me dumb. At the same time it snapped me straight.

"Yeah, what happened to my loyal little baby sister who used to follow her big bro around like a puppy wanting to swab Captain Toby's decks forevermore?"

I managed to laugh. "Oh, that one. Yeah, little Phoebe. She realized that she was swabbing her big brother's decks, all right—more like cleaning up his messes while he stole from one end of the globe to the other. Oh, and then she woke up to the fact that she was also playing lost-art sniffer dog to his partner in crime, too. That was the same little Phoebe who almost got killed over and over again by all those big bad men who thought she had to be working for the Toby and Noel art-heist duo. Is that the baby sister you mean? I'll tell you what happened to her: she grew the hell up!"

Wow, where did that come from? I had to be repressing more rage than I thought. I stood stone-still waiting for him to hang up in my ear but instead he boomed his barrel-chested laugh. "You really did grow up."

"Is that all you can say?" I was trying hard to steady my thumping heart. "And you're right: if I caught you stealing and dealing drugs again, I would put you back behind bars. I finally learned that loving someone does not mean that you have to love what they do or accept it, either. But I do love you, Toby. I'll just never accept what you did."

Silence and then: "I don't expect you to, and yeah, I feel like a shit for what I've done to you, especially for not warning you about Noel. That's the one thing I can't forgive myself for."

The. One. Thing. Everything else was fine. I swallowed. *Let it go, Phoebe.* I took a deep breath. "So, can we get back to something good again? I know things will never be the same between us but we're still blood."

"Yeah, we are. There were plenty of times I wanted to die in here, I'll admit that, and I blamed you, but I'm through that shit now. All trials and tribulation can be survived with the right tricks and a few allies. You find that out soon enough in places like this. Maybe you did save my life. Sure as hell Noel would have killed me had he had the chance. So, yeah, I forgive you, Phoeb—at least my head does—and now you have to forgive me. My heart still feels kicked to shit and obviously yours does, too, but we'll work on that, okay?"

"Okay," I whispered. It was a start, a big one.

"How's Max?"

Okay, so we were moving for steady ground now. "He hasn't quite forgiven me, either—for killing Noel, that is—but he's trying to get over it, too."

"You didn't kill Noel, Phoebe. Snakes are hard to nail unless you decapitate the bastards. Word travels around places like this and rumor has it that the snake's still alive and growing a few heads."

"What?"

"He's still alive. Nobody knows where he's holed up but watch your back."

"Oh, my God." I sat down on a chair with a thump. "I thought I killed him."

"You didn't kill him but you should have. He may come after you eventually. Word is that he's still recuperating somewhere. Seems like he's got a tricky ticker after you tasered him over the heart—nice touch that. Poetic justice. Look, time's almost up in my phone slot."

"Can we talk again?"

"Sure and keep writing those letters. I look forward to them. Did you get my last with the little sketch?"

"Yes."

"Heed the warning. Leave it the hell alone, Phoebe."

"Leave what alone? I'm not leaving anything alone. I—"

But he hung up.

2

Noel was still alive. That Renaissance sketch may be a bomb, whatever that meant. I didn't know which of those possibilities shook me the most. Probably both held equal weight for different reasons. Each carried implications for my life going forward but left me with no immediate way to assess the potential damage.

When Peaches came back an hour later, she found me staring at the walls in a state of semishock.

"Went that well, did it?" she said.

"Any time I think I've grown into a powerful woman, paid my dues and earned my stripes, something wallops the wind out of me and kicks me right back to zero."

"What are you talking about?" She dropped a bag on the table and came around to face me. "What happened?"

"As soon as I heard Toby's voice, I crumbled. I pulled myself together pretty quickly but that's not the point. For a minute I was back to being that little girl following my brother around and even felt guilty for putting him in jail in the first place. Can you believe it, after all the stuff he's done? I actually cried."

"Oh, hell, don't tell me you're human. I expected less of you. And all this time I thought you were an android." She was grinning. "Do you really think that family disfunction is a joyride? I still feel guilt for my useless brother, too, so I taped a list over my desk to remind me of all the hell he's caused. That soon snaps me out of it."

"That's not all." I gazed up at my tall friend in the crop top and skintight jeans. "He told me that Noel was still alive."

"Holy shit, no! What are we going to do—track him down, finish him off properly?"

"Nothing," I said. "We're going to get to work and forget about him. As long as he stays out of my way, I'm going to stay out of his. I mean it. I've spent too many years of my life chasing after that man and I refuse to do it again."

"Yeah, I get that but do you really think he's going to leave you alone?"

"He will for a while. Apparently he's still recuperating. I may have damaged his heart."

She slapped her thigh. "Damaged his heart? Got to love it! Is that poetic justice or what?" Suddenly she turned serious. "Are you going to tell Max?"

"Not right away. Let him enjoy his vacation. There's plenty of time to deliver the bad news, not that he'd see discovering his long-lost son still lives a bad thing. He'd probably drop everything and go after him. In the meantime, let's go to Italy."

So, I booked our flights to Rome the next day and then reread all of Toby's prior letters looking for more clues but saw nothing suspicious. He recounted boring tidbits about the food, the movie he watched on TV the night before—*The Dig*. The Dig? A story about the archaeological excavation of Sutton Hoo? Maybe that was significant.

By now, I was looking for clues everywhere and the doodles all along the margins of the page led me farther down the rabbit hole. He had sketched those inscrutable geometric compilations, a square with a series of rectangles and a circle at the end of a single thick line twice. Baffled, I took pictures of the doodles with my phone and began packing.

The flight was uneventful, which is a good thing in plane travel. Tourists filled the cabin ready for their first holiday away from home shores since the pandemic. The vaccination had made us feel invincible so that we could go back to worrying about the more mundane travel anxieties like losing our luggage or hotel booking foul-ups.

Luckily, we didn't have to worry about technicalities. Seraphina, Nicolina's assistant, picked us up from the airport in Rome. As usual she did nothing to encourage conversation despite the deluge of water that had crossed under the proverbial bridge since we had last met. As for her role in the Venetian affair, I had gleaned from Nicolina that she had forgiven her right-hand woman and had no doubt encouraged the law to look the other way. Countesses in Italy can pluck more strings than an orchestra.

The streets of Rome flew by in the early evening light with me gazing out the car window hungry for every detail. The Colosseum flashed past like an ancient birthday cake layered in an icing of monumental time and mystery. I saw the Roman columns rise bathed in spotlight before my glimpses were swallowed by the traffic and bustle of the city on a hot summer night. Everywhere people were out enjoying the evening, sitting in the sidewalk cafés, strolling hand in hand, some masked, others not. Laughter, conversation, enjoyment, *life*. Italy had regained her dolce vita.

We turned a corner and darted down a cobbled lane, Seraphina tooting at every pedestrian or Vespa that dared veer into her path. Finally we pulled into the Trastevere palazzo, the site of Nicolina's villa, without managing to hit anybody.

Peaches eyebrows rose. I shook my head.

"We arrive," Seraphina announced as the automatic door opened and she pulled into garage. "You take elevator up. I bring bags."

"I can carry my own bags, thanks," Peaches said as she climbed out of the car.

"I take bags. You go upstairs," Seraphina repeated, popping open the trunk and shooting a look over her shoulder.

I had neglected to warn Peaches about Seraphina's fierce relationship with luggage. At first, I had thought her need to commandeer bags was due to some exaggerated sense of courtesy but now suspected it more likely that she wanted to secrete surveillance devices at the first opportunity.

"And I said, I'll carry my own bags, thank you very much." Peaches stepped up to the trunk, slung both of our carriers over her shoulders, nabbed her own roller, and lunged for mine, which Seraphina had already lifted onto the concrete floor and now clutched.

Peaches was six-two, Seraphina under five feet. It was like watching a Great Dane face off with a rabid terrier. Smiling, I stepped between them and wrestled my bag from their grasps. "Thank you both but I'll roll my own roller. That's what the wheels are for. Easy-peasy."

My gaze turned pointedly to Seraphina in a challenge of my own. I didn't care if I won her affection but I would damn well demand her respect. She released the bag and stepped away, glowering at us both all the way up the elevator to Nicolina's apartments.

The moment the elevator whispered opened and we had stepped into the hall, Nicolina swept down on us in a waft of perfume. "Phoebe! Peaches! I am so excited to see you!" A flurry of air kisses followed that was like being greeted by a nymph air and fragrance. Of course she looked elegant and amazing in her cream-colored linen shift, the sleek dark hair framing a perfect oval face, but it was her eyes that affected me most. They sparkled with joy as if our arrival was the best thing that had happened to her for a long time.

"I missed you, too!" I said, and it was true. After a long and often challenging relationship, we were finally genuine friends. "This pandemic kept us apart for too long."

One perfectly manicured hand flew up. "The pandemic. Let us not speak of that. Too many losses, so much pain and fear, and the imprisonment in our homes for months and months! But now we celebrate, yes? We have planned a feast for you later tonight. Would you like to share wine before freshening up? Your rooms are ready."

The Italians lubricate life with wine but the thought of alcohol before a hefty late dinner had to be avoided in the name of articulate communication. The Europeans dined between eight and ten p.m. I ate at five, usually takeout at my desk. "Thanks, but I think I'll just wash up and meet you down here in a few minutes. Is that okay?"

"Okay? Yes, always okay. We have refreshments for you in your rooms also. Peaches, your room is across from Phoebe's. Will this suit? How are your parents in Jamaica? I ask because I have heard so little."

Peaches grinned. "Fine, all fine, thanks. Mom's collecting orchids now and Dad's settled into the life of the retired physician under duress."

After more catch-up, Peaches and I finally disentangled ourselves and made our way upstairs, Nicolina leading the way like the excellent hostess she was.

"You've decorated!" I exclaimed, stepping into my room. Once a luxurious but worn chamber of the antique Italianate style, the bedroom now spread out around me in a sweep of modern textiles fashioned after antique designs, everything new and lustrous.

"Yes, much time on my hands. When not working, I decorate." She smiled. "The drapes, the bedcovers—all were old so I changed. You will see some artifacts still not repatriated here and there. While we work to return these treasures to their owners, why not enjoy?"

My gaze landed on a female half-portrait, probably Flemish circa early 1500s, that perfectly caught the gold hue of the silk curtains without competing with the tiny fleur-de-lis design of the blue watered silk wallpaper. Another small still-life, probably much later but no less exquisite, hung across the room above the reupholstered daybed. I recognized them from the photos Nicolina had posted of her holdings over the months but nothing captured a painting like seeing it in the flesh. They were beautiful, masterful. And they didn't belong to Nicolina. "I suppose you've contacted the museums and galleries in the Netherlands?"

"Certainly. They will decide which facility will claim these pieces as they debate among themselves. They wish to send their experts to assess and I told them any time." She shrugged. "Still they do not come. I will leave you now and we will speak later."

I watched as she stepped across the hall to ensure that Peaches had everything she needed. Turning away, I wrested all those niggles to the ground or tried. I shut the door and leaned against the carved cedar surface to take a deep breath. At one time I didn't trust Nicolina. Now I'd resolved to accept that we did things differently. All of our art and artifacts awaiting repatriation in London remained locked in our basement lab or our offices while hers decorated her villa. Where was the harm in that? And yet it bothered the hell out of me.

Before I could do a single enjoyable thing, I pulled out my Evan-issued smartphone, pressed the bug app, and scanned the room looking for the latest caches of Seraphina's surveillance devices. As expected, I found five, each secreted in what I considered to be all the obvious places. I dropped them into a little china dish and vowed to return them to their owner at the first opportunity.

Up popped a text from Evan himself. *Why the need to debug Nicolina's villa? Is Seraphina up to her usual compulsions?*

I smiled and thumbed in a reply: *Of course. BTW, this business of stalking me through my phone is intrusive. Maybe I should turn on the privacy feature.*

Evan: *What privacy feature?*

Me: *My point exactly. So how's Giani?*

Evan: *Excellent. He's growing so fast. Soon he'll be as tall as I am. We've just been visiting Rupert in Capri.*

Visiting Rupert? The men worked together and now they vacation together, too?

Me: *Got to run.*

Evan: *Right. Stalk later.*

That made me smile. I hadn't seen him in the flesh since the Portuguese mission but rarely a day went by when we didn't exchange a text or an email. That connection provided just enough contact for us to stay in touch without moving our relationship anywhere deeper. Pocketing the phone, I prepared to indulge in the luxury of a few minutes alone. It was a relief to wash my face after hours of mask wearing and to relax.

I changed out of my jeans into moss-green linen pants and a silk Gucci hyacinth blouse Nicolina had gifted me years ago. When in Rome… That done, I sat down on one of the brocade chairs to knit.

Knitting in solitude with lovely yarns and a cup of tea was more restorative to me than a glass of wine ever could be. I noted, as I worked a row of purl, how this butter-yellow yarn caught the nuances in the Flemish painting across the room. I breathed in color, art, and light—all the things I loved—my muscles loosening at once. By the time I was on the right side row, there was a knock on my door.

"Come in."

Peaches entered resplendent in a long violet stretch sheath. "This place is something else. I could definitely get used to living in an Italian villa but what's with that greeting? They strike me as people who live life fully, and yet when they meet you, they kiss the air. Nicolina, you, and me have been through plenty of trauma together. Don't we deserve a hug?"

I laughed. "Maybe it has to do with a certain restrained elegance in Nicolina's case, I don't know. It doesn't mean that she doesn't care. Hey, I forgot to remind you to bug-check your room."

"Done. I found six. Seraphina has a problem. She's like some kind of bug-o-maniac."

"It's definitely a compulsion. The trick is to stay one step ahead of her." I checked my phone. "While it's still early, maybe we can see that sketch before supper?"

"Let's go for it."

Reluctantly I set my knitting aside and followed her downstairs.

WE STOOD IN NICOLINA'S OFFICE AND LAB COMPLEX, WHICH NOW occupied the basement level of her four-floor villa. Like ours, hers was newly outfitted, designed as a facility for processing lost art and artifacts. Unlike ours, hers was luxurious, if a lab furnished with spotlights, light tables, magnification devices, X-ray machines, and computer terminals could be considered luxurious. The fact that this one also showcased a range of priceless artifacts in display cases interspersed among cozy seating areas took it up several notches above ours. Everything from an ancient Gandhara bust to a 1500-year-old bodhisattva torso held court in those displays, some of which were art of Nicolina's own collection. It was like stepping into some private museum where cocktails might be served between viewings. I always bristled when in the presence of private collections but I knew that to be the skewed thinking of the poor against the very rich.

"Would you like an aperitivo before you see the sketch?" Nicolina asked.

"No, thanks," was my reply as I wandered around the room. "You know me and alcohol. I'll wait to take wine with supper."

"I'll have some," Peaches said while tapping one of the paneled walls. "Is this on the other side of the garage?"

"It is the floor below." Nicolina swept over to a table to pour a glass from a decanter. She passed one to Peaches and took another for herself. "We built a new level with reinforced steel doors and our security, as you say in English, is state-of-the-art. Seraphina takes much pride."

I turned away to study the lab. Luckily Seraphina was nowhere in sight.

"For more details, you must ask her," Nicolina continued. "She is the expert on the technical matters."

"She'd probably bite me," Peaches remarked.

They were still discussing construction specifics as I went searching for the sketch. Not a long hunt, as it turned out. I found it under a sheet of archival glass on the room's center table. Flicking on the magnification lamp, I leaned closer. "It's not worked in metalpoint, but in pen and ink on vellum," I said, "and is remarkably well-preserved. Minimal cracking except at the edges."

"Why did you think it was in metalpoint?" Peaches asked, heading toward me.

"Because of the incredible detail. Do you have whatever container it was stored in?"

Nicolina was by my side in an instant. "In a cylinder there." She pointed to a leather tube sitting on a nearby table. It did look a bit like a scroll container only longer and distinctly Renaissance in origin.

Picking up the case, I turned the worn tooled leather with the enchased brass lid around in my hands. It felt heavy, substantial. Opening the lid, I angled the interior toward the light.

"There is nothing inside," Nicolina said. "We have X-rayed. You can see the results on the light table behind you."

But I was still fixed on the externals. "Even this is in good condition for five-century-old leather. It must have been kept someplace dry and relatively safe for all these centuries because, from what I can tell, both the case and the sketch are from the quattrocento."

"Quattrocento," Peached repeated, stepping forward. "The age when art shed the modes of the Byzantine, Christian, and Gothic to embrace classical forms of Roman and Greek—or, at least, that's what I remember my prof saying. I know it mostly from the architecture side."

"You remember right," I told her. "The Renaissance broadened the understanding of the universe that had been based primarily on religious teachings and opened up our perspective to consider the great classical philosophers of the classical age." Setting the case aside, I returned my scrutiny to the sketch.

"Is it by Leonardo?" Nicolina asked hopefully.

"No. Or at least I doubt it. Maybe from the same period, though. Look at that detail on the sleeve. It looks as though the dress was fashioned in silk and couched to make those triangular patterns and yet it's what's inside those triangles that fascinates me. Every one of those motifs must have been embroidered and each is different. Do you know how extraordinary that is?"

"Not really," Peaches said.

"It means that the intricate detail of this sleeve is not due to some silk weaver's mastery. Sleeves could be the single most valuable part of the Renaissance Florentine's wardrobe and heavily regulated. At one point citizens were only allowed to wear ornamentation on the left sleeve and even then the amount of fabric allowable was measured."

"That's crazy," Peaches said.

"In a republic built upon the fabric trade, it certainly seems that way," I agreed. "But they were always at war with the Christian values of simplicity and poverty."

"But what about this sleeve is so important?" Nicolina asked.

"It seems that someone wanted to highlight a range of special symbolic images to the viewer, each one significant, each one telling a story. Pearls and metal thread would have been used to pick out the detail, and even though this is charcoal, the artist appears to have gone over just the motifs in ink. Wait." I pulled over the magnification glass on its moving arm and peered through. "Yes, pen and ink. It's like the sleeve was more important than the sitter."

"What do all those symbols mean? There are some flowers I recognize and that wasp and bee is unmistakable but what about the rest?" Peaches asked.

I pulled back to calm myself, took a deep breath, slowly exhaled, and pointed to one of the motifs. "There." My finger landed above the sleeve's central feature.

Nicolina leaned forward. "The five balls and the trefoil crest? Yes, that is the Medici coat of arms—the palle or balls, which is believed to represent money and their status as bankers. This is why I thought the artist is perhaps Leonardo since he worked for the Medici for a time."

"Yes, the six balls peg the period probably during Lorenzo the Magnificent's time since his grandfather Cosimo's crest had seven," I said, "but the Medici were patrons of many artists and sculptors, as you know."

"So this sketch is somehow related to the Medici?" Peaches asked.

"That's my guess. The subject could be a member of the Medici family, though I don't recognize her from any of the official portraits—not the

Medici sisters or wives, in any case. Then there's this motif." I pointed to an image closer to the shoulder.

Nicolina leaned forward. "The three interconnecting circles."

"I'm pretty sure those are finger rings," I said.

"If those are rings, what are those things sticking out of the top? They look like little daggers that could gouge somebody's eyes out." Peaches was leaning over the sketch, too. "With this ring, I thee stab."

"Those were probably crystal or diamonds and that type of ring was likely for ceremonial purposes," I remarked.

"But the sketch is not by Leonardo, as I had hoped," Nicolina said, disappointment in her voice.

"Probably not. This was not really Leonardo's style. Anyway, the piece is still very valuable but we'll need your Uffizi expert to assess it further."

"Which we will do in Florence," Nicolina said with a nod. "I have made the arrangements. We leave tomorrow afternoon."

I turned to face them. "Good, but, Nicolina, can you think of why my brother would call this sketch a 'time bomb' and suggest I leave it alone?"

"He said this?" Nicolina stared.

"He told me to 'leave it the hell alone.'"

"When?"

"I spoke to him the day before yesterday. He's been sketching little images in the margins of his letters, one of which was of a scroll with a comic bomb attached. That's why I asked you to post additional photos of this piece to me. He was supposedly referring to this sketch's explosive nature—metaphorically speaking, I presume. At least, I don't hear any ticking."

Nicolina shook her head. "This I do not understand. We have retrieved many priceless pieces from your brothers' hoard. Why is this one so 'explosive'?" She put the word in air quotes.

"That's what we need to know," I said. "I received this." I unfolded his latest letter and spread it on the table. "What are those supposed to mean?" I asked, pointing to the geometric tangle of squares and rectangles, interconnecting circles and lines.

Peaches leaned over. "Not his usual style, for sure."

"No, Toby's more organic than geometrical. I used to joke that he'd never drawn a straight line in his life."

Peaches straightened. "Your brother is just filled with surprises, isn't he? Toby also told her that Noel is still alive," Peaches added, turning to Nicolina.

Damn. I shot her a quick look. I had also neglected to ask her to keep that part quiet.

"Noel is alive?" Nicolina exclaimed, hands flying. "We had hoped you had killed him! But where is he? I finish him off, yes? Tell me where he is and I will do this."

That's the other thing about Nicolina: she was lethal.

"No, no—no killing," I said, holding her gaze. "No one even knows where he is, and as long as he stays out of my way, I want him out of my head, too. Forget Noel."

"Yes, but as soon as he appears—bang." She fired a finger gun.

"No, no bang. Nicolina, listen: forget Noel, I said. I spent the happiest days of my recent life believing that man was finally off my viewfinder. I want to keep that feeling. Forget him," I said.

Nicolina dropped her hands. "Yes, we forget—for now. We go upstairs and have supper."

Minutes after we returned to the main floor and Nicolina disappeared into the kitchen to check on dinner, Peaches turned to me. "Sorry about that. I had no idea you wanted to keep a lid on the Noel thing."

"I knew that as soon as she heard, she'd put a hit on him," I whispered.

Peaches shrugged. "So, where's the harm in that?"

I thought for a moment. "Good point."

SUPPER WAS THE PROMISED FEAST. ALMOST FULL BY THE END OF THE first course—bucatini all'amatriciana accompanied with crusty bread for mopping up the plate—my stomach had extended to twice its usual size by the end of the tiramisu. If it hadn't tasted so good, I might have been sensible and forgone dessert but Italy isn't about being sensible but being alive and enjoying every single moment.

"How will we get the sketch to Florence?" I asked, taking a sip of wine. Secretly I wondered how I'd get up out of my chair.

Nicolina glanced at me in surprise. "Why, Seraphina will carry it, yes?"

"Seraphina?" Peaches said while helping herself to more bread. "I'd be happy to take responsibility, me being taller."

Nicolina smiled graciously but the glint in her eye suggested that this was not negotiable. "Seraphina will take it in her carry-on luggage."

"But what if customs does a spot-check and finds us carrying a piece of priceless art?" I asked.

"Phoebe." My host smiled. "This is Italy."

I let this sink in. "Of course."

"Also," she added, "we work with Interpol and do museum business. I have certificates."

There were certificates? "Okay." I subsided into my thoughts and tried to focus on my digestion, which needed all the help it could get.

An hour or so later shortly after ten, Nicolina suggested that we all go for a stroll. By then, I was a bit buzzed from the wine so the idea of fresh air stirred with Rome was enticing.

Though we had yet to see Nicolina's assistant since our arrival, apparently she was somewhere in the villa but would not be going with us. Nicolina called her on her phone and the three of us took off on our walk.

The Trastevere area at night was a feast for the senses. Once away from the busy thoroughfares, the ancient cobbled lanes of the thirteenth rione of Rome revealed itself as if lost in time. Narrow curving paths lined with the tall faces of buildings centuries old opened up into palazzos, some grand, some cozy. Little restaurants crowded onto the cobbles with their outdoor seating areas strung with lights and climbing ivy. We crossed a bridge and traveled down an alley that opened up onto an ancient Roman ruin spotlit like a forest of marble. We gazed at it, lost in our own thoughts.

On warm nights like these, the Romans were out in droves—couples and families with young children strolled through the streets. Everyone still attempted to maintain social distancing, which had become one of the more pleasant remnants of the recent pandemic. Because of this, it came as a shock when someone bumped into me from behind. I swung around but saw nothing amiss—a couple walking arm in arm, a multigenerational group of four women farther ahead.

"We're being followed," I whispered.

Nicolina sighed. "It happens always. Sometimes Seraphina she will chase them down."

Peaches was scanning all around us. "I think it was one of those women that passed behind us. I'll go after them."

"Don't bother," I said. "Let's just head back to the villa."

Nine times out of ten these stalkers were just keeping an eye on us and nothing ever manifested, otherwise. Chasing them was a waste of energy, especially after a wine-soaked dinner. We agreed, and strolled back to the villa, relaxed and ready for bed.

Anybody can make a mistake.

3

Florence. As much as I loved Rome, I loved Florence more. Let me count the ways: the way in which the light kisses the ancient stone; the way in which a multitude of sculpture, art, and history unfolds before your eyes without ever stepping through a single interior door; the Arno at sunset. I could go on and on. Let me say only that if you love history and art, Florence is your feast. And as usual, I was starving.

Seraphina had booked us into a luxurious villa hotel in the historic center of Florence not far from the Uffizi and overlooking a garden modeled after a sixteenth-century version. My room was the kind of light-washed expanse of sky-blue watered silk, satin, and antique textiles with a carved canopied bed that made me think that I had fallen into the pages of an historic homes magazine. It was far more luxurious than even Nicolina's villa.

Surrounded by such splendor, why leave? I could while away my day checking the thread count of the Persian carpets, date the botanical illustrations on the walls, maybe even knit. Had it been in any other city, maybe I would just sit and indulge my senses. But this was Florence and one's senses were best indulged beyond the doors.

First I spent several minutes studying the enigmatic sketches in Toby's letter. The more I studied it, the more I grew convinced that he had sent me a message. This geometric jumble was so not his style. I folded away the letter and shoved it into my bag before changing into cream linen pants, a cream-colored top, and, because I would eventually have a business meeting, I folded a printed tailored sateen cotton jacket into my backpack. Admittedly, I felt a bit awed to be meeting a fellow art historian in such a majestic location. To me, it was a bit like meeting a pope at the Vatican, not that I was Catholic or followed any specific doctrine, but awe is awe. After donning what I hoped was a jaunty straw fedora, I was ready to stroll through history.

Nobody thought twice when I said I wanted to walk the streets by myself. It was still early afternoon and our appointment with the Uffizi's Giovanni Vannucci was not until 4:30. Nicolina had decided to rest after taking a light lunch in the hotel's dining area and Seraphina would remain in an adjoining room guarding the sketch, which she clearly considered to be her job. Meanwhile, Peaches was eager to climb the steps of the Duomo, its architect-cum-engineer, Filippo Brunelleschi, being one of her all-time heroes.

"The man was a genius!" she exclaimed, waving a guidebook around. "To engineer that dome under the circumstances. Do you know that it was the first octagonal dome in history to be built without temporary wooden supports? I've always wanted to see it in person so I plan to climb right on inside the dome and study every aspect. What an opportunity! Want to come?"

"No, thanks. I'm going for a walk. The streets beyond that window—" I indicated the casements opened up to the garden "—are much less crowded with tourists than usual in August, apparently." Though many visitors had returned post-pandemic, the numbers were nowhere near the usual August swarms. "I'm going to savor the city while I can."

"Sure you don't need a bodyguard?"

"No, thanks. Go meet Brunelleschi. See you later at the Uffizi."

Did I worry about being followed again? Always. The first years of my life in England I had been constantly ghosted by crooks convinced that I knew where my brother and Noel had hidden their heisted treasures. I didn't at first but that didn't stop them. Since launching the Agency of the Ancient Lost and Found where tracking lost treasures was my business, I rarely stepped outside without being accompanied by some stalker. I just knew they were there but learned to live with their presence the way one lives with flies and stinging insects. The incident in Rome just proved that they followed us everywhere.

That afternoon in Florence, I imagined that the previous night's stalker may have accompanied us here, too. I can always sense when I'm being followed. Of course, they'd be virtually invisible in the gaggle of tourists taking selfies with the sculptures outside the Bargello. It would be almost impossible to pinpoint my stalker unless I was willing to sacrifice all of my attention to the task, which I wasn't. For the first few hours alone in Florence, I craved time out to savor the history and atmosphere. I had given myself a two-hour holiday and planned to savor every moment.

I strolled across the fourteenth-century Piazza Della Signoria, once the political epicenter of the Florentine Republic whose well-worn pavers had been trod by nearly every famous personage during the Renaissance. A bronze plaque embedded into the stone marked the spot where the puritanical fanatic friar Savonarola had been burned at the stake in 1498, one year after he had orchestrated the Bonfire of the Vanities. In the name of evil excesses, he had torched works of art, gaming tables, and magnificent dresses while preaching that every form of pleasure and relaxation was pure wickedness.

In a state of pure wickedness myself, I stopped by a gelateria for a pistachio ice cream so delicious that I swear my toes curled as I continued my stroll down the famed Ponte Vecchio. It was the only medieval Florentine bridge to survive the bombing of World War Two, and that it had survived all the centuries up to that point was a miracle in itself.

Only a quarter of the way across, I looked around for a bit of shade in which to stand while frantically licking my rapidly melting luxury. It was a hot day and the only people on the streets were tourists. The Florentines were too smart to broil themselves alive in the summer heat.

Stepping under an awning, I studied the offerings in one of the pricey jewelry shops that lined the bridge. There had been goldsmiths here since the traditional butchers and tanners had been banished by decree in 1595 due to the bothersome stench that annoyed the citizens. The bridge was literally a cobbled lane of shops lining both sides up to the very center where arches opened onto views of the Arno before the shops continued to the other side.

My eyes slipped across the gold bracelets and necklaces on sale wondering which item would I choose had I the money and inclination to purchase. Maybe the signet ring with the tiny gold coin which could have been Roman or at least modeled after some classical emperor's profile—Hadrian, perhaps? Pseudo-buying expensive items was a game I often played during my relaxed moments but usually with luxury fashion magazines. In reality, I rarely bought costly items for myself unless they were textiles or yarn.

By chance, I caught the reflection of a woman standing behind me. Of all the shop windows on the bridge, why had she chosen this one to gaze into with such intense interest? Was there something particularly intriguing here not found in the other windows? I doubted that. Most jewelers sold similar wares.

I studied her out of the corner of my eye. Older than I was by a few years, oval face, blondish hair pulled back into an untidy ponytail, beige khakis, and a striped shirt with a crossbody bag, nothing about her carried the telltale signs of a tourist. Her stance—arms crossed, eyes above a mask calculating, confident—made me think she was studying me, too. This woman was all business.

Slowly, I turned, expecting to make eye contact, but she immediately bolted, leaving me to study her athletic form as she race-walked along the bridge. I had no intention of chasing her down but continued strolling in the same direction. Minutes later, I reached the center arched opening in time to see her striped shirt moving quickly along the street on the other side of the Arno. Puzzling but not alarming. I checked my watch: time to head for the Uffizi. I devoured the rest of my ice cream, cleaned my fingers with hand sanitizer, and turned back the way I had come.

The quickest way to this amazing museum of treasures was to hang a right-hand turn at the bottom of the Ponte Vecchio and proceed along the arched portico overlooking the Arno. Overhead, an enclosed corridor called the Vasari Corridor linked the Uffizi to the Medici's Pitti Palace across the river. Apparently Cosimo de' Medici preferred to remain safe and dry on his way to work in the morning in the mid-1400s while also avoiding the pungent bridge. Considering that the Florentine republic was also festering with intrigue and attempted assassinations, who could blame him?

The Vasari Corridor, named after its builder, had been lined with priceless art from the Medici collection from the very beginning. In fact, the Medici were such patrons of art and architecture that they were largely responsible for the explosion of artistic rebirth and learning that we call the Renaissance and still influenced Western civilization today. They encouraged, financed, and protected the incredible artistry of everyone from Michelangelo to Leonardo da Vinci. Oh, to be a guest at a Medici dinner table!

I intended to make several visits to my favorite museum in the world this trip, but today I planned only on keeping my appointment. As it was, I was instructed to proceed to the ticket kiosk and say that I had a meeting with one of the museum's art historians, Giovanni Vannucci, one of the many Renaissance specialists. By now, I had donned my jacket and attempted to look professional. After a quick phone call, the man at the desk directed me to a door where I met a security guard who, in turn, led me through the nonpublic corridors of the museum enclaves.

Twenty minutes early, I expected to be directed to wait somewhere until the appointed time but instead the guard took me down a floor and directly to an office down a bright corridor, ushering me along as if I were a visiting dignitary. A lean ,middle-aged man with intense lively eyes above a ready smile was standing just inside the door.

"Signorina McCabe, I am delighted to meet you." Perfect English with a touch of Italian cadence. "I am Giovanni Vannucci. Call me Giovanni, please. I have heard so much of you from Nicolina and, of course, I have read of your adventures in art."

Adventures in art? Wow. Not sure whether it was acceptable to shake hands these days but I offered mine, anyway, which he pumped enthusiastically. "I'm delighted to meet you, too, Giovanni, and please call me Phoebe." Not yet used to having fame in the art world, I felt my face flush but sensed that my host was far too gracious to notice.

"Nicolina has told me many things about the work of the Agency of Ancient Lost and Found and I have read the stories in the papers and journals. For this and because we have been many years friends, I help her identify pieces, no questions asked. I thank you on behalf of the Uffizi for the many allocations you have gifted us."

We had received thank-you letters, of course, but this personal thanks meant so much more. "You're very welcome. I hope to repatriate many more pieces back to Italy, perhaps even the piece we're bringing with us for you to study today. Have you seen a photo?"

"Not yet," he said. "I wait with pleasure." I think he meant "expectantly."

"Here, this will give you an idea of the item we are investigating while we wait for the others to join us. I have an idea of the artist but I'm no expert in Renaissance art." I took out my phone and passed it to Giovanni, who stared at the screen in silence for several seconds.

"Oh," he said, and then mumbled, "Perhaps," in Italian. When his gaze met mine, there was an unmistakable excitement there.

"Is it who I think it is?" I asked. "I mean, who I'd hoped."

He laughed. "I do not know what you are thinking, Phoebe, but come let us see this together."

I followed him out of his office to a staff elevator and into the main museum's halls, trying not to gasp and swoon at every Raphael or Leonardo we passed along the way. I could be such an art groupie. Giovanni moved with quick efficiency and I had to scramble to keep up but I guessed where we were heading, had suspected all along.

To art enthusiasts, a well-loved painting still strikes one anew each and every time they lay eyes on it. Love is like that, I've decided—the sight of the lover always kisses you with joy. That's how I felt when we stepped into the museum's new Botticelli room and stood before *The Birth of Venus*. By then, my heart was already full to bursting as I stared at that magnificent painting.

"I hoped so!" I whispered, aware that other viewers stood carefully spaced all around us. With the new protocols, it was as if air and light danced around us while we worshipped with the nymphs the magnificent image of Venus emerging from the waves.

"In this I see the mastery of composition, a similarity in the way in which the artist touches the cheek. Do you see?" He was still holding my phone, the picture of the sketch open on the screen.

"Even with the comparative restrictions of chalk and ink, I see it, yes. The way in which he shades the face." Botticelli had a delicate hand with shading, managing to create soft continuous shadow as if the full power of the Tuscan sun beamed upon his subjects.

"And here you see a hint of what I consider distinctly Botticelli but, of course, without any clear provenance, and my colleagues could argue otherwise..." Art historians argued everything. It was a favorite exercise among my profession unless a painting or sketch came with clear incontestable provenance. "But still, I think maybe."

Maybe worked for me.

In his rising excitement, he was speaking too loudly, displaying my phone screen with no effort to shield the image. I felt a ping of alarm. On instinct, I swung around and there she was, standing just meters behind us—Ms. Vecchio. I reached for Giovanni's arm to warn him but he was now speaking into his phone.

"Nicolina and Seraphina have arrived," he said. "Come, we will meet them in one of the labs." And he turned on his heels and zipped off across the room too quickly for me to intercept. My Ponte Vecchio stalker had already disappeared.

I said nothing about her as Giovanni and I descended to the elevator to the museum's labs. Now I realized her interest was serious and potentially disruptive. I needed to discover who she was and what she wanted and soon.

When we stepped into a lab much like Nicolina's and our own, Nicolina and Seraphina were already waiting and a guard was just delivering Peaches. I could tell that my friend was bursting to share her experiences at the Duomo but managed to contain herself as we watched Giovanni and Nicolina exchanging socially distanced air kisses. It was a peculiar sight, a bit like watching birds enacting a courtship dance midair. After the flurry of greetings, we quickly got down to business. Giovanni suggested we could now remove our masks, which we all did.

Seraphina carefully unfolded the sketch from the satchel she carried, removing the rolled item from its canister and offering it to Giovanni with gloved hands. He gently took the vellum to a table and beamed a magnifying light onto its surface while we spaced ourselves around him in breathless anticipation.

After a few moments of studying the sketch from every possible angle, he finally straightened and smiled. "I believe this sketch may be by Sandro Botticelli."

"I knew it!" said I, unable to suppress my glee.

"Yes!" Nicolina clapped her hands. "We thought a great Renaissance master, yes?"

"We will need to establish more detail, of course. I will invite my colleagues to further study this masterpiece, if I may."

"You must keep the sketch here for now," Nicolina said. "For safety."

"That's definitely the best idea since it appears we have already attracted some unfriendly interest." I caught Nicolina's eye. She lifted her brows in a question but I turned to Giovanni. "Any idea who the sitter may be?" I asked.

Giovanni stroked his chin. "Most puzzling but no. This is not unusual for the time. So many portraits remain not only unattributed but their subjects unnamed. Florence was not so large a city in the 1400 and 1500s by our standards. It is possible that the citizens knew one another well enough that attributions were not necessary. Perhaps we can find records to specify commissions. This will be researched, of course, but the sitter may always remain a mystery. We will attempt to date this to begin with. Do we know the provenance?"

I knew this would come up but, hell, surely he already knew some of the background? "Only that my brother or his business partner, Noel Halloren, or possibly Peaches's brother, acquired it illegally somehow. I'm sure you know the story. It was all over the newspapers. We found it among their loot in their Jamaican hideout. Probably stolen by Noel, who had—*has,*" I stumbled, "an affinity for Renaissance art."

Giovanni was regarding me with a touch of alarm. "He still lives? We had heard that you had…incapacitated him."

I sighed. "I thought so, too, but apparently he's holed out somewhere. I don't expect him to make an appearance for a while since his health is still not robust."

Don't ask me why discussing my art-heisting brother and my ex in this temple of art was twisting my gut inside out. I felt so ashamed as if I somehow bore responsibility for their transgressions, which I did to some extent. That is to say that in the beginning I had never done enough to stop them and now held myself accountable.

"This is most disturbing," Giovanni said with a sigh. "Halloran is notorious in the art world but how would he come across a Botticelli?"

"We don't know." I was so uncomfortable by now that I felt physically ill. "No doubt heisted from some private collector. He was—*is*—ruthless where art is concerned."

"And now we know he is still alive," Nicolina stated. "Somewhere."

Peaches had sidled up to me and touched my arm. "So, moving right along, any ideas as to the date of this piece?" she inquired. I shot her a grateful glance.

"Too early to say," Giovanni said, taking the hint. "I think perhaps some time between 1482 and 1486, but this I just guess."

"But what about the Medici crest and that wasp? Wasn't the wasp an emblem of the Vespucci?" I pointed to the little stinger embroidery on the sleeve. "The Vespucci were another noble Florentine family at the time."

"Vespucci is a play on words. It means wasp in Italian," Nicolina explained for Peaches's benefit.

"And the Vespuccis were allies of the Medici, correct?" I said. "Each of those motifs are meaningful and may point to the identity of the sitter or, at least, point to whoever commissioned the sketch. Perhaps the sitter is from the Vespucci or the Medici?"

Giovanni nodded. "The emblems and symbology are interesting but what do they tell us, really? This woman does not appear to be from the Medici or the Vespucci families based on the attributed portraits of the time. She appears to be of humble origin, though her clothing says something quite different. It could have been the sketch for a painting for a wedding portrait, though even that would be odd, yes?"

"Odd how?" Peaches asked.

"Odd because the sitter is not wearing jewelry or any ornamentation, which would be uncommon for a wedding portrait where the important family must display their wealth," I replied. "All that is rich here is the sleeve."

"But Botticelli does have other portraits of women dressed in plain attire. The *Portrait of a Young Woman* comes to mind," Giovanni said. "They are difficult to attribute and the best an art historian can do is take an educated guess."

"Yes, but here is a young woman dressed like a lady but apparently not one judging from her hair," Peaches said.

"And there's the *Portrait of a Young Woman*—plain clothes, undressed hair, slightly stooped posture," I pointed out. "That is perhaps the closest to this style, though there's still a huge disconnect between her clothes and her hair. The Renaissance noblewoman's coiffure was an art form in itself but this woman appears so humble in so many ways. Here she is wearing what must be a very costly dress with that magnificent sleeve and yet her hair is worn pulled back and tucked under a scarf as if she is at home or... did not have the benefit of a maid. It's almost untidy, like she was playing dress-up for an occasion she could never attend."

"Like she was doing housework," Peaches said. Catching my questioning glance, she clarified. "Back home the women always tie their hair in scarfs to keep it off their face while working. This just looks like a working woman to me. Her cheeks appear kind of ruddy...but of course it's not like I can see any color or anything." She peered down at the sketch again. "So, how valuable is it, Giovanni?"

Seraphina, who had been standing back from the table with her hands folded, issued a snort.

Giovanni seemed a bit taken aback by this familiarity but carried blithely on. "Ah, but anything by Botticelli is very valuable once attributed and benefits from clear provenance, but I cannot guess a price." He spread his hands.

"Oh, come on—give us a guess." Peaches beamed at him playfully.

No doubt startled by her brilliant smile, the historian grinned back. "Perhaps many thousands of euros."

"And what if this is the mock-up for a painting that may exist somewhere?" She asked the question I guessed we were all thinking.

"Ah," the art historian sighed, "we don't refer preliminary sketches as 'mock-ups' but 'studies.' However, if such a portrait should exist somewhere, that portrait would be a tremendous find. To discover a complete Botticelli portrait today when they are so rare? Amazing! To find anything by Botticelli is like the discovery of the century. So much has been lost."

"And Botticelli's *Portrait of a Young Man Holding a Roundel* recently sold through Sotheby's for an excess of $92.2 million dollars," I said. "They didn't know the sitter's identity there, either."

"92.2 million frickin' dollars—seriously? That's obscene!" Peaches blurted.

"Reportedly purchased by Russians," Nicolina said.

"There are only about a dozen Botticelli portraits that have survived and most belong to museums," Giovanni added. "We bid on the *Young Man* portrait, of course, but were not successful. In the art world today, it is the private collectors who possess the funds to buy such priceless pieces. Museums cannot compete. We rely on gifts. The Medici themselves indirectly gave us many of our most important pieces of Renaissance art."

"They were the ultimate collectors and benefactors," I remarked.

"Imagine an original Botticelli hanging on the wall of one's villa?" Nicolina mused wistfully.

I glanced at her while imagining the portrait of our unknown sleeve wearer gracing her walls. That made me uncomfortable.

Minutes later we bid goodbye to Giovanni with arrangements to stay in touch and to plan more meetings as the research progressed. He graciously offered to give us a private tour of the Uffizi before we left Florence and I put my request in for a guided stroll through the Vasari Corridor. Meanwhile, the museum's art historians would focus their collective knowledge on attributing the sketch and most likely we would gift it to their collection permanently.

Altogether, it was a good day's work and now it seemed that we were free to savor Florence more fully. Nicolina suggested dinner overlooking the Arno at sunset with perhaps a refreshing drink on our way back to our hotel. How could we resist?

We exited the museum, which was closing in a matter of minutes, me gazing hungrily at every passing masterpiece on our way out of the door. Admittedly, I became briefly ensorcelled by Caravaggio's *Medusa*.

"She reminds me of you," Peaches said cheerfully.

"I remind you of a monster. Thank you very much."

"Maybe not that particular painting—I mean, that's bloody terrifying—but I've seen other images of Medusa where the snakes look more like curly hair and her expression reminds me of you—I mean in the nicest possible way, of course."

I was about to protest further when Nicolina urged us out the door. The only thing that made leaving bearable was knowing that I would soon return.

Outside, the heat seemed to have intensified, the very pavers beneath our feet pulsing back hours of the Mediterranean sun's powerful rays.

We proceeded down the Uffizi's long exterior courtyard toward the

Piazza Della Signoria. Nicolina was beside me, Peaches one step behind, and Seraphina bringing up the rear, her satchel slung over one shoulder.

Suddenly Seraphina cried out and Nicolina and I swung around in time to see her falling facedown on the pavers while a woman—my Ms. Vecchio—dashed away with her satchel. Peaches bolted after the attacker while Seraphina struggled to her feet.

4

"You let her escape!" Seraphina accused Peaches as we sat at an outside trattoria attempting to restore our equilibrium. Seraphina had received a blow to the head for which she refused medical attention, saying that it was nothing. There was no bleeding, only a nasty welt. Apparently Ms. Vecchio had taken her by surprise, hitting her with some unknown object before snatching her bag and making a speedy getaway.

"I didn't *let* her escape," Peaches argued, relocating the wine carafe to my side of the table as if she planned to lunge across and throttle the smaller woman. Knowing Seraphina's abilities, that wouldn't have been wise. "She disappeared, I said. That woman must know Florence like the back of her hand, and boy, can she run. One minute I thought I had her and then—poof! Gone."

"'Poof gone? What is 'poof gone'? You are no bodyguard," Seraphina said with a sneer.

Peaches leaned over the table. "But I'm not your bodyguard, am I? I protect her." She pointed to me. "You're supposed to be the big hotshot spy-trained guard dog so why can't you protect yourself?"

Seraphina launched to her feet but Nicolina put out a staying hand. *"Sedersi,"* she told her. Seraphina sat. "This does not help. This woman she has stolen an empty container, that is all. We are very lucky that the sketch is safe in the Uffizi."

"True," I agreed, "but obviously my stalker was after that sketch. So how did she even know we had it? Since she was tracking me since this morning and possibly even in Rome, she must have already known that we had something valuable."

"Looks that way." Now settled into her chair, Peaches crossed her arms and leaned back, keeping Seraphina in her sights in case the other woman launched a surprise attack.

Our waiter arrived to fill our glasses, maybe hoping that we'd empty that carafe and order another. I smiled up at him and told him to bring us another round as I took my first sip of Chianti. Distilled bliss. "Drink up, everyone. Growling at one another is not going to solve anything. We need to find this woman. My guess is that it won't be that difficult." Yes, I was breaking all my cardinal rules about drinking wine predinner. I felt the urge to celebrate possibly finding a Botticelli sketch.

"Why is that?" Nicolina asked as she picked up her own glass.

"Because she's an amateur. She came right up behind me on the bridge this morning while I was window-shopping. An experienced stalker would know that a window would reflect her image, which doesn't make her any less dangerous. If she does her homework enough to know who Seraphina is and still jumped her, she's not afraid of much, either."

"I will kill her," Seraphina said, closing her eyes.

I shook my head. "No, you won't. We need to get information from this woman. For that we'll lay a trap. My guess is that once she discovers that she's snatched an empty bag, she'll come back for the right one and this time we'll be ready for her."

It was simple, really. I figured that Ms. Vecchio might think that she had snatched the wrong bag from the wrong person. Though Nicolina and Peaches carried smaller purses, I habitually lugged my antique carpet-upholstered backpack everywhere. Maybe she'd think that I was the sketch bearer and not Seraphina? A logical next step, then, was for her to either attempt to steal that from me or, better yet, force me to disclose where I may have hidden the sketch. Or so my thinking went. There were so many possibilities but top of the list was to put myself in her tracks.

To that end, later that evening, I sat in the garden with my knitting.

Being summer, the sun set later in the day allowing me to take advantage of the light. Nicolina had eventually insisted that Seraphina be checked out by a doctor after she began having dizzy spells during dinner so both of them were occupied elsewhere. However, Peaches lurked nearby.

The garden was a spacious walled enclosure with fruit trees, fountains, and clipped hedges set among geometric paths in the Renaissance style. I had parked myself in the center loggia, which was raised just high enough to be visible from the street. If my stalker happened to be lingering near, she could access the area through a little gate on the side with a minimum of lock fiddling.

My bag sat clearly visible while I did everything possible to look absorbed in my stitches. Actually, that wasn't difficult. Once I began knitting, time just slipped away, and considering that I'd had several glasses of wine by then, slipping of all kinds came easily. Peaches sat well out of sight near the kitchen garden in the corner. Thus, I made myself ambush bait. Yet an hour and many dropped stitches later, my attacker did not make an appearance.

"Maybe we're looking too obvious," Peaches whispered to me as I gathered up my knitting and came indoors.

"She knows that we're aware of her now," I said. "I'm going to take a stroll instead. You wait here."

Peaches laughed. "You think I'm going to leave you to wander around Florence by yourself? Not a chance. If this one doesn't get you, the pickpockets will."

"You do recall that I know self-defense."

"Yeah, but you've gotten rusty, whereas I do my practice videos every day and returned to the gym the moment they opened."

"I said I'll go alone. She'll know she's being set up if she catches sight of you anywhere near. Stay here, please. Besides, you know I can take care of myself."

"That's what Seraphina the Terrible thought before she was jumped. You of all people need a bodyguard."

"Why me of all people? Never mind. I said I'll be fine."

So I may have won that battle but whether I'd be able to corner Ms. Vecchio solo was another matter. All I could hope for was that she might take the bait.

I took off on a leisurely stroll through the winding streets away from the river this time, heading for an area where the medieval arteries grew narrower and were lined with tall stone buildings. It was like strolling through ancient urban canyons where vestibules and centuries-old niches offered multiple places to hide amid walls of stone. If I were my stalker, I wouldn't miss a chance like that. Naturally, she'd know that I wouldn't bring a Botticelli sketch along for the ride, but if she wanted to chat, here was her chance.

At dusk, most of the pedestrians had already left for home or the restaurants. Away from the main thoroughfares, a quietude descended on the cobbled streets broken only by the buzz of an occasional Vespa. Many streets were so narrow that cars were allowed through by permit only and iron posts had been installed to protect the sides of the ancient buildings. There were often no sidewalks and pedestrians had to scuttle against a wall to avoid being flattened by the occasional vehicle.

But I wasn't paying much attention to any of that. For me, it was a breathless step back into time even if those high fortress-like walls lining the streets refused to give away their secrets at first glance. Medieval and Renaissance houses were built for defensive purposes as much as for shelter. One never knew when a rival family or a band of thieves might try to scale your walls. Even though most of these stone faces had renovated exteriors, the bones of the structures remained the same.

The past absorbed me as I imagined the wealthy wool and cloth merchants that had once lived along these streets. Occasionally I glimpsed a courtyard through an iron gate and stood there for minutes picturing life in the 1400s. Still nobody tried to accost me. At one point, I became so annoyed by this total lack of opportunism that I planted myself in the middle of a quiet lane and glared back at the empty streets.

It was growing dark when I tired of the game. I resolved to return to the hotel taking a different route. This way led me down the Via San Gallo and on toward the San Marco area, a slightly convoluted route but one I anticipated because I'd be passing the famed Duomo.

I had just turned a corner off the Via San Gallo onto one of the long arteries that led to the cathedral when it happened, though I'm not sure to this day exactly *what* happened. I'm practiced at preparing myself for unwelcome encounters but no footsteps alerted me, though I'd been checking behind me every few minutes. Had I missed a flicker in the shadows?

Yet somebody grabbed me from behind, pressed a cloth over my face, and pinned my arms behind my back. Two people, I thought as I frantically struggled while inhaling a sweet pungent scent that fogged my brain. Shit! Blinded, half-shackled, I was still trying to get in a kick when my knees gave out underneath me and I dropped to the pavement.

A man's voice in Italian said, "Get her in."

I needed to call my super phone but couldn't remember the words. I was going down fast. They were dragging me somewhere.

Tires screeched to a halt followed by loud voices before I went under.

※

HOURS LATER, I FOUND MYSELF IN BED WITH A KILLER HEADACHE. FOR A moment I thought it had to be from the wine, though I was sure I hadn't had that much. Slowly, I opened my eyes. I could just make out Peaches pacing the room in the lamplight while Nicolina sat in a chair, hands folded in her lap.

"What happened?" I whispered.

"What happened?" Peaches snapped, swinging around. "I'll tell you what happened: you were almost kidnapped by a gang of deadly dudes!" She was at my side in seconds looking furious enough to singe the sheets. "I said you couldn't go off without me and good thing I didn't listen. If I hadn't been there, those two would have dragged you off."

"They chloroformed me," I said, struggling to prop myself on my elbows. "I remember that smell."

"Yeah, trussed you up like a chicken and tried to drag you into a car. You need me, McCabe, and don't think for a moment that you don't."

"Never said I didn't," I mumbled. "Did they take anything?"

"What, like your precious knitting or maybe your super phone? Not a bloody thing. I got there too fast—slugged one and knifed the other."

"Knifed?" I gazed up at her.

"Yeah, stabbed him just seconds before he tried to shoot me. Luckily I know a few tricks of my own."

"And then I arrived and finished them both off." Nicolina had appeared on the other side of my bed.

Finished. Them. Both. Off. *Hell*. "You followed me, too?"

"Yes, she did—separately—and together we got you into the car. You were out cold by then," Peaches added.

"What car?" I asked. Talk about befuddled.

"The taxi," Nicolina said. Misunderstanding my look of shock, she explained: "But do not worry, the driver will not talk. I tipped well."

"But unfortunately, the guy driving the other car still got away," Peaches said.

I was still getting hung up on the details. "Wait: Peaches, you knifed one guy, knocked out the other, and then Nicolina came along in a taxi and shot them both? And you just drove away leaving them on the street?"

"Where else were we supposed to put them—in a night deposit box? We couldn't just wait around for the police to arrive and start asking questions, could we? As it was, we think some teens down the road may have seen some of the action."

I flopped back against the pillow and closed my eyes. "How did you get me back into the hotel?"

"Just sort of half-walked you through the front door and up the elevator," Peaches replied. "I said you'd been hitting the Chianti too hard. Why so interested in logistics? You should be more worried that we've got some gang after us and not just that woman."

"Do we know they're not related?" I asked, opening my eyes.

"Who knows?" Peaches said.

"No. These men were too—what is the word?—*professional*. 'Professional'?" She turned to Peaches with a questioning gaze.

Peaches shrugged and said, "Yeah, 'professional' works."

"They had guns with silencers," Nicolina explained. "Very organized. I recognized the type."

I blinked. "There's a type?"

"Italian hired assassins."

"Assassins?" I shot up again.

Nicolina put a hand on my shoulder and gently pressed me back down. "Do not worry. They probably want only to torture you for information."

"Is that supposed to be comforting?"

"They think you know something," she explained.

I sighed. "Not this again. Thugs have always thought I know more than I do."

"But you always discover what you do not know originally," Nicolina pointed out. "This is your gift."

"My gift? I need a painkiller. I'd consider that a gift right now. Could you grab me one from my bag, please?"

"I will get it," Nicolina said.

"No." Peaches raised her hand. "She needs something natural to help her sleep and detoxify that chemical shit they made her inhale. Not more drugs. I found some valerian growing in the kitchen garden out back—cool collection of herbs. I'll make some tea, then we can let her rest."

Twenty minutes later, valerian tea liberally sweetened with honey eased me right back into dreamland convinced that everything could wait until morning.

But I didn't make it that long...

Hours later, I awoke befuddled and struggled to sit up in my murky room. With no idea as to time, my phone somewhere out of reach, I managed at least to recognize that I was still in my luxury Florentine bed. A soft predawn light half illuminated the space and a gentle rose-scented summer breeze wafted in through the open casements. Other than that, everything felt all wrong.

Vaguely, I recalled those casements being closed...

"Good. You're awake. I thought I'd have to toss water on you or something," a woman said somewhere in the shadows to the right. "I'm Zann."

I shot upright, patting the sheets desperately hoping for my phone, a gun, something my friends might have tucked away within reach.

"Forget it. Your toys aren't nearby and both of your friends are out cold. They won't be here to rescue you until morning. I drugged their tea."

5

She was American. Don't ask me why that was such a shock. I watched as she climbed onto the end of the bed, a gun in one hand, and plumped a satin bolster at her back. She then proceeded to commandeer another pillow on which to rest her gun hand and leaned back. It was still too dark to see her clearly since she was silhouetted against the early dawn light but I recognized her just the same.

"Make yourself comfy, why don't you?" I said.

"I have."

"And your name is Zann?"

"Short for Suzanna. I'm not big on formalities."

"So, Zann, is this really necessary? Why didn't you just talk to me earlier when I gave you the chance?"

She laughed. "Think I don't know a setup when I see one? Besides, you had the boys on your heels and I know enough about them to stay out of their path. Decided to choose my own time, my own way. You, Phoebe, are supposed to be some top-notch art detective but you and your friends can be pretty damn dense at times, can't you?"

"We all have our moments."

"Would it surprise you to know that I'm staying right down the hall?"

Well, yes, it did actually, but I tried not to let it show. "Seraphina would have sussed that out eventually—if you hadn't whacked her on the head, that is. She'll probably bug every room on this floor in a few days, too."

"I'm not too impressed with that one, let me tell you—too sure of herself, maybe has a screw loose—but Peaches now, she's magnificent, isn't she? But she can be a bit spacey sometimes, too. How else can you explain how I managed to drug her and Nicolina's tea earlier? Just waited until their backs were turned and dumped some sleeping powder into their mugs in the lobby—actually a bunch of mugs. I might have knocked out a few other late-night tea drinkers while I was at it but they'll sleep well tonight."

"Can we just get on with it? What the hell do you want?"

She laughed again. "You."

I turned around and made to plump up my pillows, giving myself time to think. When I leaned back again still all I could say was: "Me?"

"You. You are going to help me make the art find of the century, *my* art find."

"You want the sketch you tried to steal today."

"What I really want is the painting that's still out there."

"Why do you think there is a painting, let alone that it's yours?"

"Because I found it, or almost found it, years ago. I was cheated and now I want what's mine."

I leaned forward. "Explain."

"Long story."

"Doesn't look like I'm going anywhere and stop pointing that gun at me, will you? I'm a captive audience."

But the gun never wavered. "Okay, so, years ago I lived in Florence. My father was a visiting professor at the Accademia di Belle Arti di Firenze, a few months that turned into a few years so I practically grew up here. Eventually I went to university and was studying archaeology in Italy when Dad pulled a few strings to get me a summer job in Florence. I was working on a dig for one of the buildings they were renovating in the Ognissanti neighborhood on a street known today as Via della Porcellana. Know it?"

"No."

"So the property was bought by a hotel chain but the original structure was known to be very old—like that's a surprise in Florence. As usual, an archaeology team was brought in to excavate first since every building in this city is built on hundreds of years of history. I was only twenty-two at the time."

"And?"

"From the very moment this place captured my imagination. I had a powerful hunch. Ever get hunches?"

"All the time."

"Oh, yeah, I remember hearing about yours—something like mystical bolts from the sky that tell you where to look for art, right?"

"You watch too much TV. It's not like that at all but more as if I have a sudden vision of connecting puzzle pieces that form an entire picture in my head. It's like a blast of inspiration. I can't explain it much more clearly than that."

"Yeah, magical bolts, like I said."

I sighed. "Continue your story."

"Yeah, so the exterior had a baroque makeover like most of the streets around here but the interior was special. There was this courtyard where we uncovered the foundations of the original floor plan. We guessed that around that central garden had once been large windows or doors opening onto the light like some kind of portico. Maybe that doesn't sound unusual now but for Renaissance Florence it would have been. I thought maybe it could have been a painting studio or a workshop."

"You thought you'd found an artist's studio?"

"I thought we'd found Botticelli's studio but we had to prove it before those developers turned the place into some glorified Holiday Inn. Nobody believed me. I was only a student assistant. The head archaeologist said he already suspected that Botticelli had his studio a couple of buildings down, that site now renovated beyond recognition, and said I was following some romantic notion. He said to think like a scientist not a dreamer. Big ego."

"Yours or his?"

She was so animated by now that she didn't catch my sarcasm or notice when I flicked on the bedside lamp. Straight dark blond hair hanging in strings to her shoulders, lean heart-shaped face, bright blue eyes, a bit haggard-looking overall. Time had not been kind to her.

"But I was driven. I began to research the streets and original maps of the area on my own. My dad had access to a secret private library of one of his friends whose family had managed to obtain part of the Medici holdings long ago—don't ask me how. Nobody asks how those things happen in Italy. Dad even helped me read the texts. He had a good handle on Latin and old Tuscan. We determined that the site could have belonged to Botticelli's father, Mariano di Vanni d'Amedeo Filipepi, who by then ran a goldsmithing business in the area. If it was not his. then it certainly belonged to an artist of some kind."

"'We' meaning you and your dad?"

"'We' meaning me and my conniving snake of a boyfriend. I haven't mentioned him yet but he's important so listen up. He was also an archaeology student on work experience from another university. A bit younger, sexy, really good-looking. He acted as if I were his dream girl and followed me everywhere calling me his little 'Simonetta.'"

I almost snorted. "Simonetta as in Botticelli's supposed muse? The wife of Vespucci, who the artist reportedly based many of his most famous works on, including *Primavera* and *The Birth of Venus?*"

"Don't laugh. It was a while ago, okay? I had long blond hair then—lightened, maybe, but blond. I could have passed as Simonetta. Maybe. On a good day. In the right light," she added. By now the gun was lying forgotten on the bedcovers.

"Simonetta was actually already dead when those paintings supposedly featuring her face were painted. It's doubtful Botticelli had ever met her in person since they traveled in different social circles and even more unlikely that she ever posed for him—damn impossible actually. He painted his image of an ideal woman."

"Yeah, yeah. The point is, I was suckered. Forget the Simonetta part."

"Okay, so this charmer woos you by calling you after a famous Renaissance beauty and wiggles his way into your confidence while you research possible locations for a hidden masterpiece. You did all the legwork while he just followed you around. Am I getting the drift?"

She dropped her head and stared at me from under her brows, half chagrin, half defiance. "I'm not the first woman to get screwed by a handsome archaeologist, though, am I?"

Okay, so she knew my story. "You're not," I agreed. "Men like that should come with a warning label. So, what happened next?"

But something had changed in her bearing, dulling her enthusiasm

—*shame*. It hit so hard it may as well be my own. "So this guy followed me around, sharing my excitement every step of the way, telling me how brilliant as well as beautiful I was."

"Bastard. I mean, you probably were beautiful—still are in all the ways that count. Do we need a man to define us?—but he was just using you."

"And you know how that feels, don't you? So when I found what I was sure was a false wall, he suggested that we break into the site after-hours and do some investigating on our own. The head archaeologist wouldn't let us touch it because the stone bit was the one authentic part the owners wanted to preserve. Besides, student assistants don't get to make those kind of suggestions."

"Don't tell me you actually went in after-hours and illegally knocked a hole in the wall?"

"We did."

"Probably not the best idea."

"Stupid, ill-advised, professionally suicidal, you mean? Had I done this properly, launched a scholarly case based on the documents we'd found the way my dad suggested, and convinced all the powers that be that there was something worth investigating behind that wall, I wouldn't be where I am today, which is nowhere. Instead, I followed my handsome, sexy boyfriend's lead and broke into the dig site after-hours. We poked a hole in the wall, which caused that whole interior wall to collapse, by the way, but I was right: there was a hidden alcove behind there and, better yet, I found a leather cylinder, which contained what I knew to be a genuine sketch from the Renaissance."

"Oh, my God! *You* did find it!"

"I did but fat lot of good that did because the slimy boyfriend promptly disappeared with the sketch and left me standing in the rubble—literally."

I gazed at her in outrage. "This scumball stole your find and left you with the debris?"

"And got me expelled, landed me with vandalism charges, kicked out of Italy, and my poor dad shamed forever. But what's worse, nobody believed me when I said I'd found a canister containing a possible Botticelli sketch. Nobody believed me about my boyfriend, either. I became a vandal and a liar."

"Did you actually see the sketch?"

"Briefly."

"And what about the boyfriend?"

"Gone. Took off with the sketch and left me to take the heat."

"How in hell did that happen?"

"He convinced me that he could protect it better than I could. Said that my dad might get suspicious if I brought it home but to let him guard it overnight, that he had a friend who could help attribute it. Then he bolted."

"Didn't the powers that be think his sudden absence suspicious?"

"Apparently he'd spread the word that he was flying home the next day. I was the only one who didn't know. That bastard was crafty."

"So, did you eventually catch up with him, bring him to his knees, make him pay for his deceitful use-and-abuse tactics?"

"Like you did in Morocco, you mean? I wish I had but no."

"So who the hell was this bastard, anyway?" I demanded.

She choked back a bitter laugh. "Still don't get it, do you, Phoebe? Haven't figured it out yet. No magical bolts to make it all come together, either. And you call yourself a sleuth. Let me help fill in the blanks: the archaeologist was on a work term from the University of Queensland and he went by the name of Noel. Ring any bells?"

6

Consider that my second ambush in twenty-four hours. I stared. "You're not serious?"

"Not serious that Noel Halloren—he was going by Noel Baker then—stole my sketch and left me in that mess or not serious because we have the same bad taste in men?"

"*Had*. His type doesn't appeal to me anymore."

"What, the good-looking, sexy archaeologist type?"

"No, the criminal, conniving bastard type. And I'm not shocked that Noel did any of those things but I didn't realize he had started his criminal career so young. When was this, the `90s?"

"1996."

"That was before I knew him and I didn't realize that he had ever done a stint in Florence."

"Why would you? He was a criminal. He wasn't about to tell all the girls he screwed what he had been up to. The point is to use them to help him feed his art heist habit, right? That's what he did to you. Anyway, I want my reputation back. I want the credit I deserve for locating that sketch and more."

"Minus the wall-kicking bit?"

"I was young and easily led. Who are you to judge?"

"I'm not judging, I'm looking at this dispassionately from a legal point of view. You were still implicated for your part in the break-in. That's the equivalent of theft, any way you look at it."

"I expected more sympathy from you, Phoebe McCabe."

"Look, I'm sorry that Noel did a number on you, but even if he hadn't snatched it, that sketch still wouldn't be yours. Italy is touchy about ownership of masterpieces found on Italian soil. There would have been tribunals, legal tie-ups, and maybe still will be, should the owners of that building enter the fray."

"The building has changed hands twice since then. It now belongs to a conglomerate but I'm not after the sketch so I can hang it on my wall. I want credit for my archaeological sleuthing and to blame the real thief so I can get on with my life. I want redemption. Noel has now been outed as a notorious art thief, which works in my favor. Even dead—and thanks for that, by the way—he can be useful in clearing my name with your help."

I might have mentioned that Noel might not be as dead as she'd hoped if she hadn't kept barreling along. "I was two months away from getting my degree. I should be suitably affiliated with a university by now, taking my students out for summer digs and living comfortably on tenure. Instead, I live hand to mouth with a résumé so blotched I can't expose it to the light of day. Really, the sketch isn't the important part. I need to pick up where I left off and find that painting to redeem myself."

"What painting?"

"There's a painting based on that sketch somewhere—a Botticelli. You know it and I know it."

"But how do you know it?

"I just do."

"Not good enough."

"You're going to help me find it."

"And why would I do that? You've hardly endeared yourself to me so far."

"Because you need me. I have access to original letters and papers that could lead us to that Botticelli portrait. Well, *did* have. That friend of my dad's who obtained part of the Medici library is dead now but his son might remember me, which might not be a good thing. You, on the other hand— Phoebe McCabe, the famous art sleuth—could get in to see that collection and pick up where I left off. I'll just point you in the right direction and together we'll find that Botticelli."

"Just like that?"

"I don't expect it to be easy but since when did that bother you? I've kept up with your illustrious career and it's made me jealous as hell—just saying. Now I want some of your stardust, Phoebe McCabe. You owe me."

"How do I owe you?" I demanded.

"Because if your brother and that ass we both loved hadn't kept that sketch hidden for all these years, this whole sorry tale might be out in the open by now. Once it hit the market, its existence would prove that, first, the sketch existed like I said it did and, second, that I didn't steal it, he did, see?"

"Your reasoning is flawed and I'm not responsible for their misdeeds, in any case."

"Maybe not, but if you had tipped off Interpol when your bro and lover were stealing art, they would have been behind bars long ago."

"I thought they were stealing back stolen art to return to their owners. I was hoodwinked, too. Anyway, why all this now?"

"I'm getting to that. Do you want to find that Botticelli or not? I know things you don't; I have the inside scoop you don't. Oh, and I also know who the gang is who jumped you last night and who they work for. That might just keep you alive long enough to hit your next viral news clip—with me by your side. 'Suzanna Masters and the Agency of the Ancient Lost and Found Locates Lost Portrait of Alessandro di Mariano di Vanni Filipepi, aka Botticelli.' Get it?"

"That's too long for a headline."

"You're going to help me, I said." She was shouting now. Picking up the gun again, she aimed it at me but the door flew open and Seraphina launched into the room pointing a pistol straight at her.

"You I shoot!" she cried.

"Don't!" I flung back the covers and leaped out of bed. "We need her! Put the gun down."

"Move," Seraphina said while trying to lean past me.

Zann was on her feet, too, gun aimed at Seraphina. Had I not kept shifting back and forth trying to block one from the other, somebody might have been shot, maybe me.

And I was at the end of my last nerve. "Put the guns away, both of you," I ordered. "Seraphina, this is Zann Masters. She did not mean to hit you so hard yesterday. She was only trying to get our attention." I was winging it. "She's sorry about the concussion, aren't you, Zann?"

Zann stood legs braced, both hands on her pistol barrel, glaring.

"I said aren't you?" I demanded. "You're going to be working with us so of course you weren't intending to inflict bodily harm on one of your future colleagues."

Zann hesitated, then lowered the gun. "No, of course not. Sorry, Seraphina. I didn't mean to hit you so hard. I thought I used my plastic water bottle but grabbed my thermos by mistake. Gun's not loaded—no bullets, see?"

Seraphina didn't appear convinced and I didn't blame her but luckily Nicolina had just arrived. Holding her forehead and trying to take in the scene she asked: *"Cosa sta succedendo?"*

"Nicolina, tell Seraphina to put away the gun. Just a bit of a misunderstanding here. Meet Suzanna Masters. She's going to help us. She found the sketch originally and has valuable information we need."

Nicolina stifled a yawn and gazed from Seraphina to Zann. "You are Ms. Vecchio?"

Zann stared. "Ms. Vecchio?"

Nicolina stared back at her in a somewhat unfocused fashion.

"Yes, this is Ms. Vecchio," I said. "She has a very interesting story to tell, which you need to hear."

Nicolina lowered Seraphina's arm. "Then we must hear it. Seraphina, order breakfast for five. Add extra espresso. Meet in my rooms in an hour. Why I am so sleepy? I did not drink so much wine." Turning, she swayed toward her room at the end of the hall, her silk dressing gown flowing open.

Seraphina shot us a fierce look before traipsing after her employer, gun now safely holstered.

Facing Zann seconds later, I said: "You'd better be on your best behavior over breakfast or I can't guarantee your safety. You have a lot of convincing to do. Pass me your gun." She did as I asked. As she claimed, the thing wasn't loaded.

After Zann returned to her room, which turned out to be right next to

Peaches's two doors down from mine, I quickly showered, dressed, and took off looking for an early jolt of coffee. It was only six a.m.

Our exclusive hotel had thoughtfully set up a buffet on a carved round table that centered the marble foyer. Sunlight beamed in through the garden doors as a few early risers read their papers or tablets in the seating areas. One guy peered at me from behind his tablet—middle-aged, jeans, T-shirt, thin graying hair with a bad comb-over. Too curious to be a tourist. He was on surveillance. I pretended not to notice him.

A uniformed woman darted by asking in English if I needed help. Somehow they just knew a guest's nationality.

"Coffee?" I never let on that I understood rudimentary Italian. Remaining the obtuse foreigner could be so useful sometimes.

Smiling, she led me to a round central table ladened with a towering summer flower arrangement and indicated the selection of coffees, teas, sweet buns, coronettos, and croissants. "Americano? Cappuccino?" she asked. "I make for you."

"This is fine, thanks."

Nodding, she left me to it and I circumnavigated the central bouquet until I located a silver carafe of coffee and paper cups, perfect for travelers on the go. After filling two cups, I briefly I took a moment to inhale the roses, lilies, and unknown yellow sprigs, peering through the foliage at the guy who still stared in my direction. Right, so you're on a stakeout, buddy. Meanwhile, back to business.

On the way back up the elevator, it occurred to me that nothing about this hotel or Florence itself was safe despite its beguiling luxury and riches. I needed to stop acting as though stepping back into this beloved city had somehow transported me to my carefree student days. I'd never be carefree again. Somebody would always be after me for something. And as hard as it was to accept, I also had to face the truth that the previous exploits of the Noel and Toby crime duo had put my colleagues and me into the crosshairs once again.

But Toby would never knowingly risk my life now, of that I was convinced. What he did in his drug-addled days was different and, admittedly, he thought he could work me into the family business at one time. Something was going on here that he knew enough about to try and warn me away from but what? Something in his and Noel's past—again. And to think that another woman had fallen hard the way I had and suffered the consequences the way I had only helped to stir up suppressed memories. Would I ever be free of Noel's legacy?

Arriving at Peaches's door, I knocked several times with no response. Next, I called her on her smartphone, using one of the alarm features Evan had set up among the five agency members. Moments later, a befuddled Peaches arrived at the door.

I picked up the coffee I had sat on the floor. "Drink. We have a breakfast meeting."

"Huh?"

"Coffee, you need coffee, I said."

"Is it, uh, fair trade, sustainably sourced?" she mumbled.

I sighed. "You've been drugged. You need a double dose of caffeine to knock your brain back in line. Forget the bean pedigree."

She stared at the cup. "Drugged?"

I gently backed her up into her room and explained the whole Zann story while plying her with double doses of caffeine. While she showered, I went to the lobby and brought up refills. By then, she was fully cognizant.

"And we're seriously going to let that woman work with us?" she demanded, striding the room in her camisole and panties.

"She found the sketch originally," I said, thinking that, hell, she actually dresses in boudoir-style undies and that maybe I'd better up my game in the lingerie department. Not that I expected any romance anytime soon. "She's deep into this mess and has information we need. We don't have to trust her, but we still need her."

She turned to stare at me, hands on hips. "And she seriously knew Noel?"

"A younger, equally snaky version but apparently yes."

"Does that mean he's back to haunt us?"

"I doubt he's directly involved here. Remember that his health isn't the best yet. Toby said he has a bad heart—poetic justice, everyone says."

"Since you tasered him right over his ticker, that's justice all right. Don't know about the poetic bit."

"I'm just saying that we're dealing with the dregs of one of his past exploits here, that's all. I'm guessing that Noel tried to locate the painting but couldn't. Maybe he ditched Zann too soon, before he discovered that she might hold more clues. My theory is that someone found out about the sketch from Toby in prison. Either he mentioned something to an inmate who mentioned it to someone else or something of that ilk. They are all criminals in there so who knows? But that's where this started. Now we have to find out where it ends. Let's go have breakfast and grill Zann until she's crispy."

We entered Nicolina's rooms about twenty minutes later. I thought that my quarters were luxurious but Nicolina had a whole suite with a living area and adjoining room for Seraphina, plus a balcony. Breakfast had been set up by the open double French doors on a table set with a fine Italian woven tablecloth with matching summery green linen napkins. A server hovered nearby until Nicolina sent her away with no doubt a substantial gratuity.

"Explain why we should trust you?" she asked Zann as she lowered herself into a chair and smoothed a napkin over the lap of her lacy summer shift.

Meanwhile, Zann plopped into the chair opposite. "And why should I trust *you*?"

"Why? Because you are still alive, yes? Now you must explain everything. First, who are you, really?" Nicolina sipped her third minicup of espresso.

"I told you," Zann said while helping herself to boiled eggs and slices of ham and cheese.

"You are holding back," Nicolina insisted. "You say you know where we find the Botticelli?"

"I said that I know where to look."

"That is not the same," Nicolina pointed out.

"So who are those dudes that jumped Phoebe? Phoebe said you knew," Peaches interrupted while buttering her croissant. Seraphina sat across from her in wary silence.

"They belong to an arms cartel," Zann said. "As in very-bad-men arms cartel."

Nicolina froze, suddenly alert. "Arms cartel? Which one—Milan or Naples?"

"Does it matter?" I asked.

"Yes," Nicolina said. "It matters very much. One is worse."

"You mean arms dealers are measured by degree?" I asked in alarm.

"Bad ones and not as bad ones, yes," Nicolina explained. "Two main organizations operate in Italy with connections to Syria, Russia, and Yemen. Both finance operations through art theft and drugs. Italy is important in the race to finance arms with stolen art." She stared at Zann. "Which one—Naples or Milan?"

Zann's gaze remained focused on her plate. "Milan. The branch run by Alesso Baldi."

"Baldi!" Nicolina jolted in her seat. "This is very bad."

"Who's Baldi?" I asked.

But Nicolina was fixed on Zann. "What do you know of this man and how does he know about the Botticelli?"

Zann slowly lifted her gaze. "He's going on a lead coming out of Canada. He's got informants everywhere, including the prison where Phoebe's brother's held. Says that he has ears in every prison. Knows that I found a Botticelli sketch decades ago, that Halloran stole it, and that it's on the move again. Somebody alerted him that a priceless masterpiece related to that sketch may be hidden somewhere."

"How do you know this?" Seraphina demanded.

"Because I used to work for him."

"When?"

"Two days ago."

"What?" That was me but each of my colleagues issued a cry or expletive of her own.

"You worked for a bloody arms dealer?" Peaches cried.

"I didn't know he was an arms dealer when he hired me, okay?" Zann protested. "I needed a job and this guy was hiring archaeologists, didn't care if they had their degrees yet or not. Wanted us to dig around Roman remains on the edge of Turkey, on the borders of Afghanistan, places like that. The pay was great and he finagled me a visa into Italy under a false identity."

"And you weren't the least bit suspicious that these might be illegal digs?" I asked.

"Sure, I knew these were illegal digs but you wouldn't believe what goes on in different parts of the world. The tomb robbers in these places are desperate. They steal from the dead to feed the living. The lives of their kids are on the line, okay? Once you see how war savages civilians, you don't judge so easily. Baldi may be paying them pennies for these plundered treasures but those pennies keep them alive. Who are we to judge when people are that desperate? Anyway, I didn't do much of the digging myself, just oversaw the sites, verified them, that sort of thing."

"I'm not judging the tomb robbers but you! What's *your* excuse?" I was outraged.

"Get off your high horse, the lot of you. You've all done questionable things at one time or another. Think I don't know your backgrounds? Do you want to hear the details or not?"

"Continue." That was Nicolina. I sat back and simmered.

"So, like I said, I started working for him until I found my ticket out. You might say I resigned. Now I work against him."

Nicolina was on her feet now. She flung down her napkin. "You do not stop work for Baldi and you do not just resign. He kills you if you try. You lie!"

"There's more to the story," Zann said, looking up. "If you all just calm down, I'll tell you. You're right: I couldn't just hand in my resignation. He still thinks I work for him but I don't. He knows nothing about the secret letters. He hasn't a clue that I know so much about the Botticelli or that I ever did. He thinks I just found the sketch and that Noel hoodwinked me —poor, stupid wronged woman that I am. That's how I started working for him in the first place. He tracked me down based on a newspaper article years ago."

"Wait a minute." I held up my hand. "He knows that you found the sketch but thinks you know nothing about it? Oh, come on."

"He knows I believe that a painting exists somewhere but thinks I'm as clueless about the whereabouts as he is. Thinks Noel got away with the sketch, which he did, but knows that he never found the painting. Word got out somehow that your brother and ex had information about where the portrait might be but never followed it up. Maybe they had nothing to go on, is my guess. Meanwhile, Baldi's got the scoop on every one of you," she said, turning to me. "He thinks you may know something. Thinks Toby sent a clue to Phoebe. Wants me to worm my way into the agency's confidence and find out what."

It sounded so likely that I believed her. "And?"

"And it looks like I'm obeying his orders, doesn't it? Here I am infiltrating the Agency of the Ancient Lost and Found so the great Phoebe McCabe can lead Baldi to the Botticelli. Only, it's really the other way around. That's the beauty of my plan because I'll be the one leading you to the painting."

Peaches snorted. "Are you trying to say you're acting like some kind of double agent?"

"That's exactly what I'm saying. It will work, too, providing Baldi doesn't try to force you to tell him what he thinks you know like he did last night. Or kill me first, which is a distinct possibility. He's a very impatient guy."

"And you really expect us to trust you now?" Peaches asked.

"Let me just shoot her," Seraphina said.

"I'm telling the truth!" she protested. "Look, do you really think I'd tell you I was working for Baldi otherwise? And do you think I would just hand over my find—when I find it—to the likes of him?"

"How would we know what you would or would not do?" I said. "You have zero credibility with us. And keep your voices down, everybody."

Zann jumped to her feet. Now we were all standing facing one another, arguing over the breakfast table as Seraphina shut the balcony doors. "Think what you want about me, but I'm not after money or worldly goods. I want redemption. That's what this is about for me. I want my dad to see my name across the papers for something good just once before he dies." She paused as if trying to wrestle some emotion back in line.

"What does your dad have to do with anything?" Peaches asked.

Zann met her gaze. "My dad is ninety-five years old, in failing health, but still good. I want him to know that his daughter has amounted to something before he passes. I've hurt him so much—Mom, too, but she died years ago. I don't want him to die with that image of his only child, that picture the papers posted of me standing with the Italian police after the robbery." Her voiced cracked.

Seraphina slid her tablet onto the table. "This one? I look up article. There."

Peaches picked it up and peered at the photograph of an old black and white newspaper article—a lone young woman between two Italian officers looking frightened and confused.

"That's Simonetta busted, I take it?" I asked, and she did kind of look like some of those paintings—the hair caught in an artful tangle of scarves.

"That's Simonetta busted. And I want to undo all that shit that went down. If I follow those leads and find that Botticelli, I'll get acclaim for rescuing a hidden masterpiece against the likes of Baldi. That's all I want—credit—with the story hitting the media the way your Spanish crown event did last fall. If it hits CNN and the BBC, better yet. The portrait can go to a museum after that, I don't care. But I can't do this alone."

We all stood in silence for a moment trying to absorb these multiple bombs she'd dropped. It was Nicolina who spoke first. "Why would we help you? Why would we not find this portrait on our own?"

"Because you need me. You won't find it on your own. I have something no one else does."

"Prove it," Peaches demanded.

"Here." Zann reached into her laptop case but Seraphina whipped out her gun before she could move an inch farther.

"Let her show us what she has," I said, peering down into Zann's bag. "That's not a gun she's fetching."

Seraphina agreed with a jerk of her head and slowly Zann pulled out a plastic sheathed paper.

"Nobody knows about this—not Baldi, not Noel, nobody," she whispered. "It's a letter I found among my father's friend's secret Medici papers long ago. There were more but I never got back to study them before I was kicked out of Italy. I filched this, planned to bring it back but never got the chance."

Carefully she moved the basket of buns to one side and placed the letter on the table. "It's in old Tuscan. Want me to translate?"

"I read old Tuscan," Nicolina said, picking up the page and holding it carefully in long elegant fingers. Leaning over her shoulder, I could barely make out the blotchy script on the yellowed paper. Age had eaten through the parchment in places and foxed the surface everywhere else.

"It's written in Botticelli's hand, we think. My dad had it authenticated," Zann said.

"You tell them what it says and I see if you speak the truth," Nicolina ordered, and began reading.

"I know it verbatim. I'd always planned to make my way back here and finish what I've started. You are the first to see it after my dad and me," Zann said. "It was our secret. It says:

IN THE YEAR OF OUR LORD, FEBRUARY 7TH, 1497

DEAREST GABRIELA,

BEAUTY BURNS IN THE STREETS OF FLORENCE THIS NIGHT AND EVEN THE moon cannot hide our sins against God. Was our love of beauty truly a sin? I thought not when I lifted my goddesses from the seas and set my muses to dance in the forests of the ancients but I know that you danced in God's light, too. Have we transcribed our souls to immortal ruin? The preacher says I will be forgiven because I have confessed but I fear you will perish. You say creating beauty is not a sin but a benediction of all that is love and light. I wish only happiness for you both but would that I had your courage.

Time runs quickly through the glass. I must make haste. I will hide your painting and hope that you can follow the path to where it lays protected. Consider this my gift to you. May God forgive me but I could not send it to the flames this night, though I watched many of my paintings burn as did your much softer art. They shriveled and died before my eyes as if they were pieces of the man I once was or a soul consigned to the flames of Hell..

Tonight my very heart lay in cinders. Ash to ash, dust to dust.

Sandro

WHEN SHE FINISHED, WE STOOD IN SILENCE.

"And you are convinced this is authentic?" I asked.

Zann nodded. "As much as one can be given that this letter is, like, over five hundred years old. We had it carbon dated and the parchment is circa late 1400s. The writing matches an authenticated piece of Botticelli's. Plus, how many Sandros lifted 'goddesses from the seas and set muses to dance in the forests of the ancients'? And the references to the Bonfire of the Vanities is pretty obvious."

The art historian side of me kicked in. "Botticelli was one of the first masters of the Renaissance to be so influenced by the renewed passion of the ancient classics that he painted his extraordinary mythological allegories like *The Birth of Venus* and *Primavera*," I said. "There were many more masterpieces either lost or burned at the instigation of Savonarola. I can't bear to think what the world has lost. But who was Gabriela?"

"We thought that he must be writing to a lover—we being Dad and me—and that Gabriela might even be the sitter of our sketch since that was hidden, too. Because of their illicit relationship, the drawing and the painting had to be kept secret."

"Yeah, that makes sense. For all we know, Botticelli may have had many lovers." Peaches took the letter out of my hands.

"He would not be the first," Nicolina remarked.

"And yet from all accounts Botticelli was not drawn to women sexually but was likely homosexual. He adored the vision of the perfect sacred feminine and it was this he was trying to capture. He's like the ideal humanist."

"But how do we know, really?" Zann asked.

"True." But I was still fixed on the context. "'Beauty burns in the streets of Florence...' That has to be a reference to the Bonfire of the Vanities. It's the same date—1497," I said. "What provenance!"

"I say Gabriela was secret lover. Why else need to hide portrait?" Seraphina pointed out, finally engaged in the mystery.

"Perhaps because she was married," Nicolina said, "though this is not usually a problem."

"It would have been a problem for a married noblewoman to be involved with a painter in Renaissance Florence," I remarked. "But the identity of this woman remains unknown and if this letter refers to the sitter of our portrait, she wore a noble dress but did not look part of the nobility."

"But there has always been this story that Botticelli and Simonetta Vespucci were lovers and this certainly isn't Simonetta," Zann said. "I always liked that tale. Simonetta was supposedly his muse and posed for all those gorgeous mythological allegory paintings. He even requested that he be buried at her feet."

I turned to her. "This was the age of courtly love, remember. Men literally acted as standard bearers to noble beauties of the day. Lorenzo de' Medici bore a standard for Simonetta during the tournament held for his wedding feast to Clarice Orsini while his bride looked on. That didn't mean that he was in a relationship with Simonetta. His brother may have been but that's another story."

"Maybe," Zann acknowledged.

"Most scholars agree that it's doubtful that the painter ever met Simonetta let alone posed for him," I pointed out. "The Ognissanti was their community church. Maybe he wanted to be buried at the feet of beauty, symbolically speaking. The Renaissance thought like that—in symbols and allegories. She died young and that almost guaranteed that a beautiful woman would be immortalized for eternity."

"Like Marilyn Monroe," Peaches remarked. "Doesn't tend to work that way for black women, though, just saying."

"I still like the Botticelli/Simonetta version best." Zann shrugged. "Where's your sense of romance, Phoebe McCabe?"

I looked over at her. "Missing in action—took a direct hit. Anyway, Botticelli would already have been in his late fifties when this was written, if indeed he wrote it at all. It's said that after Lorenzo the Magnificent died in 1492, Savonarola's religious fervor took hold in Florence. Sandro himself became caught up in the friar's fiery oration and stumbled around Florence disconsolate. He must have stood by while his patrons threw his life's work into the flames, watching his masterpieces 'shrivel and die' as he says here and also supposedly added a few to the flames himself."

"What pieces survived were either protected by powerful patrons or hidden," Nicolina said.

"Or smuggled to country estates or other cities," Zann added. "These were the days of city states, remember."

"After that, his art returned to being more devotional." I studied the plastic-encased page. "Maybe this Gabriela was a secret love or maybe she was something else. Botticelli writes that she created 'a much softer art.'"

"Lovemaking is a much softer art," Peaches pointed out.

"And there would have been courtesans and sex workers in the streets of Florence," Zann remarked.

"Maybe, but I don't think so," I mused.

"Should we ask Giovanni to check with his posse of experts for any historical references to our Gabriela and show him this letter?" Peaches asked, gazing down over my shoulder.

"No," Zann said, swinging around. "Nobody can know about this and I mean nobody. Just knowing these letters exist can get us all killed."

"How would letters get us killed?" Peaches asked.

"Think, Peaches. This letter—and there are others—are the only lead we have for the secret Botticelli portrait. I've kept this one hidden from everyone, from Noel to Baldi—my insurance policy, the key to my redemption—for nearly three decades." Zann paused to gaze up at Peaches.

"Continue," Seraphina prompted.

"So, like, I knew that the moment I let it see the light of day, it could set a chain of events going that could destroy everyone," Zann said. "But we have to keep that from happening. Baldi would literally kill to get his hands on this and others like it. He's killed for far less, believe me. We have to get to the other letters to see if they will lead us to that painting without Baldi knowing, see?"

"What other letters?" Peaches and Seraphina said in unison.

"I said there were more. Weren't you listening? I said that my father's friend had a part of Lorenzo the Magnificent's library. Kept it hidden away. Clearly obtained illegally, probably by one of his ancestors, that's my guess. I didn't get to read them all."

"And your father's friend didn't notice when you stole this one?" Peaches asked.

"We're not sure. If he did, he never said anything. Signore Corsi and Dad remained friends and wrote to one another periodically after Dad returned home to New York, right up until Signore Corsi died in 2016, in fact."

"Did Signore Corsi not have his collection, um...organized?" Nicolina asked.

"Cataloged?" Peaches suggested.

"Cataloged, yes. Did Signore Corsi not have them cataloged?"

"Of course. Look," Zann said, carefully removing the page from Peaches's fingers and replacing it into her laptop case "The Corsis have the most significant collection of Medici artifacts outside of the Laurentian Library and museums, okay? An entire room has been set up in their estate to be a close proximity to what Lorenzo de' Medici's own library must have looked like circa 1460."

"Wow," I said under my breath, imagining the wealth of knowledge such a collection must contain.

"Any idea of the value of what a collection of classical Greek manuscripts scribed from monasteries all over Europe plus letters in the Medici's own hand would be? It might rival that of a Botticelli in net worth." Zann continued. "Signore Corsi was a passionate collector. Somehow he got his hands on things that he would rather not be brought to the attention of anyone but his most trusted friends—hundreds, if not thousands, of items. Priceless items on top of those he inherited. Getting my drift?"

"Got it," Peaches said.

"Signore Corsi himself was no thief but a gentleman who loved history with a passion but anything Medici was his weakness. My point is that one missing letter was not worth the family lodging a complaint that might reveal the extent of the family secret. And certainly Corsi wasn't about to mention anything to my dad either in print or by phone, was he?"

"All right, I get the picture," I said, studying her carefully. This woman was like an onion revealing herself layer after layer. What secret would she peel away next? "So where is this priceless collection kept and is it still intact?"

"I know where it was when I last saw it—in a fourteenth-century villa in the countryside that is currently run as a vinery-cum-bed-and-breakfast. Been in the family for generations. It still belongs to the Corsi family. I checked it out. The son and his wife run it now—Piero and Alexandra Corsi, with their two young sons."

"And you think the collection may still be there?" Peaches asked.

"I doubt Piero would have sold it as long as the vineyard keeps producing the Chianti Classico for which it is known. Plus, I remembered that he shared his father's passion for all things Medici. I'm betting the collection is still locked in the tower room where I saw it decades ago, still locked behind a false wall."

"So what are we supposed to do, just ring him up and ask to see it?" Peaches asked.

Zann rolled her eyes. "If only it would be that easy. So Piero knows me—we had a fling before Noel came between us. I supposedly broke Piero's heart, or so he said. But he obviously knows what I did to get thrown out of Italy. Who knows how he'd react to seeing me now?"

"I can just imagine. I wouldn't want to see you again, if I were him. Not sure I want to see you now," Peaches remarked.

"Peaches, you hurt my feelings," Zann said with a smile. "Point is, I can't just contact him and request a viewing of his secret library, especially not in the company of the Agency of the Ancient Lost and Found. You guys are all about returning stolen items to their original owners, right? That's bound to make him edgy if these things were stolen. No, have to be a hell of a lot more strategic than that."

"I know this is going somewhere. Could we just speed it up?" I asked. Really, I wasn't the patient sort. "I presume you're saying that we can't just drop by to request a viewing? Would it help if I swore upon all the swear-worthy things to ensure him that the agency is not interested in repatriating that priceless library of his? I'll quote a grandfather clause or something." But in my heart of hearts, I'd love to restore that collection to the people of Florence, the world.

"That wouldn't help," she said. "If we go anywhere near that family, it will bring Baldi bearing down on the Corsis, because if Baldi even suspects what the Corsis own those letters, that library—"

"They come in, steal collection, kill everybody, and burn villa to ground," said Seraphina.

"Always the jolly one of the bunch, aren't you?" Peaches said, glaring at her.

"But she's right," Zann said. "That's exactly Baldi's style, being a big supporter of the scorched earth policy. Roman generals are his heroes, by the way. Runs his operation like an emperor. Wears a gold medallion of Lucius Cornelius Sulla. Even quotes Roman emperors. The point is we can't go anywhere near the Corsis." She turned a shrewd eye to me. "At least not as ourselves."

7

I knew I wouldn't like what was coming next and I was right. Zann revealed an elaborate plan to digest over breakfast, most of it hard to swallow. However, she delivered it with such aplomb that we couldn't help but be impressed.

"Like I said, we can't just drive up to the Corsi estate," she said while busily cracking another egg. We were all back to sitting by then, trying to pull our group together with this new collaborator. "And we can't all travel together, either. Baldi is watching this hotel, has eyes everywhere."

"I think I saw a pair of those eyes downstairs," I remarked, watching her. Compared to our first encounter in my room, she seemed much more animated, as if her dream was all going according to plan.

"Angelo. He's been assigned to watch you now that you decommissioned Luigi and Carlo but he's no professional—probably forced to work for Baldi. Baldi's got those as well as the lifers."

"You know these guys by name?" Peaches asked.

"Just the Florence contingent," she explained. "Big operation."

"I found bugs in our rooms," Seraphina remarked. "His?"

"Those would be Baldi's, yes," Zann told her.

"We find bugs all the time, most of them belonging to that one." Peaches thumbed toward Seraphina.

73

"I protect you!" Seraphina protested.

"Oh, just stop." Peaches waved her off. "Admit it, you've got issues."

Zann was gazing at me. "So, do you use one of the fabulous smartphones I heard about, one that Evan Barrows cobbles together? It sweeps for bugs, too?"

"Look," I said, my patience wearing thin, "can we get back to the topic? You were talking about the plan."

"Right, so anyway, Phoebe and I will go to the estate tomorrow afternoon."

"Why you and me?"

"Because we can stake out the place as a pair of curious guests with American accents. We'll be playing American tourists and they won't peg your accent as Canadian."

"Her accent isn't Canadian anymore. It's sort of a bastardized British Canadian hybrid," Peaches remarked.

"As if most Italians can sort that out. Unless you tell them otherwise, they'll think you're American. Anyway, today's Thursday, in case you haven't noticed," Zann remarked.

"Which is important how?" I asked.

"The Corsis' wine delivery van comes to this hotel every Friday afternoon to drop off cases of wine and collect the empties—regular as clockwork, very old school," she replied. "You and I will hide out in the van and get to the estate that way. Baldi's eyes will never see us leave. We should arrive six-ish."

"We will be in disguise, I presume?" I asked.

"Yes, but nothing too elaborate—wigs, standard tourist attire."

Her ingenuity was impressive but I didn't relish jostling to the country amid cases of clinking bottles. Still, we were letting her take the lead here so we listened as she continued to lay out the details.

"Nicolina, Seraphina, and Peaches, you have to arrive separately also in disguise," she added.

Peaches almost sputtered into her coffee. "Are you kidding me? How do you disguise a tall black Jamaican in rural Tuscany?"

Zann grinned. "I have that all worked out, too. We need to get you onto the grounds on the sly. This is the deal: every Friday night, the Corsi estate has a wine tasting event with food and entertainment. Very big-ticket item. They hold it on the grounds for guests and visitors alike—very chichi and popular among tourists. Look it up online. Anyway, I've been in touch with the caterers and musicians. Nicolina, I have you and Seraphina on as one of the servers with the Tasty Tuscan Tours catering company, and, Peaches, you're going as a backup singer with a string ensemble called Canto Cantina. They feature an opera singer but do the jazzy global fusion thing, too."

"But I can't sing!" Peaches protested.

"And I cannot serve!" said the countess. Maybe I only imagined the look of amusement on Seraphina's usually pinched expression.

"No matter," Zann said, holding Peaches's gaze. "I told them that we would double the fee charged to the Corsis if they permit this little subterfuge. I said that we know the family and that this is all just a bit of fun."

"And they believed you?" she asked.

"For a few thousand extra euros, they'd believe anything. You'll be given lots of leeway, too. Just pretend that you are part of the group and everything will be fine."

Nicolina appeared affronted but made no further protest.

"You must have been pretty sure that we'd agree," I said.

"Just hedging my bets. So, I'll provide the addresses of both companies —they are located near Montalcino—and I have ideas for getting you there unseen. Meanwhile, I'll be meeting Baldi later today with information that should send him off to Volterra tomorrow thinking that Phoebe's picked up a lead. With a little luck, his henchmen will be off on a wild-goose chase by the time we're on our way to the Corsis'."

"Why Volterra?" I asked.

"It's out of the way with plenty of long windy roads to get there. Easy to get a flat tire," she said. "Easy to keep ahead of a tail, too."

"This is nuts," Peaches said. "If Baldi finds out what you're up to, you'll be dead."

"I'll be dead, anyway, if we can't pull this off," she remarked. "It won't take him long to figure out that I'm going behind his back. We've got to get the info we need, get back to Florence, retrieve the painting—wherever it is—and hand it over to the authorities. Pictures taken, viral acclaim —done!"

"Easy!" Seraphina said, looking as if she'd love nothing better than a good brush with death.

Again, I was stuck on logistics. "So we end up on the Corsi estate and then what? Are you planning to have us jump out of a box and announce our presence?"

Zann shot me an *oh, come on* look. "No, Phoebe, we're going to pretend to stay overnight and reveal our true identities when alone with the family later that evening. The entertainment ends at eleven on the dot."

"I do not understand," said Nicolina. "This is a bed-and-breakfast, yes? There will be other guests. How will we be alone with the family?"

"Because," Zann said, turning toward her, "we will be the only guests there in the end. Six rooms are booked as of now by a family called Masters out of New York, supposedly arriving tomorrow night. The others will cancel unexpectedly."

"And you booked all the rooms, like, how long ago?" Peaches asked.

"Okay, so I hired a hacker to bug up their booking system and to send cancellation notifications to all the legit bookers. I'll put that on your bill, too. I used Dad's card to rebook us. He'll never notice. It's under his full name, Dr. Eric D. Masters, but he always went as David back in the day. You'll have to pay for the rooms, of course."

"You're kidding?" That was Peaches again. For some reason, she was getting hung up on the money part.

"Well, you don't expect me to pay for it, do you? I can't afford that kind of thing," Zann protested. "The agency has to pay for my room here, too, since I doubt Baldi will foot the bill once he discovers he's been tricked. You'll be paying for the bonuses for the musicians and the catering group, as well—all the cost of doing business. Look, I'm working for you, get it? You have financial resources, I don't."

I just stared unfocused at a tapestry on the opposite wall—French eighteenth century—my brain racing over details, possible hitches, and all the things that could and would go wrong while I simultaneously wondered where they purchased that textile. I had trouble laying my hands on good French tapestries these days.

Meanwhile, Nicolina lifted her hand as if anointing a speck of dust. "Not important. We will pick up the tab but you must deliver," she said.

"We will go and retrieve these letters and manuscripts, retrieve the Botticelli, and give them all to Florence."

"Wait," I said, snapping back to the moment. "We're not going to steal the Corsis' collection. We're only after the Botticelli. We'll take pictures of the relevant papers and that's it."

Nicolina fixed me with a cool gaze. "Phoebe, those Medici papers belong to Florence. Lorenzo the Magnificent's nephew left what remained of the library to Florence in 1523. They belong here." Nicolina knew her history, too.

"So how'd they get from Florence to Rome in the first place?" Peaches asked.

"The Medici family declined after Lorenzo's death—more like collapsed," Zann explained. "The year they were overthrown and their palace sacked, whatever survived was smuggled to Rome where it was protected by Lorenzo's son, who was pope at the time," Zann said. "The Medicis were big on family popes—good for business as well as the soul, apparently—but I agree with Phoebe. No matter how the Corsis ended up with part of the collection, that's not what we're going for. We're after the painting."

But Nicolina wasn't letting go. "The Medici library, it belongs to Florence," she insisted. "Pope Clement, Lorenzo's nephew, had Michelangelo design the building for the library next to the Duomo. They have a home. How did the Corsis obtain these manuscripts? Perhaps they are fake?"

"Not fake," Zann said. "Dad said that the family obtained most of the collection long ago, maybe even legally for the time. The Corsis are an old Tuscan family and Florence was in upheaval, remember? Looting was a thing. Otherwise, we don't know and we don't care. That's not what we're going for. Forget the Medici library. We're after the Botticelli letters."

"I agree, we're after information to lead us to the portrait, not to steal or retrieve that collection." However, it would be useful to know if the secret collection was authentic. How could I tell? "And, Nicolina, unless the agency wants to launch a long protracted court case, removing that collection without the Corsis' permission is stealing, period."

Nicolina looked away, neither agreeing or dissenting. Her lack of acceptance of what I considered to be my obvious solid reasoning was unsettling. As so often the case with repatriating priceless items, to some extent she was right but equally and legally all wrong.

But we were already moving on to working out the finer points of our next day's subterfuge. In the end, it was agreed that we would infiltrate the Corsi estate as described and convince Piero of the need to grant us access to the secret library. I had my arguments ready while Zann planned to launch a plea of her own. We could only hope that all the moving parts of this complex strategy went off without a hitch. As if that ever happened.

For the rest of the day, I was determined to remain fixed on research while Zann took off to contact Baldi with Seraphina tailing her.

"I will not take eyes off you one minute," Seraphina told her.

"Good luck with that. Baldi has a complex method for ensuring his meetings remain private."

"Does he track your phone?" Seraphina asked.

Zann hesitated. "Probably."

Seraphina held out her hand. "Give me phone."

"What will I use in the meantime?" she asked, passing over the Blackberry.

"Buy new one. Burner."

Zann turned to me. "Hear that? Expect a new phone to appear on your bill. Anyway." She turned back to Seraphina. "He anticipated that one of us would track me. May as well be you."

After breakfast, Zann paused at the door and remarked: "Oh, and I need a few hundred euros to pay off the decoys." She paused, turning. "Eight hundred ought to do it—two hundred for each decoy." She counted out the amounts on her fingers. "I'll put the car on Dad's card and we can settle up later."

"Decoys, car?" Peaches asked.

"Sure. How did you think we're going to draw Baldi out of town? I've got to locate a double for each of you in order to lure him off on a wild-goose chase to Volterra, I said. Baldi's guys will see the car and think it's you based on the tip I'll provide. Guaranteed they'll follow this decoy car tomorrow afternoon. He already knows that he can't just track your phones. He thinks Evan Barrows is a genius, by the way, but wants to knock him dead. Anyway, hopefully we'll get what we need from the Corsis and be back to Florence before Baldi figures what's up. Do you have cash?"

Nicolina left for her bedroom and returned with a bundle of crisp one-hundred-euro notes. "Here. Eight hundred euros. If more is needed, ask."

Zann folded the notes into her inside pocket. "Thanks. Pleasure doing business with you and all that. Oh, maybe you should keep this with you in case." She handed the plastic-covered letter to Nicolina. "And his guys might follow you around today but they won't try anything now that I'm supposedly a plant. Catch up with you later—say dinner at eight and we dine here for privacy's sake?"

We agreed and off she went, Seraphina in tow.

"Order me the ravioli with sage sauce and a side of insalata di mista," she called over her shoulder as she strode down the hall.

"So are we her assistants now? I don't believe this," Peaches said the moment the door shut. "It's like we've been strapped onto a roller coaster and given no power to put on the brakes until the thing crashes. Why are we trusting her?"

"We aren't," I said, "but she has the best lead to the possible missing Botticelli. How can we not go along for the ride?"

"She's a crook, hardwired at an early age, by the sounds of things. She can blame Noel all she wants but she knew what she was doing when she knocked a hole in that wall years ago," she insisted.

"True," I said, "but I believe her when she says that it's redemption she wants. That woman is twisting with guilt. Let her have a chance to regain a little self-esteem and set things right. Everybody makes mistakes. Look at me. For years I followed Noel around believing what I wanted to believe when the evidence was right before my eyes."

"But you're different," Peaches insisted.

"Am I? I was a woman blinded by love. Now I'm setting things right the same as Zann is. Let's give her a chance."

"I agree." Nicolina turned and swept back to the table to fetch her phone. "With Baldi involved, matters are very dangerous. She has the inside track. Still, we must prepare."

I watched her photograph the letter. Thinking it a good idea, I did the same. "By 'prepare' do you mean call in the boys for support? Evan tracks us on our phones so they already know we're here."

"Why don't we tell them what's going on?" Peaches said. "Now that we have an arms dealer involved, things just got a whole lot more complicated."

"We can call them the moment things go wrong. They are only hours away," Nicolina pointed out. "Let us leave them to enjoy their holidays for now."

"Yes, let's," I said. "They aren't that far away if we need them, as you said."

"Outvoted again," Peaches sighed. "So this is officially an all-woman's job, is it? So, what's a few arms dealers among friends, right?"

She had a point. We were treading into dangerous territory but, so far, I figured we could handle things without bringing in Evan and Rupert.

Nicolina excused herself and got ready to meet Giovanni at the Uffizi. "He called to say he has information," she told us.

※

THAT AFTERNOON, PEACHES AND I HAD AN APPOINTMENT AT THE Biblioteca Medicea Laurenziana or the Laurentian Library, as it was known. Designed by Michelangelo, the building housed the Medici holdings. Built in a cloister not far from the iconic Florence cathedral formally known as the Cathedral of Santa Maria del Fiore, I had yet to pay my respects. This would be my first visit to the Laurentian Library ever. How did I let that happen?

"You know that we're being followed," Peaches whispered as we threaded our way through the leather vendors who set up shop along the streets leading to the cathedral complex.

"Of course. Angelo?" I asked.

"Possibly. Never saw the guy myself. Short, well-dressed, thinning hair, and shifty-looking, bit of a hobbling gait?"

"Sounds like him. Which reminds me, we had no fallout from that incident last night—no police visits, nothing."

"I've heard that gangs like Baldi's have crews that can clean up a crime scene pretty fast."

That was a possibility. In any case, Angelo didn't worry me. His tail actually suited my purposes. Baldi would expect me to be researching a Botticelli painting so why not begin in an archive? After the Uffizi, a library holding contemporary Renaissance manuscripts would be a logical place to start. The key was to ensure that he didn't discover my true intentions.

Most of the priceless Medici manuscripts had now been digitized. There were approximately 11,000 in total including incunabula, papyri, and prints available for study on computer. Still, I carried this romantic notion of settling myself down in one of the booths designed by Michelangelo himself to view the venerable tomes with my own eyes. Old books held a certain magic of their own and are best served without a technological barrier, at least for my purposes. But this was the dreamer talking. In reality, I was seeking something much more concrete.

In the meantime, I had no intention of accessing the library in the company of a tour group and this wasn't the kind of place where you could just drop in. Instead, Nicolina had called ahead to request a private tour. Whether it was because of our reputations or Nicolina's string-pulling, we ended up booking with a registered guide named Francesca Abruzzi. "I hear she is very good," Nicolina said. "She will help you."

As Peaches and I approached the imposing long rectangular exterior of the library that afternoon, I marveled at what a contrast its gray stone made against the glowing white and green marble facade of the cathedral beyond. The building almost seemed unfinished by comparison, a stony break against the creamy glory of the cathedral.

We met Francesca on the steps. Short straight hair, a ready smile, crinkles at the corners of her eyes, and animated features, I liked her at once. "Come, I do not wish you to miss even a minute, Phoebe and Peaches," she said. "The next group begins in less than an hour and I must get you through the highlights before they arrive. The last group is ten minutes ahead. Let us enter through the main door."

Following her up the steps, I turned before entering to shoot a glance toward Angelo.

"He's there hiding behind a map pretending to listen in on a tour to the right," Peaches whispered.

"Maybe he'll learn something, the bastard," I said. "Do I see him wearing a sports jacket in this heat?"

"Looks that way. Let him sweat."

Scurrying after Francesca, we stepped into a tall marble vestibule and for a moment I was overcome. It was like standing at the bottom of a waterfall of smooth, flowing stone, the steps leading up to the reading room having been designed by the master to create the illusion of wonder. We could be gazing up at what looked to be the outside of an imposing classical building thousands of years ago.

"It reminds me of the library at Ephesus," Peaches whispered. "But different. Wow, I had no idea it would be so...majestic."

"Majestic, yes," Francesca said. "Michelangelo followed the classical rules. Florence was in the grip of a powerful rebirth that celebrated Greek and Roman literature and art."

"But he only followed the rules long enough to break them," Peaches said, scanning the structure with an engineer's eye.

"Yes, that is true!" Francesca laughed. "You believe you understand how it goes but then you see how he plays with the proportions. He breaks the rules." She waved her hands, her expression registering wonder, serious contemplation, and delight in quick succession. She was a woman for whom history never got old.

"Yes." Peaches nodded. "Look at those columns and pediments. It's so dramatic!"

While they enthused over the architecture, I carried on up the stairs, eager to take my first step into the ancient reading room above completely alone. Give me a few seconds to stand in this cathedral of knowledge, I thought, and feel the weight of centuries bearing down on upon my shoulders. History is best savored in the deep respect of solitude.

But the long empty reading room hit me in unexpected ways—walnut booths on either side, a high carved ceiling overhead, the mosaic floor warmed in reds and toasted golds, with tall windows illuminating all.

After the monumental drama of the vestibule, the reading room seemed almost welcoming by comparison but no less awe-inspiring. This was a holy hall of knowledge, books being one of the most valuable items you could own in Renaissance Europe—hand-scribed, illuminated with gold and precious pigments, and containing knowledge almost lost to the centuries. If it hadn't been for the Medicis, many of these ancient texts would have been lost forever. Lorenzo had such a passion for ancient Greek philosophy and knowledge that he collected with devotion.

When Francesca and Peaches stepped in seconds later, I was sitting in one of the booths, my hands palms-down on the slanted wooden reading shelves, communing with the centuries. I turned when they entered and, just moments before the door closed behind them, I caught a glimpse of a man's shadow—lean, slightly stooped.

Angelo had actually followed us inside? How did that happen with security guards everywhere? I stood up and linked my arms with Francesca's and Peaches's. "Quickly—we have been followed," I whispered.

"Followed? But that must be one of the security people. I will explain the—" Francesca began.

But I was race-walking her down the length of the long room. "He's not security. Where can I speak to a librarian, archivist, scholar, curator, or whatever they have working here?" I whispered.

Francesca cast a bewildered look over her shoulder. "But I have not described all the features of the reading room, of Michelangelo's most brilliant design—"

"It's all right," I said. "We'll come back."

Peaches was retracing our steps toward the entry door. "You go ahead. I'll track down Angelo."

"But that is not allowed," Francesca protested. "You must remain with me at all times!"

"Consider this extraordinary circumstances, Francesca. That's a criminal following us," Peaches told her.

"Then we must tell security!"

But we had already reached the opposite door. "Please, Francesca, while we have time, introduce me to an expert so I can ask a couple of quick questions. After that, you can call all the alarms you want."

Her reluctance was palpable but she agreed to take me downstairs from the reading room to another part of the building which I assumed was the working part of the library. It definitely had a scholarly air. Desks were arranged behind which sat several knowledgeable-looking people checking computer screens while talking to what I assumed were scholars in hushed voices.

"These are all scholars or archivists. Wait here," Francesca said, but no sooner had she approached the desk when a stylish silver-haired woman stepped up to her. They engaged in an intense discussion, with the silver-haired woman shooting me sharp glances from over the top of her wire-framed glasses. Shortly afterward, Francesca introduced me to Dr. Silvestri and may I just say that, in Florence, the archivist wore Prada. I recognized the design from one of the windows in the couture shops we'd passed.

Francesca and I followed the woman to an anteroom where she shut the door behind us. Silvestri spoke English but said that she preferred to converse in Italian because it was the language of the learned. Since I didn't yet trust my spoken Italian, I let Francesca translate. Silvestri studied me over the top of her couture glasses and I sensed that I did not pass muster, either academically or stylistically.

"Dr. Silvestri knows of you," Francesca told me, trying to smile away the doctor's contempt. I had picked up phrases like *pseudo scholar, an affront to art history*, etc. from Silvestri's opening comments.

I smiled. "First, thank you, Dr. Silvestri, for taking the time to speak with me. I have several quick questions. I need to understand what an authentic Medici document looks like. How can it be identified? Are their seals or telling markings? Old documents can so easily be forged but are there any distinguishing features I could look for?" Actually, it was a simplistic question but my intention was mostly to draw her out.

Francesca translated. Dr. Silvestri turned her shrewd gaze to me. "There are many features that a skilled archivist or Medici scholar such as myself can use for identification purposes. I have both doctorates in fifteenth-century Italian Renaissance history, an undergraduate degree in classical languages, and am a professional archivist."

She paused as if waiting for me to spew my qualifications in return but knew I couldn't measure up. "How wonderful," I said. Damned if I was going to play that game.

"May I ask what you are hoping to find, Signorina McCabe?" she asked after a moment. "If you locate a valuable manuscript, I presume you will contact the nearest authority in Florence. I will personally make myself available."

I wonder how the good doctor did with arms dealers? Still smiling, I replied: "As an art historian, I assure you I would take the proper measures should I encounter an authentic Medici document. However, is it possible for you to provide a brief summary of what a book belonging to the Medici family might look like?"

Now I saw something like alarm rising in her aquiline features. "You

THE FLORENTINE'S SECRET

believe you have located authentic Medici manuscripts, Signorina McCabe? For this you must contact us immediately."

Hell, what have I done? "No, no," I assured her. "I have definitely not seen any such manuscripts. I am only asking how I could identify such a piece if I were to come across one. If you know anything about me at all, you'll know that my agency frequently recovers lost objects. I wish only to be prepared."

"You are seeking a logo or a label, perhaps?" So the double doctor did sarcasm, too.

I smiled. "Subtle clues are fine, thanks."

Turning, she led me to a glass case along one long wall in which many old books sat encased in what I recognized as a humidity controlled environment. "Here, you see samples of the Medici collection. This volume is from Di Lorenzo de' Medici Ode brevis. He sought out priceless classical manuscripts from the monasteries across Europe and would have then had them copied out by his scribes. He was also a poet of some note."

I peered down at the speckled vellum frontispiece with the elaborate engraving of vines, leaves, and what appeared to be frolicking angels. In the center of the page was a circle encased in a quatrefoil motif containing four balls or palle around a square design.

Angels rode horses amid waves at the bottom of the page, everything linking to everything else in a complex rhythm of vines and motifs. My gaze skimmed across the rest of the opened books, taking in illuminated letters, intricate colored pages still aglow after all these centuries, the italic script clearly legible. Lorenzo had deviated from the church-sanctioned Latin and embraced his Italian roots by using Tuscan.

Stepping back, I turned to Dr. Silvestri. "Besides the palle, are there other motifs that signal that a manuscript could be from the Medici library?"

"Many books and manuscripts were destroyed in 1497. If you should discover others, it would be a significant find," she stated. "But there are common motifs that may distinguish such a Medici volume. Here you see the cover of Lorenzo de' Medici's collection of sonnets." She was pointing several volumes down, to a closed book—deep mottled red leather with ornate gold filigree corners and a central crest featuring six gold balls. "Lorenzo in particular enjoyed illuminating his collection with various and

85

unique symbols beside the Medici crest. He was a poet as well as a collector of ancient manuscripts."

I knew that. There was more than a touch of condescension in her tone that her native tongue did nothing to suppress. "Would wasps, rings, flowers feature?" I asked.

"I have seen many things in the pages of this collection," Silvestri said, studying my face as though she'd like nothing better than to slap me silly.

"Are letters part of the collection?"

"By letters, do you mean correspondence?" she asked.

"Yes, like letters back and forth between, let's say, the Medici and the artists they patronized."

"We have many such pieces but this is a library," she said curtly. "We carry mainly books and incunabula, even papyri dating back to the ancient Greeks and Romans. Many letters did not survive the centuries. Many books did not, either, especially after the fall of the Medici. If I knew what you seek, perhaps I could assist you better."

"Thank you. You've been most helpful. One more thing: should someone approach you regarding our discussion, I'd appreciate it if you didn't disclose my questions."

That was a misstep. She glared at me as if I'd just requested that she break her oath of allegiance to F.A.K., the god of Freely Accessible Knowledge.

"Let's go," I said to Francesca, who kept in stride with me as I beat a hasty retreat out the door.

"I am sorry that she did not appear helpful. Research is very important to Florentine scholars. Everything follows the rules. I could set up an appointment with the chief archivist for you, if this is helpful?"

"No, thanks." I didn't want to disclose that I may have already dropped too many bread crumbs for a Baldi minion to follow. I'd been careless and could kick myself.

The sound of alarms ringing through the building chased all other thoughts from my mind. We arrived at the vestibule in time to see Peaches handcuffed between two polizia.

8

It took all of Francesca's persuasive powers to get Peaches released from the Piazza Santa Maria Novella police station hours later.

"He accused me of being a pickpocket who had been stalking him all the way from the Duomo!" Peaches sputtered in outrage as we stood in the piazza.

"I am very sorry," Francesca kept saying.

"Did you tell them the truth?" I asked.

"I am so sorry. This is not the Florentine way." That was Francesca again.

"What, like he was really the hoodlum, not me?" Peaches said. "I told them that he had been following *us* but they didn't believe me. Who are you going to believe—the white Italian male or the tall black foreign female? Note that I deliberately emphasized the black part."

"He said he was a scholar and introduced himself as Dr. Angelo Ficino," Francesca explained. "He had a very fine vocabulary and claimed he was studying the style of Attavante, a scribe hired by Lorenzo de' Medici. It seems he was very convincing, this man."

Peaches and I exchanged glances. Could it be that Baldi had scholarly thugs on the payroll? Well, why not? He had Zann, not that she was either a scholar or a thug, exactly.

"The worst part is that he just strolled away and I'm the one left in custody." Peaches thumbed her chest.

"Please forgive us. I speak on behalf of all Florentines." Francesca was now clasping her hands as if begging for absolution.

"Francesca, it's not your fault," I said, patting her shoulder. "You're just the best. Thank you so much for all your assistance but you'd better give us a wide berth from here on in. I had no idea it would go down this way, believe me."

After further protests and offers to assist us any way she could, Francesca finally took off to meet her next tour group, leaving Peaches and me to fester.

"Come on," I said. "We need to lick a gelato along with our wounds. I'm told it can cure anything."

Not long afterward, we strolled toward the Duomo licking panettone and pomegranate flavors. I chose the panettone for a sense of creamy magnificence to soothe my bruised ego. It was almost as good as milk and cookies.

"So, tell me, did you get what you came for?" Peaches asked, trailing her tongue around the circumference of her double-scooped cone.

"Yes and no. I forgot what academia can be like sometimes. Had I been a student, Dr. Silvestri probably would have bent over backward to help me. Had I a couple of doctorate degrees she might even have been courteous, possibly respectful. As it was, she treated me with undisguised distain. The agency's activities are obviously being met with disapproval in some scholarly quarters."

"So, between racism and academic snobbery, we both took a hit today. We'll survive."

"Dr. Silvestri treated me as if I was the equivalent to art history's version of a game show—all glitter and no substance," I continued, having a bit of a vent. "She wasn't going to tell me anything unless I revealed my reasons for asking, which I couldn't do. I mean, I don't blame her, really. What am I but an upstart when it comes right down to it?"

Peaches paused licking to snarl. "Knock it off, Phoebe McCabe. We don't bow down to the disapproval of others. If it weren't for us, many pieces of priceless art would be lost forever. Think this Silvestri is out there busting her snobby butt to save history against gunrunners? Leave the scholars to do their business and we'll do ours. We're about saving art, not our reputations."

She was right. I gazed around. "I don't see Angelo lurking anywhere so let's go to the Medici Chapel and check out Michelangelo's tomb while we're at it," I said.

"Yeah, a tomb is bound to cheer us up."

Though the tomb didn't cheer us up, exactly, it certainly distracted us, which was nearly as good.

"What's with those boobs? Did Michelangelo even know what a naked woman looked like?" Peaches whispered, gazing up at the marble image of the reclining *Night*. It was safe to say she had to be in a bad mood to criticize the master.

"The figure is supposed to be mythic and not based on a real woman," I replied.

"Good thing."

After an hour of studying Michelangelo's extraordinary mastery and discussing the factors that led to the explosion of artistic brilliance we call the Renaissance, we finally decided it was time to head back to the hotel. For that, I took us on another route.

It always amazed me how the streets away from Florence's city center emptied out by seven o'clock or earlier. It's as if a button had been pushed and everyone just disappeared.

We were strolling along one of the long narrow arteries leading away from the cathedral when my neck hairs prickled.

"We're being stalked again," I whispered. "Probably Angelo."

"Bastard. I've had it up to my neck with him," Peaches said.

Behind us, I saw nothing but a row of parked Vespas and a few ambling pedestrians strolling toward the Duomo.

"Tricky bugger," I said under my breath. Unlike last night's encounter, this Baldi bad boy probably only meant to keep an eye on us rather than inflict bodily harm but his presence was annoying.

"Is this bastard really a doctor?" Peaches said with a hiss.

"Let's ambush him and find out," I whispered.

We turned a corner and ducked into the alcove of a shuttered farmacia. "No knifing," I warned, "no killing, either." I waved my phone. "Leave this to me. I'm about to try Evan's stun app set on mild."

"Why not let me do it? After all, I'm the bodyguard and I've got a bone to pick with this scrawny con man."

"Okay, you do it but set the app to stun."

Peaches grinned and held her phone. "Stun app engaged—mild."

Several minutes later, Angelo rounded the corner keeping his head down and appearing like a local heading home from a long day at work. His shuffling limp was now much more evident. I almost felt sorry for him.

We watched him for mere seconds as he gazed down the street, pausing when his quarry wasn't in sight. He kept his back to us, giving Peaches time to lunge out and zap him between the shoulder blades. He half turned before sinking to his knees. In seconds, he was sprawled on the sidewalk, semiconscious.

"Feeling shocked, are we?" I muttered, leaning over him.

"How long do these micro stuns last?" Peaches asked, checking the street for pedestrians or cars. Empty.

"I have no idea but you've got to love Evan's tool," I whispered, staring down at the back of the man's balding head.

"Yeah, you might love his tool, all right, if you'd ever let things get that far."

"I'm referring to his apps, not his... Oh, just stop. Let's get out of here. Did you find his wallet?"

Peaches was patting his pockets while Angelo tried to push himself up from the pavement. She shoved him back down.

"Got it and his phone, too. *Arrivederci, bastardo.*"

"Let's go," I urged.

We left him struggling to sit as we walked rapidly down one of the adjacent streets. Halfway along, Peaches dropped his phone down a drain in case he was being tracked.

Our stalker wasn't killed, he wasn't even harmed—unless waking up with a headache and weak knees counted—but it felt good to zap the rotter. Consider that our little payback. Yes, we can be that childish.

"We should have knocked him off. You can believe he'd do the same to us if Baldi gave the word," Peaches said.

"This wasn't self-defense," I pointed out.

"You and your code of ethics."

Once we were safely near Santa Croce without alarms going off or foot-

THE FLORENTINE'S SECRET

steps beating the pavement behind us, we leaned against a wall in relief. Peaches fished Angelo's wallet from her bag and we stared down at his driver's license.

"His name really is Dr. Angelo Ficino?" I said in amazement, staring over her arm.

"Baldi has doctors and archaeologists on the payroll? And look, he has a card for our hotel tucked in there, too."

"And look at that wad of cash," I noted.

Peaches whistled. "Wonder what Dr. Ficino is willing to do to line his pockets with all those euros? Should we take the wallet with us?"

"Yes. I have an idea."

We arrived back to the hotel in time for a quick shower and change before our dinner meeting, but first I stepped up to the desk and passed the wallet over to the clerk.

"We found this in the street near the Duomo," I explained. "Poor man must have dropped it. The hotel card tucked inside suggested that this Dr. Ficino may be a resident here. May I leave it in your care?"

Peaches nudged me. Angelo was now stumbling through the front doors. "Must have caught a cab. See you upstairs," she whispered before bolting.

I watched as Dr. Ficino—slightly wobbly, definitely limping, and hastily smoothing strands of thin hair back across his skull—arrived at the desk. He spoke Italian to the clerk, requesting money to pay for his cab. He'd been robbed, he said. When he caught sight of me, he blanched like a ghost.

"Why, could this be the man on the driver's license? Yes, I'm sure of it. What a stunning coincidence that we're both in the same hotel," said I. "Dr. Ficino, I'm Phoebe McCabe." I pumped his hand enthusiastically. "You think you were robbed? But I found your wallet near the Duomo and had just this moment left it at the desk. Sorry for checking inside but it seems that you have both cards and money in there so it can't have been a robbery, correct? You must have dropped it." I beamed my full set of teeth at him. "Just carelessness. It happens." I shrugged.

Dr. Ficino seemed at a loss for words. *"Sì, grazie,"* he mumbled.

"You're welcome. Aren't you glad there's a few honest people left in the world?" I headed for the elevator, waving at him as I went.

Minutes later, I was on my way up the lift, congratulating myself for a job well done. Sometimes the smallest thing delivers the biggest punch of satisfaction.

But I needed to shower and change before our dinner meeting. However, first I stood in my room checking my messages. Not surprisingly, a text from Rupert was at the top of the list.

Rupert: *You would tell me if there was any excitement afoot, wouldn't you? It wearies me to be sitting about on recliners by the pool in Capri all day. I could use a dose of excitement. RF*

I replied at once: *Dear Rupert, enjoy your vacation. We are here on the business Nicolina told you about. No need for you to rush away from your recliner just yet. PM*

And then as if they'd planned a relay between them, in came a call from Evan. Admittedly, my heart gave a bit of a leap when I saw his name on my screen, but otherwise I answered with restraint. "Hello?"

"Phoebe, I see that you engaged the stun app at 6:36 this afternoon. What are you up to?"

He could not only track the use of every application activated on one of his super smartphones but knew the exact time, too. "Just incapacitating a stalker with the stun app, Evan. Works perfectly, thank you very much."

"Good, glad you like it. What kind of stalker?" he asked.

That voice. "What kind? The one that follows behind you, of course. You know they are a dime a dozen in our business. All's good now, though. Nice to hear your voice, by the way. Are you enjoying Capri with Giani?"

"Actually, I need to return him to his mother. As soon as I drop him off at the train station tomorrow, I thought I'd meet up with you in Florence."

Yes, tempting—strolling the streets of Florence with a handsome, charming, fascinating, and adoring man. "Great idea but we'll probably be finished up by then. Oh, sorry—have to run. Talk later." I pressed End and stood there feeling as guilty as hell. He deserved better. Maybe I did, too.

Seconds later he texted: *You don't fool me.*

Damn. Pulling myself together, I headed for the shower. As much as I was strongly attracted to the man, thought him wonderful in every possible way, and teetered on the edge of desire every second of every day, I steadfastly resisted the temptation. My heart was still not open for business.

Twenty minutes later, I emerged fragrant with the complimentary bath

THE FLORENTINE'S SECRET

products, donned my hydrangea print Gucci blouse, snatched my Ode to Melancholy wrap from the chair, and proceeded down the hall. It was almost eight o'clock.

Nicolina was sitting by the window swathed in a long blush-colored silk shift. Nearby, the table had been set for dinner with fresh flowers arranged in a Majorca bowl. A fragrant breeze stirred the air.

"Phoebe, I am glad to see you. That blouse does suit you. I will buy you one from this year's collection. Did you have a good day?" she asked, rising.

We exchanged summaries of our day's exploits where I learned that the Uffizi experts did, indeed, believe that our sketch was a probable Botticelli. Of course, they would not easily commit to an absolute statement since it remained unsigned but at least the possibility remained strong.

"Do they think that the sketch is a study and that there may be an existent painting somewhere?" I asked.

"No word on that. When they see the letter, they might think yes. We will leave the sketch with the Uffizi unless we find evidence that it should go elsewhere. And this Angelo is truly a doctor?" She was as surprised as we were.

"Apparently."

I checked the time on my phone. "Where are Seraphina and Zann?"

Nicolina poured us each a glass of wine. "Seraphina texted to say that she had lost sight of Zann just before three o'clock this afternoon and attempts to locate her still."

I stared at the wine glowing gold in the glass. "That's not good. On the other hand, Zann did say that Baldi wouldn't easily give away his location."

When a knock came at the door, we both turned expectantly but it was only the servers delivering dinner, Peaches sweeping in behind them.

"Howdy, gang," she greeted, now dressed in a long floral sleeveless silk dress that furled around at her ankles, all pink roses on an inky blue background. She twirled around, exposing her new strappy sandals. "Dolce and Gabbana, very midnight gardenesque." She beamed. "Saw it in a window today on sale so dashed over and got it this morning. You like?"

"I like," I said.

"It's beautiful," Nicolina agreed.

Peaches stopped mid-twirl. "Of course it's beautiful and I look like dynamite—a mirror image of Beyoncé or maybe Naomi Campbell, since

93

she's Jamaican, too—just in case that was on the tip of your tongues. What's with the long faces?"

We waited until the servers left before answering, one of them whispering, *"Bellissimo!"* to Peaches on the way out.

"Seraphina and Zann are missing," I said.

"Zann is missing and Seraphina looks for her," Nicolina clarified.

"Well, damn." Peaches did not sound too concerned as she helped herself to a glass of white wine from the silver chill bucket and checked herself out in the venetian gill mirror. "Those two can take care of themselves but maybe we really should get Zann an Evan phone while on the case. That way we can track her properly. Are we doing white wine tonight?"

I did not mention the call from Evan to avoid a lecture on missed chances, a few good men, etc. However, when I had told Nicolina earlier she understood my reluctance completely.

Half an hour later, we were still sitting around the table picking at our salads, waiting. It was almost nine o'clock when the door flew open and Zann lunged into the room, Seraphina at her heels. We sprung to our feet, our questions dying on our lips as Zann collapsed on a nearby chair, refusing to meet our eyes.

"I found her," Seraphina said, sounding winded, "in back alley."

"You did not *find* me," Zann said, glaring up at her. "I was coming toward you when we collided."

"You were on ground!" Seraphina insisted.

I stared at Zann—a bruise under her eye, a cut lip, a ripped shirt. I crouched in front of her. "What the hell happened?"

"What do you think happened, Phoebe McCabe? I didn't give boss man what he wanted." She glared. "So he had me roughed up." My look of shock made her emit a strange coughing laugh. "Did you think Baldi was some kind of self-help guru? This is what happens in the world I live in: if you don't deliver, you pay."

"What were you suppose to deliver?" I asked.

She stared at me with one eye, the other nearly swollen shut. "You asked somebody at the Laurentian Library about Medici manuscripts today, apparently."

"I did." *Silvestri.*

"So Angelo informed Baldi. I was supposed to know what you were after but didn't have a clue, did I? I'm supposed to be infiltrating the agency so how come I didn't know what you were up to? he asks. Was I holding out on him? When I denied knowing anything, he slapped me around."

"Shit," I said.

"I told him nothing. He still thinks we are off to Volterra to check out a lead on the Botticelli tomorrow but now he suspects there may be a connection to Lorenzo de' Medici. After keeping the letters secret from him for years, you threw him a lead."

"Damn," I whispered, blaming Silvestri but, deep down, realizing I was the guilty party.

"I will kill him," Seraphina growled.

"Look," Zann said, gazing up at us each in turn. "This may not be the first time Baldi's hit me but I swear to God it will be the last. Tomorrow we'll find that Botticelli and leave the bastard in the dust. If you do manage to kill him along the way, I'll consider that a bonus."

9

The next morning was spent preparing our various disguises and alternative identities. Typically, Zann had planned every last detail right down to wigs and clothes that had been smuggled up to our rooms. By 11:30 a.m., four people who looked vaguely like us trying not to look like us left by cab for Volterra.

"You've got to be kidding. That was a man dressed up like me," Peaches protested after peering out behind a potted olive tree on the roof garden.

"Baldi's men don't know that," Zann said as we gathered in Nicolina's room later. "Those guys are looking for a six-foot black woman with a topknot wearing purple leggings and a tunic with a matching mask—check. She's accompanied by a willowy elegant Italian woman and a short snippy-looking sidekick with cropped hair—check times two."

"Snippy-looking sidekick?" Seraphina glared.

Zann ignored her. "Baldi's men have the descriptions I gave them. They'll follow that car to Volterra, as planned. Meanwhile, the three of you will make your back-door exit."

Which they did an hour later. Nicolina, Seraphina, and Peaches left out the delivery door to sneak away in a cab to their bogus workplaces, leaving Zann and me to prepare for our own getaway.

THE FLORENTINE'S SECRET

The moment they exited, Zann turned to me. "I have FaceTime with my dad in ten minutes. I really want you to meet him."

Minutes later, I was gazing down at a man sitting under an umbrella on a patio in a large garden. Seated in a wheelchair, the man seemed alert and eager while, in the distance, I glimpsed other seniors in groups or reading in the sun.

"Hi, Dad," Zann greeted him, holding her tablet so that we could both see the gentleman with me remaining in full view. "This is Phoebe McCabe. Remember me telling you about her?"

"Phoebe, how very good it is to meet you at last." He peered at the screen to get a good look at me while Zann avoided the camera completely. "Suzanna has told me so much about you and all the wonderful things you do for the preservation of art and antiquities. Stellar work. Brava." He softly clapped his hands.

"Thank you and lovely meeting you, too."

I planned to tell him more but Zann quickly intercepted. "Have to cut this short, Dad. We have work to do. Talk soon."

"Good bye, darling!" he called as she hit End.

"Well, that was abrupt," I said as she slapped the cover of the tablet closed.

"I didn't want him to see my black eye. I'll make it up to him next time. Besides, we have to get ready."

"How much did you tell him, anyway?"

"Not much. Just that I was helping you with something."

I soon forgot about Masters senior as we went into camouflage mode.

I stared at my image in the mirror, now transformed by a straight blond shoulder-length wig, sunglasses, and a tiered pink sundress that made me feel like a birthday cake. The wide-brimmed sun hat and bright pink lipstick ensured I was almost unrecognizable even to myself. I'd always dreamed of iron-straight hair. Now I realized that might look best on an iron-straight body. The only piece of the outfit that was mine was my undies and the capri leggings I wore under the dress. "And you say we're from New York?"

"Upper New York state—no raspy New York accent necessary. If anyone asks, say you went to school in Canada. Mixed North American accents always throw the Italians off." Zann was leaning toward the hall mirror applying thick foundation over her black eye. A bit of makeup sleight of hand had all but covered the evidence of the prior night but I knew her wounds lay much deeper. Otherwise, her black bob and chic ensemble made her look like the polar opposite of her usual self—sophisticated, pampered, and rich rather than beaten, wily, and desperate.

"I don't know how you stuck with Baldi as long as you did," I remarked, studying how the woman flipped from battered to gorgeous with a few props. Maybe Noel calling her Simonetta wasn't such a stretch, after all.

"Because I had no choice, obviously. As Nicolina said, he'd kill me if he knew I was leaving him. May still. I figured that if I waited long enough, one day I'd see my escape hatch."

"And here I am."

"And here you are," she agreed, straightening.

"But there are bits that still don't make sense. For instance: supposing we manage to retrieve the hidden painting without Baldi finding out and even get it to the authorities without mishap—unlikely but possible. You then get your redemption photo and your father is happy, you're happy. What then? Baldi says 'win some, lose some,' shrugs, and goes on about his business as if nothing ever happened, leaving you to live happily ever after?"

She smiled lopsidedly. "What's your point?"

"My point is that it doesn't add up. Your impressive planning only goes so far before falling into a mess of unanswered questions."

"Obviously, I do my planning in stages. First, accomplish this task, then worry about the aftereffects."

"The aftereffects being certain death? Unless I'm totally misreading Baldi, he doesn't sound like the forgiving sort."

"He isn't."

"So you must have a plan since that's how you work. Tell me your endgame. How do you plan to escape Baldi?"

She dug her hands into her hips. "I told you my endgame: get the Botticelli and achieve redemption for my dad."

"Baldi isn't going to let you just walk away."

"What do you think of the bag and shoes?" Turning, she staged a slightly wobbly walk across the room in her red high-heeled Ferragamos, the matching bag swinging from her fingers. I inwardly cringed at the bill she'd present us with at the end of all this. "We're going as two women who can afford to shop a swath through Florence. Everything comes from a secondhand shop but they don't need to know that. And we're sisters."

"Sisters?"

"Yes, Peggy, sisters. You can call me Sandy. Oh, don't look so surprised, McCabe. We are all sisters under the skin."

I wasn't about to wade into that one. Meanwhile, I hadn't ruled out the possibility that she was still working for Baldi and that this was all a ploy. If she was working for him, that would explain her reluctance to disclose her final plan. On the other hand, if Baldi already knew about the Medici papers, why not just steal everything from the Corsis and be done with it? And surely with the experts he had on the payroll, they, too, could piece the puzzle together leading to the possible Botticelli. Where did we fit in? At the root of it, I believed she really was after redemption and some part of me was cheering her on. That didn't mean that I trusted her.

"So, are you in a relationship with Evan Barrows?" She was standing in front of me now, studying me from under her glossy bangs.

The question took me by surprise. "Why?"

"Why not? Aren't we two sisters talking about guys? Isn't that what sisters do?"

"We're not sisters," I said carefully. For an instant, I glimpsed another facet of her complex personality: loneliness. My circle of women friends must seem like an impenetrable clique in her eyes but I was determined to maintain my boundaries without being unkind. "We're tentative colleagues, at least for the duration of this case. Personal questions don't apply, but just for the record, no, I am not in a relationship with Evan Barrows. Why do you ask?"

"Just curious. Wondered if you ever recovered from the Noel debacle."

"Recovering from a bad relationship doesn't necessarily mean jumping into a new one—at least not right away. There's a certain power in remaining in my own orbit."

She smiled with difficulty. "I get that. You're kind of like my hero. After you tasered that bastard, I thought: 'Now there's a woman who doesn't let them grind her to the ground.' I've studied you, kind of like a fangirl but not in any creepy way." She was grinning now, her still puffy lip slightly destroying the effect.

"Being held at gunpoint in my bedroom fits the creepy category, just so you know," I said. "Why so interested in my love life?"

She crossed her arms, now standing with her legs spread, again completely ruining the fashion plate mode. "Even after I was over Noel, I still wanted to kill him."

"Then you weren't over him."

"I am now because you killed the bastard for me. Wish I'd seen it, wish I'd been hovering over your shoulder watching him writhe in the dust. Did he writhe in the dust, by the way?"

"He literally never knew what hit him. Look, Zann—"

"Too bad. Anyway, he's off my radar for good now—done, toast! I'm moving on with my life. Once we find the Botticelli, I'll be free."

"About Noel—"

But she was tapping her watch. "Damn! We're here gabbing away without watching the clock. We've got to get down to the delivery bay. It's almost time."

So we hastily grabbed our bags—I had briefly traded my textile backpack for a large couture Fendi bucket bag that held a night's worth of necessities in the interests of disguise—and made our discreet path down the back stairs to the basement level.

And yes, I could have forced Zann to listen to the facts about Noel's probable nondeath but I didn't have the heart. Let her live with the belief that he was gone for a while longer. Just because I had to carry the burden didn't mean she did or at least not right away.

We arrived at the basement level, a route Zann must have plotted out in advance since it involved weaving between laundry bins and sneaking behind shelves of complimentary toiletries and she performed it with practiced efficiency. We then had to wait in a storage closet until we could descend unseen yet another flight of stairs to the wine cellar. There, loading bay doors opened to the back of a panel truck, were four guys standing around talking and smoking.

"They're already here," Zann whispered.

Tugging me behind a corner, we huddled out of sight watching as the men chatted. Two I gathered from the uniforms were hotel staff, the others the Corsi delivery crew—young men in their early twenties. Though I could only hear every second word floating down the hall, I caught enough to know that the topic centered on women and sex. Apparently Nico, the driver, went out the other night with a girl named Bianca, whom all the men knew about. He took her to his grandfather's farm and they drank wine and drove around on his Vespa until… His voice dropped. His companion, Markus, howled with laughter.

I poked my head out far enough to catch a few lewd gestures and see Nico being slapped on the back.

"Same old same old," Zann whispered, pulling me back. "The 'boys will be boys' shit."

We listened for a few minutes longer until we heard bottles clinking. "Finally. They're exchanging full cases for the empties. Once that's done, Nico and Markus will go to the back room with the other two, belt back a shot of something—probably grappa—and then hit the road. This is their last stop of the day."

She'd obviously been checking these guys out for a while. I didn't have time to protest the drinking and driving bit because in seconds we were slipping across the concrete loading bay while the sounds of laughter bellowed out of a back room. Up the loading ramp we scrambled, Zann removing her heels and padding up in her bare feet. Mine weren't full heels but strappy dressy numbers but I removed them just the same. It took almost a minute to make enough space between the cases to slip through to the back.

At last we settled down on a ledge of boxes while trying to organize the surrounding cases in such a way that nothing would topple on us should the van brake suddenly.

"Won't they notice that the boxes have been scrambled?" I asked.

"Doubt it," she said. "It's Friday afternoon. They'll just want to get home after this. Nothing back here but empties, anyway."

It was stifling in there. I leaned against the back of the cab wall, fanning myself with a map I'd stuffed into my bag.

"It will cool down as soon as the van starts up and the air-conditioning kicks in."

"They air-condition the back of a wine truck?"

"Heat destroys the wine."

That made sense. Luckily, I'd had prior experience with traveling in the back of trucks so expected it to be more about endurance than comfort.

JANE THORNLEY

I'd brought water, a sweater, a change of clothes, a pair of sneakers, a gun (Nicolina had finally convinced me), my decoy phone along with my real phone, and an assortment of overnight necessities.

"Did you buy a burner phone?" I whispered.

"No time, remember? I got beat up before I had a chance. Shh. Here they come," Zann warned.

We heard laughing. The back door slammed shut plunging us into total darkness. Then the engine rumbled up and we lurched forward while a radio blasted Italian pop music loud enough to vibrate the walls. The guys seemed to be singing along. This was going to be a long ride. According to my GPS, at least an hour and a half of back-of-truck endurance training.

With all that noise, talking was out of the question, or so I thought. Only I had that niggling sense that I had forgotten something critical. A battery charger? Check. Extra ammo. Check. I ran down my mental list confident that I had packed every necessity. So what was I missing?

"So have you given up on men?" Zann asked after maybe forty minutes of stop-start city driving followed by a stretch of smooth road accompanied by blaring music.

I had been tracking our route on my phone's GPS so knew we were somewhere between Bagno a Ripoli and San Casciano. I couldn't bear to imagine all the scenery we were missing. "Pardon?" I could see her profile in my phone's screen light.

"Men, have you given up on them after Noel?"

Back to my love life again. Why did this keep coming up? I turned away and sighed. "No, I haven't given up on anything. I'm just taking a break, I said." The next step was for me to ask the same thing of her but that would only open a proverbial can of worms. "And you?" Blame boredom.

"I don't waste my time anymore. Women are so much more interesting, don't you think?"

For a moment I didn't answer. "Interesting people exist in all genders. You already know that so I'll just add that I'm still attracted to men. That's not a judgment, just a fact."

"Okay, thanks for the honesty. What about Peaches?"

"You'll have to ask her but she seems very interested in the opposite sex, too."

"Nicolina?"

I couldn't believe she was considering us as a dating source. "I have no idea. Again, you'll have to ask her. Haven't you tried a dating app?"

"I don't do dating apps—too tricky in my business. Anyway, she probably wouldn't be interested in the likes of me. Glad that we can talk openly." She stared straight ahead. "It's hard finding partners in our business."

Our business—were we in the same line of work? We kept quiet after that, lost in our own thoughts, but I swear that the music grew so loud that even thinking became difficult.

An hour or so later, the truck jerked to a stop, the engine cut, and the back door flew open all in a matter of seconds. We sat stone-still as the guys began lifting the cases from the back, the light slicing through the stacks bright enough to make my eyes water.

This was the moment I'd worried about and I'd even rehearsed a stowaway explanation. Only twelve cases remained between us and the open doors when somebody shouted Nico's and Markus's names. Crunching gravel followed as the two guys headed off. I caught Italian for "pile of trouble."

"What's happening?" I whispered.

"I arranged for the boys to get a phone call from the cops. Don't worry, it's bogus. I hired a guy to call. Should give us enough time to get out of here."

She'd thought of everything.

In minutes, our stiff legs were taking us down the loading ramp. We donned our shoes and scrambled across a graveled drive up a pathway between tall cypress trees beside a modern building painted a butter yellow with wraparound glass windows on the upper floor. To the left, I could just see a cluster of gray stone buildings tucked behind a wall far off on a wooded hill while behind us rolling hills of vineyards could have come right out of a Tuscan tourist brochure.

"This is the wine tasting center, a new building the Corsis put up maybe ten years ago to handle bus groups and the like," Zann whispered. "Wasn't here when I knew Piero. He was always big into modernization but his father resisted. Up there is the Corsi villa and hamlet."

"The medieval walled village," I whispered, looking up. I did my homework, too.

"The Corsis renovated all the old cottages up there into B and B rooms over the years. Did you check the website?"

"Thoroughly," I assured her. "Those walls are thirteenth century and Dante is supposed to have visited the hamlet after being exiled from Florence. Can't wait to see it. The villa itself is considered a recent addition."

"Yeah, the fifteenth century is so yesterday."

"Is that medieval tower I see where the Medici holdings are hidden?"

Zann turned to peer up into the trees. "Providing the Corsis haven't moved it. It's thirteenth century, too, and looks to be a ruin but that's all a facade. We'll check it out later. Now we've got to blend in with the wine tasters and plant ourselves here for the evening."

This part of the grounds was practically deserted. The only person we saw as we wound our way toward the front of the building was a man watering flowers. We pretended to be lost and merry tourists as he pointed us farther up the path beside a march of potted olive trees.

Nodding and laughing, we followed his directions until we arrived at the front where a tour bus stood parked in a gravel parking lot amid cars and three vans. No sign of a catering or musical troupe van in sight but they probably parked below.

"Shit, we're late," Zann said while hastily reapplying her lipstick. I didn't bother.

The sound of a woman's voice projected through a microphone led us to a set of huge double wooden doors where a young man stood guard. He smiled behind his black mask as we drew near, a grin that grew wider after Zann produced her tickets for the event. I glanced down at the stubs surprised to discover that the wine tasting extravaganza cost two hundred euros each.

"Are they serving caviar with a side of gold-embossed truffles?" I whispered as we swept through the doors.

"Probably," came her answer. "Have to pay for the entertainment and food, remember."

Inside, a spacious wood and concrete facility blended a touch of old-world high beamed ceilings with gleaming stainless-steel modernity. About thirty-five people stood in six-foot intervals around two wide concentric marble and steel counters placed steps below the other, theater-style.

Between these curved counters, three young uniformed women delivered wine samples to the guests while another described the offerings in both Italian and English from a raised dais at the front of the room.

Zann and I were directed to our own bit of marble real estate where we were permitted to remove our masks. Each person had a little sink for spitting the samples as well as our own little tray of snacks—bruschetta, smoked salmon, something that looked like mushrooms on top of cheese...

I leaned toward her. "Would you recognize Baldi's men if they were here?"

"Maybe, maybe not. I don't know everyone—big operation. Besides, how could they be here so soon?"

I pulled back and studied the treats. Suddenly, I was starving but tried not to shove the tidbits in my mouth without pretending to sample the wine first. I objected to spitting out beautiful wine in principle but these tastings had their protocols.

"The finest Sangiovese grapes anywhere in the world," the hostess was saying. "These grapes are Chianti's hero. I invite you to sample our 2018..." Let me just say that that vintage was particularly delicious.

I watched as a young blonde woman delivered an inch of rich red wine to my glass next. Another vintage tasted with relish—exquisite—and duly spat it into the sink before devouring my tidbit of porcini on bread. Six more wines came along with six more snacks plus a sampling of the family's own limoncello and even olive oil. I probably swallowed once or twice but I'm sure liquor is absorbed through one's tongue by osmosis. Otherwise, I couldn't explain how relaxed I suddenly felt.

By now everyone was chatting and laughing across the spacing protocols, a sure sign that some of the brew had gone down the proverbial hatch. The German family to my left were toasting me. Zann was requesting a refill of her favorite vintage. Our server complied while directing her to the shop next door to buy her very own bottle after the tasting ended.

Meanwhile, this sip and spit dance went on for almost an hour longer while I studied my fellow tasters from the corner of my eye—a mix of national and global tourists including Japanese and Kenyan, judging from their accents—a good mix, one big happy international family. Hopefully international criminals weren't among the guests.

Once all the vintages were sampled, a hush descended over the room as an attractive man probably in his early forties stepped into the circle to stand beside the hostess and welcome us all again to his family winery—Piero Corsi.

I almost choked on my last bite of bruschetta. The man was gorgeous, as in film star gorgeous, with a charming graciousness as smooth as his family's Chianti and just as intoxicating. His English was impeccable, no doubt well-practiced along with his hospitality.

"My family is delighted to have you as our guests. Consider yourself our friends this night as I invite you to proceed through those doors to our gardens where the evening's entertainment will continue under the stars. A magnificent Tuscan feast has been arranged for your dining pleasure, which I hope you will enjoy as our guests."

Paying guests, that is, but why quibble? I watched as the attractive Piero swept his elegantly dressed self—caramel-colored linen slacks, an open-neck long sleeved shirt, and woven leather loafers that hinted of money worn casually but with great style—out of a set of glass doors toward a back corridor, ushering his slightly tipsy clients along with him.

I caught Zann's eye and grinned. "You gave up on men before you tried life with that one?" For a moment I gazed at her, shocked. I couldn't believe I'd just said that. How superficial, as if I regarded men as mere objects. "That's not me talking," I said quickly. "That's a society-conditioned fossil embedded in my cranium floating up from the alcohol."

We gazed at one another in silence before she burst into laughter. "Have you been knocking back the samples?" she asked.

"No!" I think I may have, actually. Read the part above about osmosis. I took a swig of the complimentary water and followed her out the door.

Outside a huge curved patio with potted olive trees, fountains, and vine-covered pergolas looked out over the family vineyards. For a moment all I could do was stand and inhale the view—rolling hills punctuated by rows of cypress trees, an old chapel tucked away in the distance, along with other villas and wine estates amid the rolling hills. Here was quintessential Tuscany, so beautiful that one could almost believe that it had been magically staged for tourists while knowing that was impossible.

The sun was hanging low in the sky and somehow I'd ended up with another glass of vino in my hand when I set off looking for Zann. In the time it took me to inhale that scenic vista, she had disappeared.

Weaving through clusters of laughing guests, I followed the sounds of an orchestra warming up. There, under the shade of a raised pergola-cum-stage, Peaches could be seen dressed in a sleek black suit with pants far too short for her long legs, chatting with a tall bald black man who was setting up a kettle drum. Slipping into a vine-shrouded corner, I waited until I caught her eye. In seconds she was beside me.

"That's Luigi, the drummer—great guy. The man standing in the tux is Mario," she whispered. I glanced toward the barrel-chested gent in the bow tie who appeared to be spritzing his throat. "He's from Siena and tells me he's multitalented and can sing anything, including opera."

"Wow, and modest, too. Have you seen Nicolina or Seraphina?"

She grinned. "They were here when we arrived. Try the kitchen. I tell you, before the night is over, I wouldn't be surprised if Seraphina doesn't stab somebody with a fork and Nicolina may swoon from being forced to serve the minions. What are you doing with a glass of wine in your hand?"

I glanced down at the glass. "I'm not even sure how it got there."

"Well, that's not good, is it? You need to stay away from that stuff, woman. You're like a fairy who gets knocked over by mere fumes. Give that to me. Go find some coffee. Luigi's going to teach me how to play the cymbals now. Catch you later." She took the glass from my hand and strode away toward the band.

Minutes later, I followed one of the servers through a set of automatic glass doors into a spacious kitchen where Nicolina was being passed a silver tray of tiny bruschetta bites. Dressed in a navy-blue cotton uniform with a matching cap and apron, she was almost unrecognizable. Turning, she caught my eye, lifted her chin, and swept past me without a word.

"How's it going?" I whispered, following after her.

"This uniform scratches," she said. "How do they stand this? Cheap clothes! For more hours I will be scratched to death. Pink is not your color."

"Do you know where they're serving coffee?"

"Not until later. Before then we eat."

She swept off to deliver more bruschetta while I slipped up a set of stairs to a large empty dining room overlooking the vineyards. From this vantage, I could gaze down at the guests, at the view, and even glimpse the family hamlet far up on the hill. Imagine owning a thirteenth-century hamlet, even if it had been now converted into an inn?

What really interested me lay up there, not at this wine-infused Tuscan production. Still, I had more hours to play this game before we appeared at our lodgings and revealed ourselves to Piero. I was eager to do a little reconnaissance in the meantime. So far, everything appeared to be going according to plan. Presumably Zann was keeping an eye out for Baldi but now I had to keep an eye out for Zann.

I found her on the patio, circulating among the guests. "All the hired hands have been paid and I walked right by Piero and he didn't recognize me," she whispered. "Saw Seraphina in the far pergola growling at a customer who dared ask for a wine refill."

I laughed. "So we made it here without Baldi knowing. Good planning." Only, I still worried that I had forgotten some crucial detail.

"We're not out of the woods yet. Just heard from my contact that Baldi's thugs now know Volterra was a ruse and are gunning it back to Florence. Just pray that we kept our tracks well-hidden until we get what we came for tonight."

"Which is?"

"Who knows? Something about Botticelli."

I left her to stroll around the patio. By then the fairy lights strung through the pergolas were glowing, lanterns flickered around the space, and groups were claiming their tables for the Tuscan feast to follow. I found my name with Zann's—Peggy and Sandra Masters, both of us divorced and returning to our maiden names—and took my seat across from a young newlywed Dutch couple. A pair of married guys from Verona arrived just as the band struck up a medley of instrumental pieces. Soon Zann joined me to chat with our table mates while I listened in to our supposed backstory.

"So you are both divorced sisters on a trip together and your friends join you also?" Vincent from Verona asked in broken English, and flashed me a bright smile. If possible, he was even more stylishly dressed that Piero.

"Right. They'll be along later." Zann sipped the house Chianti while flinging an arm around my shoulders. "Pegs here is just the best but both of us were dragged through a wicked divorce. This trip is a promise to ourselves. Bet you have better divorce laws in Holland and Italy compared to the US."

Ria cast a shy grin at her husband. "We are just married so we don't know these things. Divorce, what is that?" Gales of laughter.

"We had to be married in Denmark," Vincent explained. "Laws not so good in Italy—very Catholic."

And on it went. I learned that I was a real estate agent and Sandy an accountant, fascinating details of a life we hadn't lived. I hoped I could remember it all if the time came.

The setting was magical, the company fun, the music superb, and the food that began arriving delicious—ribolita, pici with duck sauce, tortilla stuffed with pears and pecorino cheese with butter and sage, pappardelle with boar sauce... By the time the warm chocolate pudding arrived, I was done. One really can have too much of a good thing, even in Italy.

Zann was chatting about motorcycling through Europe when I plotted my escape. Excusing myself, I took my glass of limoncello and drifted across the flagstones, my gaze fixed on the walled hamlet above. Like all these old buildings, the stone was uplit by spotlights tucked along the base and, again, like everything in Italy, the aspect was divine.

Drifting to the edge of the patio, I gazed up through the trees just as a full moon rose above the tower and Mario burst into tenor magnificence. I followed the perimeters of the patio until I found a lit path leading up through the trees. By that time I was beyond caring about anything but that path.

Halfway up the trail, I slipped from my stacked heels into flat sandals and carried on, my limoncello still in hand. Mario, a powerful tenor, was singing a song I recognized from Andrea Bocelli—*"Sogno"*—and if I listened closely, I could just hear a cymbal reverberate at every passionate crescendo. The moon was riding high above the trees and I was a little drunk. Now you'll understand why I diverted from the plan or maybe you don't even care. At the time, I certainly didn't.

The lane took me to a smooth dirt road that carried on up the hill and, between the music and the wine, I may as well have been floating. I arrived at the ancient archway that opened onto a narrow cobbled street winding through a cluster of stone houses. Lights were embedded into the walls every few hundred feet. The buildings were rustic, many multistoried, and built of warm sandy-colored stone with red doors and window boxes spilling spotlit geraniums. Clearly the basic structures were rustic medieval, cleverly restored to both capture the ancient spirit of the place while still accommodating the modern traveler. The Corsis knew what they were doing.

I could just see the main villa ahead. A lovely fifteenth-century cream stucco building with a top-floor porticoed balcony and an ivy-covered watchtower of its own, every second window alight. The only thing that indicated this was a hotel was the discreet bronze sign almost lost in the ivy by the front door. I presumed one entered the open arches to register inside but I kept on walking. No one seemed to be around.

Since we were to be the only guests that night, I wasn't concerned about bumping into anyone and, if I did, I was merely a resident checking out the place. Zann had emailed the desk to say that we would be along later. Of course, they would be expecting many more guests than the handful that would eventually arrive.

Mario was singing *"Canto Della Terra"* as I followed the cobbles around the villa toward the medieval tower. Passing more little houses, an ancient well, a building labeled *Olive Press* in two languages, and a little stone chapel, I finally arrived close to the tower or as close as I could get.

For a moment I gazed up at a six-foot wall. The tower was in an enclosed walled garden. That's what the map on my phone said. Unlike the rest of the hamlet, which seemed to keep every door open, the garden was not only gated but locked. Odd.

I didn't need to touch the door to recognize an electronic mechanism. I engaged my phone's X-ray app and ran it over the lock. As I suspected, it was alarmed. Next, I activated the infrared app and ran it along the wall, confirming that it was strung with the equivalent of an electronic tripwire.

Backing away, I stared up. Appearing deceptively ruined, I could just detect what looked to be signs of a plate glass inside one of the tiny arrow slits near the tower's crenellated roof. Not so ruined, after all.

I actually considered deactivating the alarm and breaking the lock, but even with my tools, it would be complicated—breaking into the gate and the tower door, trying to locate the secret room, all dressed in a sundress even though I wore stretch capris underneath. Better to wait. Besides, the moment I used that app, Evan would be notified and did I really want to draw Evan into the action? Well, honestly, under a Tuscan moon while being serenaded by a tenor, the combination of Evan and action held a certain allure but for all the wrong reasons, all the wrong action.

Something like a branch cracked behind me. I swung around, staring hard at the deserted path. Lights fixed near the corner of each building illuminated everything in sight and the doors directly in front of me were flush with the wall. No place to hide. So where did that sound come from?

Switching on my motion detector app, I strode down the lane.

10

I swept the enhanced camera feature back and forth across the cobbled lane, the radar grid forming bright green lines across the screen. No red heat signature detected. Running the app three hundred and sixty degrees around me revealed the same—no warm-blooded creatures within range, either, not even a cat. Apparently I was alone in this part of the hamlet, yet I didn't believe that. Still, I had things to do.

Keeping my phone open, I returned to scrutinizing the tower. But the sound, whatever it was, had jolted me from my stupor. I couldn't afford to be lulled by wine and Tuscany and I couldn't afford to simply break into the tower unless it was absolutely necessary. We had planned a more under-the-radar approach for a reason and I needed to return to the plan. Besides, breaking into the tower would be messy. That could wait.

I sent a text to Peaches and copied it to Nicolina: *Am up at the hamlet and will wait for you there. Doing reconnaissance. Pls let Zann know in case she goes looking for me.*

Messaging Zann directly was impossible since she hadn't picked up a burner phone. Peaches did not respond immediately, presumably because she was busy playing the cymbals with Mario, but Nicolina got back to me right away.

Nicolina: *Back in my own clothes and now a guest. What do you seek?*
Me: *Anything relevant. Will catch you later.*

That done, I scoped out the hamlet. It was small by any comparison—a cluster of ten stone buildings enclosed by a twelve-foot-high wall with one rough cobbled street curving up through the gates, past the villa to the tower garden, and down around the other side. Plenty of little lanes jutting between the buildings plus storage buildings and a garage, an overview gleaned from the Corsis' handy website map.

All of the cottages were lit as if waiting for guests to arrive so I checked every one, counting a sleeping capacity of at least twenty. Each building was different. Some had two stories with bedrooms and lounges, others were tiny with a cozy bedsit arrangement. All had kitchens and modern bathrooms but otherwise the beamed ceilings and simple country furniture kept the rustic mood alive.

I peered into the olive press with its floor-to-ceiling windows revealing a dining room with tables and counters. The map labeled it as a breakfast room. Not much of interest there. Next, I tried the chapel door, finding it locked. That surprised me. Why lock a church when all the resident rooms with their stocked amenities were left open? Of course, chapels weren't churches, exactly.

Unlike the tower, entering the chapel seemed relatively easy. After one quick check around using the intruder app, I dug inside my bag for my tools and was about to pick the lock when I realized that it wasn't as straightforward as I expected. Instead of a basic cylinder lock, this one had a sophisticated combination mechanism meant to be disengaged by both a code and a key. That usually meant an alarm, too, but why alarm a chapel?

Now I had to see inside, regardless of the consequences. Scrolling through my super phone's apps, I located a key-shaped icon. Here was a deactivating device designed to send a jolt into the system to disengage an electronic alarm.

In seconds, I had scanned the phone over the lock, which caused something to beep multiple times before going silent. Good. Next, I picked away at the lock until a satisfying click followed. Done. Then I grabbed the handle and pulled the door open, noting that the heavy oak was spring-loaded and would slam shut the moment I let go. I propped the door ajar with a loose cobble and slipped inside. Dropping my bag several pews in, I voice-commanded the flashlight feature to engage.

And gasped. This rustic thirteenth-century stone chapel with its single nave and wooden trussed ceiling held an extraordinary secret: every inch of wall had been covered in once-brilliant frescos, some of which had almost completely flaked away. Angels and saints below, Mary and Jesus above, plus a gathering of richly robed citizens making a procession along the lower walls toward the altar.

The style of the clothing, as faded as it was in places, retained enough glorious detail to peg the citizens as fifteenth-century Florentines, meaning that the entire procession must have been painted at least a century later than the chapel's construction. Though it was not unusual for exceptional frescos to dazzle the interiors of simple country chapels in Italy, I had never known one to depict wealthy Florentines so far from home. And the clothes were extraordinary.

I stepped closer, magnifying the surface of one of the ermine-lined robed men who was bearing a gift of a gilded box. Further along almost at the altar stood a woman represented in profile, her head flaked away but standing straight-backed, hands folded demurely over her waist, and wearing a magnificent gold embossed giornea or sleeveless overdress over a gown of shimmering cream silk. Most of the sleeve had disappeared but for a tiny bit by the wrist—a tantalizing glimpse of a triangular motif that could have been embroidered and accented with pearls. My eyes dropped to the tangled jeweled vine trailing along her gown's hem.

Briefly, I forgot to breathe. The clothes indicated the work of a master tailor who employed every possible guild to embellish his client's garments but it was no less a feat to depict that glory in the first place.

Along the procession, men were garbed in what must have once been brilliant red cioppas or cloaks lined in fur. Though it was difficult to tell in a painting so faded, I guessed that those crimsons were kermes dye, the most expensive dyestuff available at the time. The Florentine republic had an entire hierarchy based on the color red alone and only the wealthiest citizens were permitted to wear it, let alone afford that deep kermes dye in the first place.

More women followed behind the men, each adorned in unique ways, some young maidens with flowers in their hair and simply dressed, others probably married with their hoods thrown back to reveal stunning headdresses including the strange horned hats popular among the nobility. Most of these were citizens of wealth showing their clothes as proof of their standing, marching around the base of a tiny rural chapel in the woods dressed in as much splendor as could be seen anywhere between Florence and Rome.

Yet, as one grew closer to the altar, some of the clothing simplified. Still lovely, still intricately embroidered, but made of what appeared to be plainer fabrics—wools instead of silks, no rich damasks, and very little fur. The frescoed surface of many procession members had been so badly flaked away that only their legs showed and the man standing beside the yellow-robed lady had nothing left but a pair of red legs. Both their faces looked deliberately eradicated as if chipped away.

And then there was the background—tangled trees in a strange fantastical forest. I could see a similar landscape to what currently surrounded me—rolling hills and what could be the hamlet itself way up on a wooded hill—but what about that stack of books tucked away under rocks, branches growing out from the pages? And was that Zephyr and Flora running through a field of flowers toward the gathering with Mars swooping down from above as if late for a party? What was going on here in this amazing scene?

Stepping back, I swept the light across the walls while taking several deep breaths to still my thumping heart. I couldn't believe what I was seeing: to find a fresco by a Renaissance master disintegrating in a tiny chapel far from an urban center. Who was the artist? I had an idea, of course, but my guess made no sense.

I began taking pictures and even ran a video all around the walls until my phone began flashing a low battery warning. Bad timing but at least I had a charger with me. The phone went dark just as I'd finished photographing the nave. Behind me, the propped-open door provided enough light for me to find my way back to my bag, that is before it slammed shut. I was halfway down the aisle when it happened.

For a moment I stood stunned. I'd tested that door; there was no way it could shut by itself. And now I stood in total darkness with a dead phone. Someone had deliberately shut me in but why? Unless my stalker planned to blow up the chapel with me in it, locking me in could either be a warning or an attempt to get me out of the way. I had to alert the others.

I shot up the aisle, counting every row until I reached the third pew from the door where I'd dropped my bag. After fumbling seconds, I gripped my battery recharger. It took more fiddling before I could get the attachment into the tiny port and then all I could do was wait for the charger to do its magic. It would take at least fifteen minutes before I could get enough juice to send a text, but in the meantime, my team could be in danger.

Setting the charger on the pew, I grabbed the handle and shook the door until it rattled. My app had broken the electronic current earlier and deactivated the alarm, something that couldn't be restored without the alarm company. That meant that someone had physically barricaded me in from the outside. No amount of pushing could budge the thing.

Shit! I swung away and paced the floor, panicked over what could be going on outside. After a few moments of senseless fretting, I realized that Mario had stopped singing, that there were sirens blaring away from somewhere down the hill. I started calling for help, yelling at the top of my voice, even while knowing it would be useless. Whatever was going on at the bottom of the hill would detract from a faint wailing up here.

I stopped that and hovered over the phone waiting for the red flashing light to turn green. The moment it did, up popped a text from Peaches. *Where the hell are u? Bloody chaos down here!*

I thumbed an answer: *Up on the hill locked in the chapel. Somebody shut me in. What's going on?*

Peaches: *Lots of guests are being rushed to the hospital—suspected food poisoning. Nicolina and Seraphina are looking green around the gills but they're not as bad off as some. We're all waiting around to be questioned by the police. As soon as they finish with us, we'll be up to get you out.*

Me: *And Zann?*

Peaches: *She's sick, too, but not as bad as the rest. They think it was one of the canapés. Everyone who ate them got sick—something porky with a spicy Italian name. The band didn't get a chance to eat anything but most of the servers did and plenty of guests. They're all busy retching now. It's a mess. The Corsis are in a panic. How'd you get locked in a chapel?*

Me: *Long story. Just get here as soon as you can.*

I sat down in a pew to wait, thinking that the food poisoning event couldn't have been an accident. Someone deliberately tampered with the canapés as surely as they locked me in the chapel. But why? Because they needed to get my team out of the way. Baldi had to be on the premises because nothing else made sense.

A message from Evan came in: *I suppose you'll try to convince me that using the lock deactivator is a perfectly normal day in the life?*

I typed my reply: *Considering the business we're in, yes, but I'm currently barricaded inside a thirteenth-century chapel with a brilliant fresco possibly by Filippino Lippi to keep me company. How far away are you?*

Evan: *Approximately twenty miles to the south.*

Me: *Arrive undercover. Somebody got to us first.*

As usual, the man had perfect timing.

11

Peaches and Zann released me from captivity about an hour later. The door had been barricaded by a huge potted olive tree that must have taken two men to budge.

"Who the hell did this?" Peaches asked, gazing around. She'd just run a quick reconnaissance around the hamlet but found no human activity except inside the villa.

"The same people who poisoned the capicola, I told you," Zann said, leaning against the wall clutching her stomach. "It's Baldi. I thought for sure he'd never track us here but he must have had his dogs on our heels all along. Damn, damn, damn!"

Her wig askew, clothes rumpled, and lipstick smeared over one cheek, it was safe to say that her disguise was slipping.

"Where's Nicolina and Seraphina?" I asked.

"At the villa. Nicolina insisted they be taken to a suite inside the main house to recover. Got them run off their feet," Zann explained.

Peaches grinned. "She mentioned something about a lawsuit so Signora Corsi seemed more than willing to give her anything she wanted."

"She almost played the countess card until Peaches gave her the look. We've got to go there now to get ready for the big reveal," Zann said.

"Can't waste a single moment in case Baldi—oh, crap, not again. Excuse me: got to run."

We watched as she lurched over to the opposite cottage and bolted through the open door. The retching sounds that followed made me think she might not have made it to the bathroom.

"Won't be staying at that one," Peaches muttered.

"Any idea who the poisoners might be?" I asked.

"Nicky said that a couple of kitchen helpers disappeared halfway through the evening—a man and a woman."

Minutes later, a wan-looking Zann stumbled out of the cottage. "Sorry 'bout that. Jeez, I only had one of those damn canapés." She had straightened her wig and reapplied her lipstick. A wet spot damped the front of her chic little dress. Looking down, she added: "Spillage. I tried to get it all out."

"Didn't you bring a change of clothes?" I asked.

"Just jeans and a tee." She glanced down at her dress and shrugged. "Considering what just went on down there, they probably won't even notice. Let's get to the villa."

Gripping our bags, we strolled up the lane, scanning in all directions as we went. "Baldi's crew must be lurking around here somewhere," Zann whispered. "They'll be after you, Phoebe. He's always wanted to kidnap you and force you to disclose everything you think you know about the sketch."

"Think I know? Did he say that?"

"Yeah. He's afraid you've sniffed out something he hasn't yet. Drives him nuts."

"But why didn't he take me when he had the chance? I've been locked in that chapel for over two hours."

"Probably had their hands full with the poisoning bit. That must mean that the bastard only has a skeleton crew here and isn't on-site himself yet. Must have sent his minions as a last-minute thing once he realized what I was up to. This has all the signs of a rushed job. What happened down the hill was messy and Baldi doesn't like messy."

"If Baldi's only got a handful of men here and hasn't yet arrived, we still have a chance to get what we need and bolt, even if we've already got two of the team down," Peaches said.

"That must have been the idea—poison our crew, including me—but I blew the plan by coming up here. The poison can't be fatal, just incapacitating," I mused.

"Yeah, sounds like Baldi: knock you off your feet and then kidnap you. When he kills you, he prefers to take his time. Must have sent his minions in a tailspin when you went off script." Zann was angling her phone so she could see her face in selfie mode. "I look ghastly. Okay, ready?"

We had arrived at the villa entrance and spent a few minutes adjusting our disguises before entering. Peaches had already changed into her own pants. Straightening our various couture accessories, we stepped into the villa's foyer just as a maid dashed out, arms filled with what I guessed to be soiled linen.

Zann caught sight of the slender woman with the brown curly shoulder-length hair and frazzled expression standing in the hallway first. "Signora Corsi, hello. We are your guests for the evening—Peggy and Sandy Masters and our friend Lulu. We have reservations. We were just down at the gathering."

Signora Corsi had been turning one way and then the other as if unsure what to do next. About thirty-five and slender, she wore a sheath dress and high-heeled sandals perfect for a soiree under the stars but not so much for managing a household full of retched guests. At first, she barely glanced in our direction. The sound effects coming from upstairs explained her distraction.

"Signora Corsi?"

The woman swung toward us, hands clasped before her as if trying to hold herself together.

"I said we're your guests, the Masters from New York?" Zann repeated.

Signora Corsi looked startled but quickly pulled herself together. "You were at the Wine and Starlight event, yes? I am so very sorry. This has never before happened. My husband, he is with the police now but the caterers are the best in Tuscany. How could such a thing happen?"

"All very odd," Zann agreed, stepping forward. "You have two others from our party staying upstairs."

"The countess?"

So Nicolina had reverted to her true identity. "Yes, the countess," Zann agreed. "How's she doing? Not too good by the sounds of things. I so sympathize."

"Very bad in the stomach. We call a doctor who says what to give but he says she will be fine after she...purges."

I considered paying her a visit but, considering the noises coming from upstairs, decided to wait. Knowing Nicolina, she'd rather not be seen until after the intestinal drama was over. So far, she hadn't even answered my texts.

"Show us to our rooms so we can freshen up after our ordeal," Zann demanded. There was an urgency in her tone that made me think she may be on the verge of another digestive event herself.

"Of course. So strange. Everyone they just cancel last minute and then you book. Happy you are here, of course, though not such a good night in the end, yes? Leave your passports, please, and we will show you to your rooms." She was already turning her attention to the two young boys—ages somewhere between ten and fourteen, I guessed—who had just entered the foyer. She spoke quickly to them in Italian, the equivalent of *Go back to your rooms, please.* The boys turned and left the way they had come.

Peaches and I exchanged glances. We had forgotten that hotels in the EU are obliged to collect passport information from each guest before registration and, of course, our pseudo identities wouldn't match. Zann, however, looked as if that was the least of her worries. She was back to clutching her stomach.

"Paola?" Signora Corsi called. A young woman appeared from behind us wearing a staff name pin. "Please show our guests to the Forrestere. I hope you are comfortable there. Paola will take good care of you. Please ring us if you need anything. Now, please excuse me for I must check my husband." Signora Corsi dashed away with a phone pressed to her ear.

"We'll be back later for the cocktails," Zann called after her.

"Cocktails?" Peaches whispered.

"In the brochure," Zann explained.

The young woman standing before us smiled. "I am sorry for the problems. Please give your passports and I will register and then take to your cottage."

Zann threw up her hands. "You've got to be kidding! I've just been barfing my brains out because I've been poisoned and you want me to hand over my passport? I need a shower, and unless you want to mop up the hall next, you'd better take us to our rooms now!"

The young woman's eyes widened. "Um, yes, of course. Follow me."

In minutes we were led to one of the two-floored stone buildings just down the path from the main villa. I'd checked it out earlier—three bedrooms and a separate lounge with a huge fireplace and very rustic furniture everywhere. Paola had no sooner delivered us through the door when a cell call sent her dashing off again. Zann had already bolted upstairs for the bathroom, slamming the door behind her.

"That one's going to need some extract of wild strawberry leaves to settle her stomach. I saw some on the way up the hill," Peaches remarked. "I knew that her best-laid plans would capsize pretty fast."

I was pacing the room, my technique for thinking being motion-activated. "As soon as Piero returns, we'll gear up for act two."

"With Baldi's thugs hiding somewhere?" Peaches was digging around in her bag.

"Evan's on his way and, with a little luck, Piero may help us locate what we're looking for, especially once he hears about Baldi."

Peaches paused her rummaging. "Evan's coming?"

"Yes, he texted me."

"How far away is he, exactly?"

"I didn't have time to look but not far."

"I'll check the group map feature." Phone in hand, she opened up her own Evan super smartphone, tapped an app shaped like five little heads, and up popped a map. I gazed over her shoulder at the two green dots heading from opposite directions toward the big green dot that I figured must be our location. "He's somewhere just outside the closest town and it looks like Rupe is closer still."

"Rupert's coming? Good, we need all the help we can get."

Peaches put away her phone and pulled a pile of neatly folded clothes from her bag. "What are we looking for, exactly?"

"I still don't know." I caught her eye and stopped pacing. "Okay, so everything is a long shot but there are plenty of strange skeletons rattling around in the Corsi family closet. I think they may hold a key to the missing Botticelli, whether they know it or not. That chapel has what's left of an extraordinary fresco by Filippino Lippi, or I think that's the artist."

Peaches whistled. "Isn't that the guy who was a priest and kidnapped a nun?"

"That's probably the most audacious story in Renaissance art history. Everyone seems to know it but you're thinking of his father Fra Filippo Lippi."

"Seriously?"

"Fra Lippi did become a bit too up close and personal with a nun, one Lucrezia Buti, but thanks to Cosimo de' Medici's intervention he ended up marrying her. Filippino, their son, was also a master painter. He's the suspected artist of the frescoes I just saw and, furthermore, Filippino was once apprenticed to Botticelli. Sort that one out."

She stared at me. "Filippino and Botticelli were connected and that artist's son who was Botticelli's apprentice may have done a fresco in that teeny-weeny chapel?"

"He was a prodigy. Apparently he was painting masterfully at only twelve years old."

She gazed up the stairs. "Makes you wonder what was in the water back then. And the only thing differentiating the handles of father and son were a couple of letters? And they call Jamaican names quirky. I'm just going to place my clothes upstairs in whatever bedroom is closest to the door. Keep talking."

"Confusing, isn't it? Plus Botticelli had once been an apprentice in the father Filippo's workshop when he was young, too, so there are double, *triple* connections," I said as she ran up the stairs.

"What's it all mean?" she called down.

"That's what we need to find out. Hopefully Piero can tell us."

In seconds, Peaches was back in the lounge. "Right, so I've got to get the extract of wild strawberry to Nicolina and Seraphina before some Italiano doc pumps them full of the equivalent of intestinal cement. I'll make some for Zann, too. While it steeps, I'll do a once-around the property and keep an eye out for Evan and Rupe. Meet you at the villa later," she called on her way out the door. "I'll text when I see Piero arriving."

"Wait—do you have your phone charged? I got caught out in the chapel."

"Charged it while I was with the band—I've also got my gun and knife, too. Don't worry about me. You two watch your backs on your way to the villa. Keep your intruder app on."

I saluted her as she dashed out of the building. Now I had a few minutes to brush up on my research. Thankfully the Wi-Fi was worthy of any urban connection. By the time I'd finished, Zann had emerged from the bathroom looking considerably better than she had when she'd entered. She quickly put her wig into place, only now wore her own clothes instead of the couture props.

"I know I messed up," she said while reapplying her makeup. "Baldi must have had a tracker on one of us. Can't think of any way he'd have tailed us otherwise. I've been racking my brain trying to figure out how this happened."

And then it hit me. I jolted up from where I'd been propped on the arm of a chair. "He *was* tracking you. We forgot to debug you after you returned from Baldi last night. Peaches, Nicolina—all of us—are automatically debugged by our smartphones. Not you. Damn!"

She turned. "Had you debugged me earlier?"

"Of course. I do it every single time I'm in your presence, but after last night's excitement, I forgot." I began running my phone over her person, her bag—everything. Predictably, I found two trackers, which I ground into the terrazzo-tiled floor. "Damn. Damn. Damn."

Her shoulders slumped. "It's not my fault, then. I don't want any more blame on me, you know?'

I stared at her. "Anyway, it's done. The important thing is to get what we need and out of here before Baldi comes down on the Corsis, that is if it's not already too late. Are you ready? It's 10:15."

By the time we arrived at the villa, Peaches had texted to say that all was clear with no sign of interlopers. She also informed me that she had dosed Nicolina and Seraphina with her natural medicine and had left a cup of extract for Zann in the kitchen. *I'll take one more trip around the hamlet before joining you. Oh, and Piero is back home now*, she added. *Lots of strange bird calls around here. Do you know anything about Tuscan birds?*

Not in the ornithology mood, I texted back. *I know the Tuscans used to eat songbirds as a delicacy.*

They just dropped a notch in my books.

Zann and I entered the villa expecting more of the agitation witnessed earlier but it was as if the Corsis had mustered their resources to appear as if normalcy had been restored. I pitied them.

Paola ushered us across the vaulted hallway into the salon, a gracious butter-colored room with a modern frescoed ceiling softened by lamplight. Piero and Alexandra Corsi sat together on a brocade love seat opposite another couch and four easy chairs. A low table set with glasses and snacks sat in the midst of the seating. At the sight of us, Piero released his wife's hand and rose.

"Ladies, welcome," he said, stepping forward with a dazzling smile. "I apologize again for the unfortunate events of this evening. The police believe it to be sabotage by two servers who have since disappeared. They give chase now." He spread his hands, his expression shifting to chagrin, every nuance enhancing the man's good looks. "Our caterers believe that rivals from another event company must be the cause. It is regrettable. It is also criminal, and I assure you that those responsible will be met with the full extent of the law. Meanwhile, we ask that you allow us make this up to you. A glass of wine perhaps, a bite to eat?"

I couldn't bear the thought of more. I thanked him but helped myself to a glass of water.

"Yes, please help yourselves," Alexandra added, now radiant in a loose rose-colored silk top and skinny jeans. "I was very upset when you arrived. I hope I was not rude. It was just so distressing."

"Of course," Zann said brightly as she took a seat. "No problem." She waved away Alexandra's offer of wine and sweets with a grimace. "Water's just fine with me, too." She helped herself to a small bottle of the fizzy water provided.

"Actually, we need to speak with you, preferably in private." I looked around the large room which probably served as a guest lounge. "Could we shut those doors?" I pulled the double doors shut without waiting for permission. When I turned, Zann was sitting across from the Corsis staring at Piero.

"I don't understand," Piero said, gazing from Zann to me. "Why must we speak in private?"

"You don't recognize me, do you, Pietro?" Zann said.

No, no—this was not how I saw this unfolding. I stepped over to sit beside Zann, placing a warning hand on her arm.

"Sorry for the intrusion. We're actually undercover agents assisting a police matter," I said, not quite truthfully. "We are attempting to locate a lost Botticelli, the key to which we believe may lay in your Medici library. The only reason we entered in disguise was because there's a criminal element after the painting, too. We need your help now. It's urgent, but I promise you, we're not here for any purpose other than to retrieve information. I apologize for dropping this on you now but I'm afraid that time may be running out."

Piero had gone ghostly pale. "How do you know about the Medici library? Who are you?"

"I'm Phoebe McCabe and—"

Zann pulled off her wig. "And I'm Zann. Don't you recognize your old flame, Pietro? It's me, your little Suzanna."

The man looked stricken. "Suzanna?"

"Who is this Suzanna?" Alexandra cried, looking from one to the other. "What is going on?"

"It's complicated," I began, trying to calm her. "I'm Phoebe McCabe from the—"

"Suzanna Masters?" Piero was on his feet. "You dare come into my home after everything you have done to me and this family?"

Now that was unexpected. Apparently time does not heal all wounds.

"It's not what you think, Pietro," Zann began.

"Stop calling me that! I am not your '*Pietro.*' You stole from me and now you return to take the rest, is that it?"

"I didn't intend to break your heart. It's just that Noel—"

"I do not refer to my heart but the letter you stole from my father's library. How dare you return here. You were extradited from Italy and now you return to finish the job?"

"That's not what happened or what's happening now," Zann protested. "I always meant to return the letter and now I will. We're here to track down what I started before Noel Baker—you remember Noel, don't you, the bastard who stole my sketch? There's a lost Botticelli portrait hidden somewhere and those letters of yours hold the key. I intend to clear my name for my dad's sake."

Now Zann was standing, too, the hair plastered around her head giving her a somewhat deranged appearance. Meanwhile, Piero strode toward the door and Alexandra glared at each of us in turn.

"I will call the police immediately! You will not steal from me a second time!" Piero threw open the doors.

And there stood Peaches holding a mug with Rupert Fox standing at her side.

"Good evening, dear chap," Rupert said, extending his hand. "I am Sir Rupert Fox of the Agency of the Ancient Lost and Found. Would you happen to have a spare room available tonight and possibly a pot of proper British tea for a road-weary traveler?"

12

Rupert pumped Piero's limp hand like he was trying to pump air into a tire. Piero stood frozen as if in shock. "I daresay this all comes as a bit of a surprise, dear chap, but there is a bit of urgency to our presence. I have it on good authority that your premises have been infiltrated by unsavory individuals who mean you harm. Indeed, those involved in the food poisoning incident are undoubtedly from the same nefarious clutch. Now, do you mind terribly if I take a seat so we can discuss this more thoroughly?"

Piero stepped back, his mouth agape as he watched Rupert take a chair next to mine.

"Do join us, Signora Corsi. We have much to discuss," Rupert added mildly while helping himself to a plate of cheese and crackers. "Not the tainted snacks, I presume?" He smiled at Alexandra, who vehemently shook her head.

Piero walked back to the couch. "You had better explain quickly before I call the police, sir." He was still standing.

Behind him, Peaches shut the door and passed Zann a mug of brackish liquid. "Down the hatch," she whispered.

Rupert turned to Piero. "The police have already been made aware of the situation. You do know that the Agency of the Ancient Lost and

THE FLORENTINE'S SECRET

Found are affiliated with Interpol, do you not? As for the explanation, it is a bit complicated and best digested with a calm disposition and a side of tea. Please do sit lest I develop a crick in my neck, there's a good chap."

Piero returned to his spot on the couch, his wife having now scooted to the opposite end as if putting as much space between them as possible. Zann leaned toward her and whispered, "It was a long time ago," but Alexandra only averted her eyes.

"Excellent, thank you," Rupert continued. "You have heard of the Agency of the Ancient Lost and Found, have you not?"

Piero hesitated. "That is a television show, yes?"

"Oh, perish the thought!" Rupert pitched his voice to his most Oxfordian sounding vowels. "We are an agency established for the retrieval of lost or stolen works of art, and quite famous, I might add. Surely you've heard of the lost crown of Prince Carlos or our recent work in Venice? We made the international headlines. Indeed, the renown Phoebe McCabe sits right before your eyes," he said while unfolding a cocktail napkin. He shot me a quick look and frowned.

That would be Phoebe McCabe in the blond wig, electric pink lipstick, and frothy candy-colored dress. My credibility factor had taken a nosedive. "We haven't had much of a chance for introductions after Zann revealed her identity but I—"

"Providing background, that's all," Zann said after downing the last of Peaches's elixir and making a face. "Sorry for dropping a bomb on you like that, Pietro, but I promise that I'm not here to steal. I'm working with the agency to solve a mystery and we need your help. When the countess revives, she'll pass you the letter. I gave it to her for safekeeping. Forgive me for everything that went down long ago, okay?"

Alexandra sprang to her feet. "Would you like tea, Mr. Fox? I will get it."

"Oh, yes, thank you, and it's Sir Fox."

But Alexandra had already swept from the room while Zann remained fixed on Piero. "I was young and foolish but I never meant to steal from you so much as borrow that letter to help me locate the Botticelli painting."

"Is that supposed to excuse your actions?" Piero asked.

"Probably not but please hear me out. I know the portrait exists. I tracked down the sketch that creep stole from me and one thing led to another and here I am. I need to retrieve that painting so that my dad will know the truth. He didn't deserve any of that stuff that went down years ago. You know that, don't you? He is a good man." Her voice hitched.

Piero remained silent.

"He and your dad were such good friends, remember?" she pressed.

"A friendship that you betrayed," he said between his teeth.

I jumped in. "We have reason to believe that there may be more letters similar to the one Zann borrowed that may lead us to the portrait's hiding place," I said quickly. When Zann tried to interrupt, I held up my hand. "Your Medici library may hold clues, and if you know of other letters written to or by Botticelli, I'd appreciate you letting us view them. In fact, anything referencing Filippino Lippi could be of interest, too. Please trust us. We mean you no harm."

Rupert turned to me. "Filippino Lippi?"

I held Piero's gaze. "The Corsi family's private chapel appears to be decorated with an amazing fresco possibly by that artist. At least, he's the only Renaissance painter I know to have had such a unique way of capturing the clash between paganism and Christianity so rife in this period of the Renaissance. His backgrounds are animated with mysterious trees growing from books and mythological figures appearing to dash across the fields to join what looks to be a Christian procession. The fresco may have been painted between the years 1485 and 1487 when Savonarola was stirring up religious unrest in Florence in response to the wave of classical knowledge flooding the homes of the nobility. It could be an important work, though badly in need of restoration."

Piero stared. "You broke into my property and ask for my trust?"

He had a point. "I apologize but there is such a sense of urgency in this matter that I couldn't waste a single moment. The criminals Sir Rupert referred to followed us here—in fact, they chased us through Florence trying to kidnap me and abscond with the sketch Zann located long ago. Here, this is a photo of that sketch recently assessed by experts at the Uffizi who believe it may be an authentic Botticelli. It's in their hands now."

I passed over my phone and watched as Piero studied the screen.

"Since this may have been hidden during the artist's lifetime, there's a good chance that a corresponding painting may be hidden, too," I continued. "As you know, a Botticelli portrait is worth a small fortune on today's market and a ruthless bunch of art thieves would do anything to obtain it. We want to ensure it is preserved for all."

A deep anger simmered in his eyes. He passed the phone back. "And to obtain a portion of Lorenzo de' Medici's library also. How much would that be worth to these thieves or to you, Phoebe McCabe? My family have guarded this collection for centuries and you bring them to my door!" He leaped to his feet. "I want you off my premises immediately. I will take my chances with those criminals but I will not tolerate hosting your variety of crook under my roof for a single moment longer."

"Crook!" Rupert said, affronted. "Dear fellow, name calling is most unnecessary. We have only your best interests in mind, I assure you."

Piero picked up the house phone from the side table and in seconds was striding away saying, *"Polizia? Pronto polizia?"* over and over again. Halfway across the room he stopped and turned back to us. "You have cut the line?"

"Not us," Peaches answered. "Don't you have a cell connection? Landlines are so passé."

But Piero was pounding the buttons on his phone like he wanted to shake it into operation.

"Signore Corsi, do not be hasty, I implore you." Rupert was on his feet now, too. "These types are not to be trifled with and the local constabulary is ill-equipped to deal with their insidious ways. We are gathering resources as we speak. Please exercise patience."

"Patience?" Piero glared at him. "You want my library and now ask for my patience, too?"

"We don't want your library," I assured him, "just a chance to study it, honestly."

He scoffed, whether at the honestly part or my entire statement. "It has been my family's secret for decades—no, centuries—and she betrays my confidence a second time!" Piero said, pointing to Zann.

Then the doors flew open and in came Paola carrying a tray of mugs and a teapot with Alexandra following close behind. Catching sight of her husband, she stopped and hissed something in Italian. I thought I caught the words *miserable lying swine* or an Italian equivalent thereof. In seconds the couple darted from the room arguing all the way.

Peaches turned to Zann. "You just love to contribute to domestic bliss, don't you?"

Paola set the tray on the table and made a hasty exit, too, shutting the door behind her and leaving the four of us alone.

"I daresay, Phoebe, had you handled this differently we might be much better positioned to convince this family of a good intent," Rupert said, gazing down at me, his bristled eyebrows giving the impression of colliding caterpillars.

Yanking off my wig, I freed my curls from captivity. "Okay, so maybe I should have alerted you sooner but I truly thought it was straightforward... until it wasn't. Everything happened very quickly. Where's Evan?"

Peaches peered at her phone. "He's nearby, as in very nearby, but for some reason he's staying undercover. The tracker points to him somewhere beyond these walls."

"The lad will remain hidden until he can attest to the exact location of Baldi's gang," Rupert said, heading for the tea fixings. "He is using strategic maneuvering based on his extraordinary MI6 training and will guard the perimeters accordingly. Actually, he is testing a new device that creates an electronic fence around the walls. I must say, Phoebe, I cannot believe that you have run afoul of Andre Baldi, the most notorious arms dealer and drug lord in Italy, possibly the world."

Peaches caught my eye. "I filled him in on the details," she said.

I watched Rupert pour each of us tea whether we'd requested it or not. "Then I presume you know also about Suzanna Masters. Allow me to formally introduce you: Zann, this is Sir Rupert Fox, one of the members of our agency, and, Rupert, this is Suzanna Masters—"

"—one of the members of Andre Baldi's gang," Rupert said without looking up. "Yes, I know you by reputation, Ms. Masters, and admit to being alarmed when I heard that you were involved with our team."

"And she whacked Seraphina with a thermos and held Phoebe at gunpoint," Peaches added with grin. "Our kind of gal." I shot her a look but she only shrugged.

"It wasn't loaded," Zann protested.

"What, the thermos?" Peaches quipped.

"And were you not responsible for the appalling plunder of Afghanistan's Roman ruins and more recently took part in the heist of the Temple of Neptune on Corsica?" Rupert asked, eyes fixed on his mug.

Zann, who was just beginning to regain her natural color, lost it all over again. "When you are working for Baldi, you do what Baldi tells you. I was obeying orders."

"And now?" Rupert asked.

"And now I'm not. Now, I'm getting out from under the rock he's shoved me into for years. Finding this Botticelli is my only chance. I must succeed."

"You mean *we* must succeed, don't you?" I asked. Without waiting for a response, I turned to Rupert. "Did Peaches fill you in about Noel, too?"

"Indeed." Rupert took his first sip and sighed. "Never as good as English tea, of course. The Italians fail to grasp the finer nuances of brewing the proper cup and no doubt left the bags in the pot entirely too long, but to your question, yes, Peaches explained the distressing news that Ms. Masters also had an entanglement with Noel Halloren or Noel Baker. My, but that boy did get around."

So Peaches had left the critical part for me to tell.

"Entanglement—is that what you call it?" Zann began. "More like—"

I held up my hand. "I'm not just referring to the unfortunate romance but to the fact that Toby has alluded to the sketch during a recent phone call and in our letters back and forth. He called it a 'bomb,' Rupert, a *bomb*. Now I realize why."

"Indeed, it appears as though your brother may have had some inkling as to the location of the painting."

"That's what I think, too. All those years ago when Noel took off with the sketch, he must have left the portrait in its original location because he simply couldn't find it. I like that idea best. Bastard never could find the really challenging puzzles without me."

"Yes, that is what I am deducing," Rupert remarked. "Certainly the fellow had plenty of opportunities over the years to return to Florence and retrieve that painting or possibly smuggle it from Italy, but if he couldn't find it that explains why it may still exist."

"Maybe it's not even in Florence," Peaches said, "but someplace he couldn't easily access."

"Baldi thinks it's in Florence," Zann remarked.

"And how much does Baldi really know, pray tell? Rupert asked, turning to Zann. "Or could it be that he has not disclosed all his information to you, Ms. Masters?"

Zann dropped her gaze. "I have no idea what Baldi knows. He certainly didn't tell me. Bastard plays his cards close to his chest but that's not a luxury his minions get. He beats stuff out of you if he thinks you're holding back but deep down he also believes women will just crumble under him." She coughed a kind of laugh. "Blind macho stupidity or what? All the times he's slapped me around, I still never told him about that letter or the Corsi library."

"Then how did he discover it now?" Rupert asked.

"He tracked us," I said. "I found the tracker in Zann's purse but not soon enough to prevent this. He also had one of his minions ghost Peaches and me to the Laurentian Library yesterday.'"

"The point is that Baldi has people working for him who are totally cowed into doing things they wouldn't do otherwise. Some are hardened criminals, of course. Some are like me." Zann's head lifted, proud defiance flickering in her eyes.

"It's not easy being a 'Baldino', obviously," I remarked, liking Peaches term.

"It's hell," Zann agreed. "He practically beats his men senseless—cuts off their toes to make a point—but never the women. Us he just roughs up a bit. Thinks we'll capitulate that easily but I never did." A small smile crossed her face. "The whole time I've been plotting to steal him blind. I swear, he's not getting that Botticelli even if I have to die to prevent it."

We all gazed at her in silence for a few seconds. Rupert cleared his throat. "Yes, well, let us hope that no one needs to die in this situation. Now, back to Toby and Noel for a moment. Phoebe, did you mention something about sketches in your brother's letters?"

"More like cryptic doodles. I think Toby knows the approximate location of the painting, too, and has sat on the information for all these years —both of them have. If I could meet my brother in person, he'd tell me, I think, but so far he's just sending me doodles."

I handed him my phone where I'd photographed each drawing separately. Rupert stared at the images for a few minutes, turning the drawings in all directions. "How odd. Indeed, I recognize the style from his video game productions but these little rectangular creations almost look maze-like."

Peaches leaned over his shoulder. "Or like a knot garden. All those square compartments were a Renaissance thing, after all, but the rectangles within boxes baffle me. Is your brother into puzzles?"

"Definitely," I explained. "Toby's old video games were all puzzle-based but not like this. His designs were far more organic and this is more geometric. That's why I believe he's trying to send me a message."

"What about the maze idea?" Zann added, studying my phone.

"That's like no maze I've ever seen," I remarked. I pulled away and stood listening. "Anybody notice how the house has gone a little too quiet all of a sudden? We'd better fan out and check to make sure we know exactly who's here. Let's all meet back here in twenty minutes. Zann, you come with me."

I didn't want Zann's company particularly but I figured I might be the only one able to handle her, not that I'd managed that so far. Either way I considered her my responsibility.

"I'll check outside again," Peaches said.

"And I will seek out the Corsis. The last I heard, the couple appeared to be arguing in the kitchen and I heard the serving woman call out goodnight on her way out the door." Rupert patted a gun in his jacket holster. "Best to keep a firearm handy lest the villa has been infiltrated."

"Don't worry, I've got mine. Zann and I will check the upstairs. Keep in touch by text, everybody," I said.

We spread about the premises, Zann and I heading for the first landing.

"How well do you know the layout of this place?" I asked. The decor held the right balance of authentic fourteenth-century villa style and what was essentially a public place. Nothing could be easily pilfered from the huge Majorca painted vases to the occasional landscape print or decorative plaster.

"Doesn't look like they've changed much since I was here. Added a lick of paint, maybe. Looks like Alexandra may have brightened things up here and there. This is the floor with all the guest bedrooms. The top is the family quarters and the kitchens are on the bottom level with the lounge."

We crept down the hall, checking each guest bedroom, en suite bathroom, and wardrobe, all of which had their doors ajar. At the end of the hall next to a bathroom with lights blazing, we found Nicolina's and Seraphina's bedrooms side by side.

We entered Seraphina's first, finding the woman sleeping deeply in a comfortable but not luxurious bedroom. A lamp glowed on the nightstand where sat a collection of glasses and an empty sludge-lined cup. Her phone lay nearby faceup set on intruder mode, flashing "1 Intruder + Phoebe McCabe." At least her phone was active. I guessed the combination of concussion and poisoning would keep her in a deep sleep for hours longer.

Backing out, we tiptoed into Nicolina's considerably more spacious bedroom where I slipped up toward the pale figure on the bed. I only made it a few steps before the patient sat up and pulled a gun on me.

"Oh, good, you're awake," I said. "How are you feeling?"

"Phoebe?" The gun hand dropped and the other brushed away a lank lock from her forehead. "Very bad still but better. No more retching. Peaches's medicine is very effective. Never again I will tease her about those boiled leaves. What is happening?"

I filled her in. "We're going to continue checking out the villa and then try to convince Piero to let us into that library again. I don't want to have to break into that tower but I will if I must."

She leaned back against the cushions. "Maybe you should not wait. If Baldi is on his way, it is better to get the information now."

"Good point. First, we'll make sure that his honchos aren't here already and then I'll do exactly that, with or without Piero's help. Will you be all right?" I asked.

She waved her gun and smiled wanly. "Yes, for I am armed and dangerous."

"Never doubted it." I grinned and left her to rest.

A few moments later, Zann and I had checked every one of the bedrooms once again before heading up to the family's level. Rupert texted me that Alexandra and Piero were in the kitchen and that he would attempt again to urge them to cooperate. Peaches informed me that there were no signs of unusual activity—in other words, heat signatures—within the hamlet walls and that she was going to scout out the woods in the immediate vicinity. She had heard from Evan, who was still setting up his detector equipment. I needed to text Evan myself but that could wait.

On the top landing, we followed the sound of voices to the end of a corridor where we found the two Corsi boys lounging on a couch playing a video game. Zann flicked the ceiling lights and both kids leaped to their feet.

"Hi, don't be frightened," I said in very bad Italian. "We're here to help."

Zann refused to permit me to mangle another Italian sentence and translated after that. "It's important that you two be extra careful. There are some very bad men on their way here and maybe a couple on the property already. Do you have a place you can hide?"

The boys looked at one another. "We know places," the eldest said.

"Okay, great. At the first sign of trouble, run and hide, okay?" Zann held their gazes until the boys agreed, after which followed a battery of questions we didn't have time to answer.

"Are our parents all right?" one said.

"What do these men want?" his brother asked in English, which turned out to be excellent. I spoke to them directly after that.

"As soon as we can, we'll answer your questions," I said. "Right now we have to hurry to make sure these bad guys are not already hiding in the house, but yes, your parents are fine. How do we get to the lookout tower from here?"

The eldest kid, Enrico, delivered us to a staircase at the end of the corridor that was locked from the stairwell side. Apparently guests were welcome to use the stairway door from the guest level to take tea or drinks up to the tower balcony.

"There is nothing up there but chairs and a table. Shall I turn on the light?" he asked.

"No, thanks. We'll use our phones," I told him, waving mine around.

But minutes later, we climbed the narrow steps to the lookout tower finding it was just as Enrico said—empty but for chairs and a table, a lovely place for drinks on a summer evening. We spent a few seconds studying the view from every direction but saw no suspicious lights anywhere in the surrounding woods. The nearest village seemed far away.

I decided that this was the best time to text Evan. I hastily keyed in my message: *Where are you?* The response came immediately.

Evan: *In the forest behind the olive press. Just tracked down a man dressed in an apron attempting to scale the walls. He won't be poisoning anyone again.*

Me: *Dead?*

Evan: *Very. Don't worry, Phoebe, he had a painless end. I have an app for that.*

Me: *But he might have been some innocent minion obeying Baldi's orders.*

Evan: *If he's sneaking around this property armed, he's not innocent by my definition. I'm after the second one now.*

Me: *The woman?*

Evan: *Nicolina sent a description—slight build, short black hair, and female, yes. Criminals don't become less so by gender.*

Would he kill her, too? Had he ever killed a woman before and why in this age of female empowerment could I even think like that? I had to let it drop.

Me: *Meet me by the tower in fifteen. I've got to get inside that library and find those letters. The Corsis are not cooperative.*

Evan: *I'll be there.*

"I'll be there"—words that caused my heart to lurch, as if I had time for heart lurching.

"You want him to spare one of Baldi's gang because she's a woman —seriously?"

Zann was peering down over my shoulder again. I jerked away. "Stop that!"

"I just can't believe you're a bleeding heart over these assholes based on gender. I know most of the women on the payroll and they're ruthless bitches."

"Maybe some of these ruthless bitches are like you, Zann—some screwed-up woman who made one mistake too many and now can't break free. Being female can make it that much harder to escape in the power game."

That shut her up.

"Come on," I said. "We need to join the others."

The boys were waiting for us on the second floor. "We could stay guard up in the watchtower and let you know if we see danger," the youngest, Vincenzo, said. "Like in the old days, we could be the tower watch."

"Sure," I said, seeing a way to keep the boys occupied and possibly out of harm's way. "Lock the door, okay?"

THE FLORENTINE'S SECRET

"We will," Enrico said excitedly.

We air-dropped our contact information and dashed down the stairs to the lower level where Rupert was again sitting in the salon across from Alexandra and Piero. Though the couple were side by side, I could tell from their expressions that he'd made no headway with our request.

"Alexandra, Piero, your sons are in the watchtower keeping an eye out for intruders."

"The intruders are already here—you," Piero said.

I ignored that. "One of the poisoners has been captured by a team member while he was attempting to scale the walls. Another is still at large," I told them. "If you won't help me access the tower, then I'm going to do it without your help. We believe the mastermind is on his way here with reinforcements. Please reconsider. There's not much time."

Piero leaped to his feet. "You cannot possibly break your way into the tower! I have installed the most modern of security systems. You will fail but go ahead and try." He waved his hand. "I hope you are caught in the act when the police arrive."

I nodded. "I hope so, too. We could use their help. Rupert, would you keep the Corsis company? Nicolina and Seraphina are still recovering."

"Most certainly," he assured me.

"Excellent. Come on, Zann."

We left the villa but I held Zann back in the doorway. "Keep to the shadows," I whispered as I engaged my phone's detector app. Currently there was no way to run two apps simultaneously, such as activating the detector scan at the same time the laser feature was engaged or read texts at the same time as anything else. Frustrating. I made a mental note to remind Evan to keep working on that one.

The two of us crept along the edge of the villa avoiding exposure under the stark moonlight. Except for the cry of an owl and some little animal squealing in the night, all was still. We kept to the shadows until we reached the edge of the villa. At that point, we needed to dash across a narrow alley to reach the next block. Only then could we work our way down to the exposed lane that separated the buildings from the tower.

"How are you going to get inside?" Zann whispered as we paused to do a three-hundred-and-sixty-degree scan.

"Technology," I said.

"That phone of yours, you mean? I want one of those."

"Shh! We have company." The detector app had picked up movement ahead. I stared at the screen at what appeared to be a figure slinking through the shadows along the wall. My guess that it was female by the shape. Too short to be either Evan or Peaches. So where was Evan going to meet us? I switched over to the text feature and shot him a quick: *Where are u?*

Evan: *On the other side of the wall chasing some bastard with an AKA.*

Me: *An automatic rifle? Baldi must be here! I've just spotted somebody, too. I'll deal with that one.*

Evan: *My intruder circuit picked up two more. I'll get to you as soon as I can. Zap to kill.*

Zann was looking over my shoulder again. "Smart guy."

Switching over to the taser feature, I set the slider to the milder end of the spectrum. I'd knock the Baldino unconscious. "Here." I passed Zann my gun. "It's loaded. Cover me. I'm going out."

"By yourself? Are you crazy?"

"Just do it!"

I stepped under the moonlight, my eyes fixed on the deep shadows around the wall, phone held up before me. The phone was vibrating, alerting me that a text message that I had no time to read was coming in.

"Hello? Anybody there?" I spoke the inane statement deliberately: let the enemy think that you play in stereotypes so you can deal their assumptions an unexpected blow.

A figure stepped from the shadows into the silvered light. I blinked to make sure I wasn't hallucinating. A female action hero in camouflage? A leaf-patterned jumpsuit, goggles, and a single dark braid hanging down over one shoulder rounded out the effect. She could have climbed out of the pages of a video game but the assault rifle pointed at me looked deadly real.

"You are Phoebe McCabe," she said in a thick accent, possibly Eastern European.

"I am, and you are?"

"Irena. I take you now to boss."

"I am my own boss, Irena, and I have things to do. I'm not going anywhere. How many of you are there?"

She took a couple of steps forward. "You do as I say."

"I don't think so." I lined up the big red dot on my screen so that the beam would hit her mid-shoulder.

She laughed and lifted the rifle to aim straight for me. "What, you take picture now?"

Good, she didn't know about my super phone. "Is it okay if I take your picture, then? I mean, you're pretty amazing looking, like some super chick."

She grinned. "I like that—super chick. You take one more step, I shoot you but not with picture," Irena said.

"She won't shoot you," Zann called behind me. "Irena's been told to bring you in alive."

Irena's rifle swerved to the right. "Zany? You I can shoot!" But a shot blasted behind me, hitting Irena straight in the chest and knocking her over backward. The woman landed faceup on the cobbles, limbs splayed.

"What in hell did you do that for?" I cried, swinging around as Zann dashed from the shadows.

"She was going to shoot me!" Zann yelled. "You saw that. It was self-defense! You wouldn't feel so stricken if you saw what she did to that village in Afghanistan, she and her sister, Lana, who is twice as vicious."

I whipped the gun from her hand and shoved it deep into my bag. "If you'd stayed put I would have just stunned her. Goddamn it!"

"And she would have shot me eventually." Zann picked up the rifle.

"Leave it," I said.

"What, you leave assault rifles lying around now?" Zann was already holding the thing as if she knew how to use it.

Leaning over Irena, I checked for a pulse but I already knew she was dead, shot through the heart. Mental note: Zann was a crack shot.

At that moment, a gunshot blasted in the woods followed by another and another. I straightened, seared with anxiety for Peaches and Evan. No time to text them, either. Just in case I lost my bag, I shoved my phone deep into my bra, the thing still vibrating with incoming messages.

Zann held on to the rifle. "Hear that? We have to get out of here!" she hissed. "Baldi's arrived." She grabbed my arm and dragged me into the bushes.

"Head back for the villa," I whispered. No time to break into the tower now. Time for defensive maneuvers.

We were halfway along the side of the villa heading for the front door when a male voice barked behind us.

"Drop your guns!" British accent this time.

We froze and turned. Three men were marching out from the side lane, rifles trained on us.

13

"Meet Peter Dunbar, super bastard," Zann whispered. "Baldi's praefectus castrorum, European division."

Baldi really did organize his team like a Roman army.

"Step out from the shadows, ladies," the man called. "Lay your guns and bags down and your hands up."

We did as we were told, stepping out under the moonlight. One of the three men—a thin red-haired guy—took my bag while a thickly built blonde hulk with a Viking physique complete with long braided hair whipped up the rifle. That left Peter Dunbar to study us from his position of power. It was a strange relief to see that at least he was not dressed as a Roman centurion but in jeans and a T-shirt.

He stepped forward, whistling through his teeth. "Still in your party dress, I see, Phoebe McCabe. And look at little Zany. So it's true that you've been working against us." Mid-thirties, short brown hair, boyish good looks, scar across his left cheek. "The emperor has been right all along. 'Someday Zany will be very useful,' he said in a mock Italian accent. 'She will reward us for our patience.' Right again. For the record, I didn't believe a word of it myself. I thought you were a liability from day one."

Zann spat at him. "Wrong again, Dunbar. You should start taking lessons on how to stop being such a brown-noser for once."

He smirked, but before he could respond, a woman dashed up behind him. "They kill Irena!" she cried. "She is dead! They kill her!" She was sobbing hysterically, wailing at the moon like a runaway banshee.

I stared in disbelief. Here was a mirror image of Irena only the braid hung down her back instead of over one shoulder—same camo outfit, same everything. Twins. *Hell.*

Dunbar shot out an arm to silence her. The sobs switched off like a faucet. "Bloody tragic," he said. "Damn regrettable. Irena was a good soldier. Now pull yourself together, Lani. If you hope to have Baldi let you have your way with her murderer, turn off the waterworks. Which one of you ladies did the deed?"

Dead silence followed as the four of them stared down the two of us.

"Oh, come on," Dunbar said. "Baldi will get it out of you eventually. Much better just to 'fess up."

"Me," I piped up after a second, convinced that admitting that Zann had pulled the trigger would get her killed on the spot. Me they had to keep alive.

"Then I kill you." Lani lunged forward.

Dunbar held her back. "Discipline, girl. Now move, you two. We're off to see the boss."

Every rifle pointed at our backs as the men herded us forward like stray sheep, Dunbar whistling, *"We're off to see the wizard, the wonderful wizard of Oz..."*

I thought maybe we'd detour to one of the guest houses, but no, we headed straight for the villa. That wasn't good. In seconds we had crossed the threshold and were steered into the salon, gun muzzles shoving us along.

Inside we found Rupert sitting beside the Corsis with two men standing with combat rifles pointed at them. Two other men sat across from the hostages in armchairs, one of whom I recognized to be Angelo staring morosely at his hands. The other sat legs crossed, enjoying a glass of wine and smoking a cigarette, blowing the smoke up toward the painted ceiling. Seeing us, this one stood and raised his glass. This had to be Baldi.

"At last, here is Phoebe McCabe, who they say can find lost art like magic." The man grinned, revealing a space between his teeth. "The lost-art sniffer dog."

How did Baldi know that term? Had I ever once referred to myself as that publicly? It was my tongue-in-cheek name for myself.

"I am glad to meet you at last," Baldi continued. "You see I have your friends in my care and the two ladies upstairs rest comfortably with my men to keep them company. That leaves us to talk."

Baldi in the flesh was not what I expected. Blame word association but I thought he'd be bald. Instead, he had plenty of thick gray-streaked black hair growing in close-cropped curls against his skull. Wiry tuffs emerged from the top of his short-sleeved shirt and more crawled down his arms. About mid-height with a stocky build, I pegged him to be around fiftyish. The glint in his small dark eyes made me doubt that he had a compassionate bone in his body.

He ignored Zann as he stood sizing me up, dragging on his cigarette and blowing the smoke into my face. I coughed, trying to wave away the fumes. "Haven't heard the news yet that smoking's bad for your health, Baldi?"

"Haven't heard the news yet that crossing Baldi is very bad for yours, McCabe?" He laughed. Passing his empty glass to the skinny red-haired guy, he slowly walked around me, sizing me up like a prize cow.

"That one, Phoebe McCabe, she kill Irena, boss," I heard Lani say behind me. "Kill her dead!" she sobbed.

"Ah, too bad, so sad. Maybe I let you have her when I'm finished, my girl."

"But—"

"Silence!" Baldi continued to walk around me while Dunbar and his troop formed a line standing side by side in military formation.

"How did she make the kill, by gun or phone?" Baldi inquired.

"Glock G17 standard," Dunbar told him. "Don't worry, we disarmed her."

"If you did not take her phone, you did not disarm her. Where is the damn phone?" Baldi barked.

He was standing so close to me now that I could smell the nicotine on his breath. I stood still, hoping like hell he couldn't hear the phone vibrating in my bra. Zann was frozen to the spot beside me as if solidified in fear.

"Check her bag!" Baldi yelled.

The Viking strode past me to dump the contents of my tote onto the floor. Out tumbled my change of clothes, zippy of hair products, undies, map of Florence, and my decoy phone, which slid across the tiles to stop inches from my feet. Viking was about to pick it up when Baldi yelled, "Halt," in Italian: "Do not touch!"

Pushing past me he pulled out a gun and shot the phone to smithereens before kicking away the pieces of tile and circuitry. I noticed another mess of electronic debris in a pile under a chair across the room—Rupert's, I guessed. Was that his dummy or the real one and had they slaughtered Nicolina's and Seraphina's phones, too? I risked catching Rupert's eye. His guarded expression communicated caution. I looked dismayed.

"There," boss man said, grinning at me. "No tricks now. I hear about these phones—very dangerous. True burner phones." He laughed at his own joke. "Where are your friends—the boyfriend and the big black one?"

I stared as if unable to grasp his meaning. "Boyfriend? Big black one?"

"Don't play with me, Phoebe, for you will lose." He turned to Dunbar. "Find Barrows and the black girl. Kill them both and find those two boys. Are you an idiot that two kids escape you? And what about the road?"

"Rigged with explosives as per your command, sir," Dunbar said. "Nobody's getting in or out in one piece."

"Excellent. Take your troops back to their posts. Lars, stay."

The Viking remained in position by the door. When Baldi fixed me with those cold dark eyes, I understood Zann's fear. It was like staring into the abyss. "So, tell me, Phoebe McCabe, why are we here?"

I sensed that he'd know if I was lying, which meant I had to balance on the tightrope between fact and fiction. "I don't know exactly," I said carefully. "I had a lead that a clue to the Botticelli painting may be here. So far I've found nothing."

He assessed this statement and nodded. I could just make out the glint of a gold medallion nested in his chest thicket, a laurel-wreathed profile of an emperor clearly visible. "A clue that drew you to the Laurentian Library after you delivered the Botticelli sketch to the Uffizi. Too bad but it's the portrait I seek. What did you want at the Laurentian?"

"Anything. The library seemed like a good place to start since I didn't have time to comb the official archives."

A sharp shift in his eyes. I'd misstepped. "You know why you went there and you know exactly why you are here. You do not come to this place for wine holiday." He walked back and forth before me, his gaze never leaving my face. "There are important items here—books, manuscripts, yes? I have informants, too, and they say the Corsis hide valuable papers. So far, these fools tell me nothing but they will. You want to study these papers for clues about the Botticelli, and you, Phoebe McCabe, have a clue yourself."

"Me?" Was he referring to Zann's letter or something else? "I don't know what you're talking about."

A slow cold smile crept across his face. "Your brother gave you a clue. That is why you are here."

"My brother? I haven't seen my brother in years. How could he give me a clue?" Oh my God! He did know about Toby! Everything Zann said was true.

"I said do not play with me." Baldi lifted one hand and I watched aghast as Lars leaned over the table and dragged Alexandra to her feet by the hair, the two other gunmen leaning in with rifles pointing at Rupert and Piero. Piero made a lunge for Lars but Rupert held him back and simultaneously cracked a hand across the gunman's arm when he tried to slug Piero with a rifle barrel. The gunman swung his weapon to Rupert ready to shoot.

"Stop!" I cried.

Baldi lifted his hand. "Stay."

The men froze.

"Talk," Baldi said to me.

But Piero spoke first. "We have a Medici library here with many of the Medicis' private correspondence and other manuscripts—books, as well. You can have anything you want but don't hurt my family! Please don't hurt my family!"

Baldi jerked his head at Lars, who released Alexandra so quickly she fell back into her husband's arms. The two huddled together, Piero comforting her while saying: "Zann stole a letter from our library decades ago and that was what led them here. There are other letters, too, which they hope will lead them to a presumed lost Botticelli, but we never found any such clue among those papers. All nonsense, like my father said, another of Suzanna's crazy ideas."

"She stole a letter and did not tell me?" Baldi turned slowly to Zann, who I sensed was trying to shrink herself invisible. But not that invisible.

"So what? You expect me to tell you everything? You think you know me so well, Baldi bastard?" Zann said in a low fierce voice. Her whole body trembled.

When Baldi strode toward her, I knew what was coming. I stepped between them. "Don't touch her. I need her alive and well. If I'm going to figure out the location of the Botticelli based on the Corsi manuscripts, I need her knowledge of the Florentine streets in the fifteenth century. As an archaeologist, she's a valuable asset."

Baldi grinned, that space between his teeth annoying me for some reason. "I give her stay of execution only. She will be dead soon enough. You will find the Botticelli for me, and if you do, I let you live."

I choked back a laugh. "You won't let me live. That's not how you work. You intend to kill me once this is done."

He shrugged. "I give you a choice: you find the Botticelli, I let you work for me and then you live. If you do not find the painting, you die. If you refuse to work for me, you die. Simple."

"Yeah, so simple. And my friends?" I asked.

He shrugged. "Maybe I give them a clean death or maybe they work for me, too. Only the successful work for Baldi so you must be successful. I do not let failures live. Do you understand?"

"Of course." How could I not understand that?

"Excellent. You I see are no coward and that is good, for 'cowards die many times before their actual deaths.'"

Great, so now he was quoting Caesar. "And 'as a rule, men worry more about what they can't see than about what they can,'" I said, also quoting Caesar. I was desperately relieved that I didn't need to repeat anything in Latin or dredge up any more pithy emperor-speak.

Baldi grinned. "I like you, Phoebe McCabe. You would make good member of my legion, perhaps be my magister equitum someday. My current one weakens. I need fresh new blood."

So he had a magister equitum, too. The Roman legion counted their mounted soldiers as the highest ranking class, making the head of the cavalry a high-ranking officer—not Dunbar, in other words. He must be one of the regional commanders. I doubted they used horses, either.

"You will find what I need whatever it takes, understand? No tricks. First trick, I kill her." He pointed to Alexandra. "Second trick, I kill Fox and your two sick lady friends while you watch. I let Lani do the deed. She likes slow deaths and has ax to grind. Third trick." He fired an invisible handgun at me. "Bang but only after Lani is finished with you. Understood?"

I nodded. "Understood."

"Good." He snapped his fingers. "Corsi, you let us into library. Angelo, come here."

Angelo, who had been sitting huddled into his linen jacket, unfolded himself and shuffled over to stand by me.

"You and McCabe will be locked in tower. Zany will wait outside with Lars. The first one who finds the location of the Botticelli lives. The failure dies. With this lost-art sniffer dog and my Medici scholar, the location of that portrait will be found."

"And if we both fail?" Don't ask me why I needed to hear him say it.

"Then everyone dies." Baldi shrugged.

"And if we work together?"

"Then maybe I let you both live."

14

Zann, Piero, and I were herded from the villa at gunpoint with Baldi, the Viking, and Angelo at our heels. I considered launching a disarming maneuver but it was too risky as long as armed men held the others hostage. If I only knew where Evan and Peaches were...

I stumbled over my own thoughts.

"Move!" Baldi said behind me.

We marched down through the hamlet toward the tower. As we drew close, Piero was ordered to step up and open the gate, which he did with a device as slick as any TV remote control. The thick wooden gates swung open, revealing a tidy knot garden lit with low lights embedded in the myrtle. Of course I longed to see that pattern but with a little luck I could do exactly that once on top of the tower.

Not that I longed to be locked inside a tower with Angelo, but at the same time, the thought of laying eyes on part of Lorenzo de' Medici's own library held an almost taboo-like appeal. I tingled at the thought, despite the circumstances.

The tower's exterior had the convincing appearance of a crumbling thirteenth-century watchtower with the exception of another electronic alarmed door that opened at a press of Piero's device. Inside, a curving stone stairway led upward, lights embedded into the well-maintained steps.

We climbed single file, Piero first, then Baldi, me, Zann, and Lars. The stairs were narrow and claustrophobic but a sweet breeze blew in through the lowermost arrow slit. By the time we passed three more, glass covered the openings. When we reached the top floor, puffing and panting, the interior temperature had cooled enough for me to recognize a climate-controlled environment.

Piero, Baldi, and I squeezed into the well-lit top landing, Zann and Lars still on the upper steps since there was no room for everyone at once. Again I considered launching an attack. If I could just pull out my phone and activate the stun feature, swing it around in time to nail Baldi, maybe beam over Zann's head at the Viking—but all the imagined disastrous consequences nixed that idea. All it took was one error and retrieving my phone from my bra might be hazardous enough. Instead, I watched in breathless anticipation as Piero unlocked the door and pushed it open. Lights in the ceiling illuminated a sight I could have only dreamed about.

"My father, he designed the library to the same specifications as original Medici library according to contemporary accounts."

I stepped in behind Baldi and gasped. The room couldn't have been wider than four or five meters, a compact space with a painted white, green, and deep red barrel-vaulted ceiling inset with pot lights that illuminated terra-cotta roundels for each month of the year. Cupboards were built into the walls, each inlaid with wood and semiprecious stones. Forward sloping shelves all around showcased books in tooled leather bindings, some jeweled, others open to reveal illuminated manuscript pages in glowing colors, and countless other tooled leather bindings embedded with semiprecious stones.

"My father believed these tiles were the original by Luca della Robbia, the master tile maker of the Renaissance."

I looked down to where Piero pointed, amazed to see that the tiles did look authentic and beautifully preserved. "But how would he have obtained them?"

"The Corsis have had a long history here. Filelfo Corsi had been a close friend of the Medici and reportedly arrived on the scene shortly after the palazzo was attacked."

Baldi whistled between his teeth. "This must be worth a fortune." He shot a quick glance at Zann. "And you kept this from me?"

"If I hadn't, it would have been destroyed by now, ruined the way you ruin everything," Zann said without looking at him. "I would have done anything to keep this from you."

Baldi tsked-tsked. "Instead, you deliver me straight to it. I should reward you for your stupidity. Enough! Where are the letters, Corsi?"

I snapped out of my awe to watch Piero remove something from a cupboard which turned out to be a thick leather-bound binder with pages encased in clear archival plastic. "Here." He set it down open on the room's single central table. "Take it and leave us alone."

Baldi chuckled. "I will not leave you now, if ever. If you are lucky and these three find what I seek, maybe I let you live but for that we must wait." He pointed to me. "You and Angelo sit. Zann, stand outside with Lars. If they need you, you come."

He then proceeded to stroll around the room, flicking open cupboards, poking through books, peering at glass-encased manuscripts while tapping something into a calculator. Bastard was doing a value assessment.

Meanwhile, I sat across from Angelo, the binder between us. His eyes never met mine once. It was as if he'd found something fascinating in the hands he folded on the inlaid table. The Viking pushed Zann back into the landing to stand against a wall beside him.

Baldi returned to the table and fired a question at Piero. "What do these letters say?"

"Nothing relevant," Piero assured him. "My father translated the Latin and old Tuscan texts and had them transcribed onto typed pages that accompany each sheet. There are accounts of family ledgers, discussions by various Medici members as to purchases like clothing, a business meeting, a thank-you letter, that sort of thing. Nothing mentions Botticelli or is in the artist's hand except for the letter Suzanna stole."

Baldi turned to Zann. "Where is that letter?"

"I gave it to the countess for safekeeping," Zann said.

"I will get it. Tell me what it says and do not try to cheat."

Zann proceeded to read it from memory, ending with the remark: "That and the sketch is what started it all."

"So," the boss man said, turning to me. "The sketch is a clue, yes?"

"It just indicates that there may be a corresponding painting somewhere. That in itself is not proof that such a painting exists." I wasn't about to tell him my thoughts about the sleeve symbology and, as far as I knew, he had never laid eyes on the actual sketch.

Something shifted in Baldi's cold dark eyes again. "So you think the sketch unimportant?"

"I didn't say that," I said, gazing up at him, deciding that his eyes were the color of an icy brown peat bog, the kind that contains the mummified remains of ancient people. I wondered how many corpses lay behind those orbs. "I just meant that the sketch gives no clue as to the possible painting's location."

Why didn't he ask to see a copy earlier? He must have realized that all agency members had copies on their phones, including Nicolina and Rupert, not that they would have showed him willingly.

In seconds, I had my answer. Baldi pulled a printout from his jacket pocket and tossed it in front of me. It was a photocopy of the Botticelli sketch. Where the hell did he get that?

"So these motifs on the sleeves mean nothing, is that what you say?"

Before I could respond, he slammed my head down on the table with enough force to scramble my vision. When he yanked me back up by the hair, it was to sneer into my face. "Do not lie to me and do not think you can outsmart me. No one outsmarts Baldi. I come, I see, I conquer. Do you understand?"

In the midst of dizziness, one thought screamed at me: *play submissive female.* Zann had implied something about Baldi's assumptions and I needed to use them.

"Sorry," I whispered. "I don't kn-know what the symbols mean yet," I stuttered. I needed to squeeze out real tears, too. That would be harder. "I mean, I recognized the symbols like flowers and fruit but don't know how they come together."

Still holding my hair, he turned to Angelo. "Angelo, say what you have found."

Angelo cleared his throat and began in a flat tone. "I have deciphered many symbols from the sleeve including the Medici crest, the oak leaf to indicate endurance, the plum for fidelity or independence, the bee for order and work, the goose for vigilance, and the sparrow indicating someone lowly. There is also the wasp, which may refer to either the Vespucci family or to trouble. It is an unusual selection of motifs on a piece of apparel of such obvious cost and workmanship. I have not yet deciphered their combined meaning."

A tear trailed down my cheek. Damn, I was good. "You forgot the lemon and the peach—marital fidelity and silence, respectively," I whispered. "Those two are located near the sleeve hem, almost invisible."

"True," Angelo stated mildly.

"Do you know the identity of the woman?" Baldi demanded.

"No," I squeaked.

Baldi released my hair and my head fell forward. I pressed a hand against my forehead where a bump would soon form. "May I ask how you came by that photocopy of the sketch?"

"No," Baldi replied. "Instead, you may ask how you can decipher the symbols on that sketch and use this library to locate the Botticelli. That is the only question important now and I suggest you work quickly to find the answer."

"We can't concentrate with you hanging over us," I said. "It's too small a space."

He dropped a phone-sized black box onto the table. "I leave you but will listen to everything you say. Do not play tricks, McCabe. Remember, the Corsi woman will pay for your first mistake."

"Please, no!" Piero cried, begging me with his eyes. "Leave my wife alone. Take me, do anything you want with me but leave her alone!"

"I will do whatever I want with you both," Baldi said with a smile. That gap between his front teeth again. "Maybe I will even let one of you live."

As if we would all just walk away from this; as if our lives depended solely on my good behavior. But I smiled encouragingly at Piero before turning to Baldi. "I'm on it." I would have added a trembling lip if I could have pulled it off. The tears had been hard enough.

Baldi seemed satisfied. He turned to Piero and said: "Move. Back to villa. My men and I need something to eat. Tell your wife to get into kitchen and fix us something." He pulled out his own phone and barked orders to somebody on the other end.

I risked a single request. "May we have coffee?"

"Stay alert, so coffee, yes!" Baldi responded. In seconds he was nudging

Piero before him down the stairs and soon we heard the tower door slam shut, leaving Angelo and me sitting across from one another, the other two staring in at us from the landing.

Angelo had already taken the binder and begun to read the first of the letters.

"May I?" I asked, indicating the binder. Without looking, he shoved it toward me. I flipped over the next plastic sheet and peered down at the accompanying typed translation. "It's in Italian," I said.

"We are in Italy," he replied.

So this was how it was going to be, was it? And my translator app was tucked out of reach. I looked over to Zann. "I need your help."

Zann left Lars's side and entered the room to stand by me.

"Please translate these for me," I asked. I could read basic Italian but didn't trust my abilities on something this important. The last thing I wanted was to miss significant nuances.

"He tell you what it says," Lars said from the door pointing to Angelo.

"Angelo prefers to play solo so Zann will have to help me," I said. "Angelo doesn't buy in to the collaboration thing, apparently."

Lars shot a searing look at Angelo, who ignored him—ignored all of us—and kept his head down over the letters. Zann pulled up the only other remaining chair and proceeded to translate the documents, one by one, reading aloud and referring to the Italian transcription of the Latin where necessary.

We went through twenty-three letters in all, most of which were as Piero said, primarily domestic communication between the Medici family across many generations with various business associates and tradesmen. Some were penned on vellum, others on parchment. Several were in Lorenzo's own hand such as a thank-you letter for services rendered and a clothing order to his tailor. Others were by his father, Piero, his wife, Clarice, and another from Lorenzo's grandfather, Cosimo.

I returned to Lorenzo the Magnificent's over and over again, not just because I could stare at the handwriting of the famed maestro of the Renaissance but because one letter dated 1479 in particular intrigued me. At first glance, it was no more than an order to a tailor, a one Antonio di Domenico from whom Lorenzo requested several bolts of cloth in a particular shade of the finest red to fashion a travel tunic with embroidered sleeves and a fur-lined cloak. A travel tunic. Lorenzo was going somewhere. The date was too obscured by what appeared to be a damp stain to read but it was clear that his destination required the finest clothes.

Another was an order from the same tailor for a gamurra. Since a gamurra was a woman's over-gown, it seemed odd that the patriarch of the Florentine republic would invest time in ordering women's clothing. Why not leave the task to his wife, Clarice? I had never understood him to be a domestic micromanager like some of the noblemen of the time. Here he made special reference to a ricamatovi and ricamatrici, who would have been the embroiderers of the day, most of whom did piecework at home, and he referenced a design of which he seemed keenly interested, one that clearly he and the tailor had discussed many times.

As always, Lorenzo wrote, *I leave this to your capable hands and artistry. Know that you will be well rewarded. I require the garment to be worked exactly as we have discussed and for the same assistant to oversee the details and attend us for the fitting.*

It had to be for Clarice and must refer to one very special dress, too. Why else would he single it out? I had read many accounts where patriarchs of wealthy Florentine families had ordered clothing for their households including one contemporary Medici ledger that I had studied for my thesis back in my art history days. That account had described clothes required for Lorenzo's own wardrobe, including an astounding amount of yardage for tunics, cippas, manitellos and cappucios, which were all standard menswear for the time, but never descriptions for women's apparel except by the women themselves. In the Medici household, the needs of most of the womenfolk landed in the lap of the wives or sisters.

This man, like all of his wealthy contemporaries, did spend a great deal on clothes and must have appreciated them as an art form like all the other masterpieces he collected. Though Lorenzo dressed down for his civic duties, when entertaining in his palazzo or appearing in public on feast days, it was important to his standing that he flaunt his riches. All Medici women did the same only their apparel was even more ornate and designed to showcase the family's wealth and standing. I had read nothing about Lorenzo being actively involved in his wife's wardrobe before this. He was, after all, a busy man—poet, statesman, art collector, banker, warrior, diplomat, patron of the arts and sciences...

THE FLORENTINE'S SECRET

"What are you thinking?" Zann asked.

"I'm thinking that perhaps we're looking at this from the wrong angle. The only item of clothing considered to be so significant as to engage the head of the family would usually be a wedding trousseau. This was the age when a noble family saw a bride's trousseau to be of the utmost importance. Many families were willing to break the bank in order to properly outfit their daughter's bridal garb. A single dress could be equivalent to half a year's income to some families. If they couldn't afford to outfit a daughter properly, they'd often send her to a convent. One scholar estimates that at least seventy-five percent of the young women in Florence's forty convents of the day were from noble families sent there because papa either couldn't or wouldn't fund their dowries."

"Seriously?" Zann said. "But why is Lorenzo's letter so important? Obviously, he could afford to outfit any daughter."

"Or sister or wife, but look at the date: 1479, one year after his brother, Giuliano, was viciously murdered in the Piazzi conspiracy. Lorenzo rallied the city, who avenged Giuliano's death by lynching the perpetuators from the walls of the signoria."

"One of the insurrectionists was the archbishop of Pisa, if I recall," Zann remarked.

"Yes, and dangling him from a window didn't endear Lorenzo to Pope Sixtus IV, regardless of the archbishop's crimes. As a result, Florence was excommunicated and the Holy Roman See seized all of the Medici assets they could lay their hands on."

"Yeah, and didn't Lorenzo end up in prison while trying to make matters right?"

"In Naples, where he was imprisoned briefly by King Ferdinand," Angelo said without looking up. "Lorenzo requested an audience with the pope and traveled to Rome where he stated his case and won."

I glanced at him. Maybe he was warming up. "In other words, Lorenzo had his hands full and here he is ordering cloth?"

"For his travels, perhaps," he said. "This is not important."

"Yeah, and Clarice was a 'good wife—'" Zann put the term into air quotes "—who even hand-sewed the family's personal linens sometimes, right? She could have handled that part if there was a marriage in the works."

"But in 1479, none of Lorenzo and Clarice's ten children were getting married. The children were still young and wouldn't marry until the next decade, but here is Lorenzo in the middle of a crucial time ordering cloth and lining up fittings?"

"You waste time on unimportant details," Angelo said. "This has nothing to do with Botticelli—too many years between the dates."

We looked over to find him glaring at us. His sharp-bone unshaven face made him look like a rabid ferret.

"We'd figure out this puzzle so much faster if we all work together," I pointed out.

"I will not work with you or be led down the wrong path. I will stay alive while you he will kill. This has nothing to do with Botticelli."

"Maybe not directly but I believe it fits in somewhere. What if Medici was using this portrait as a kind of message where each of the symbols impart some meaning?"

"If this is true, it is for another time. For now we have only to *find* the portrait. We do not need to interpret its meaning," he said.

Zann sighed. "Angelo, you're so not a fun guy. Very tunnel-visioned."

Angelo waved us away. "You distract me with your chatter. I must concentrate and suggest you do also."

I glanced at Zann, who caught my gaze and held it for seconds, or at least until the moment a man arrived with a tray of coffee, another keeping him company with his gun in hand. While the second guy chatted to Lars at the doorway, the coffee bearer set two mugs down on the table, leaving the third on the tray. Turning to Zann, he said in Italian: "The boss says you are to go back and stand with Lars and leave these two to work. Take coffee with you."

I looked over at Lars, who seemed to have scored an entire thermos filled with the brew along with a snack of some kind. Zann slid out of her chair, grabbed the mug off the tray in passing, and returned to stand beside the Viking.

"Boss says not to dribble over merchandise," the man said before making a hasty exit out the door.

That left just Angelo and me. Angelo kept his head down, rereading the correspondence and ignoring me. I kept staring down at Lorenzo's letter, almost in a trance of concentration as I sipped my coffee.

I studied the photocopy of the sketch Baldi had left. At the center of the drawing with its mix of symbols was a dress—a sleeve, actually. Lorenzo put great importance on clothing. Was this sleeve significant in some way, an intended gift to somebody with a message embedded in its symbology? But what did Botticelli and this Gabriela have to do with it? Was Gabriela Lorenzo's lover? Somehow I doubted that. Lorenzo did supposedly have a lover but she was reportedly a great beauty and her name was not Gabriela. What was going on here?

I got up and began to pace around the small space, my brain turning over ideas. There was Filippino's extraordinary fresco in the chapel with so much detail lavished on elaborate gamurras and cappucios, embroidered hems and tunics. Why? Clothing played a part in this mystery, I was sure of it, but Angelo was right about one thing: the immediate task was to locate that portrait. I thought of Toby's doodles. They had to mean something, too.

"You distract me," Angelo said.

I stared at him. He didn't bother to look. Quietly I stepped over to one of the forward sloping shelves. These were mostly holding red-bound leather books that looked very much like those in the Laurentian Library. One shelf showcased a brilliant blue velvet Book of Hours with a lapis lazuli cabochon embedded into the cover. I carefully opened the pages to gaze in wonder at the illuminated content. Then something else caught my eye on the shelf below. Not as brilliant as the illuminated pages, not as stunning as the carefully scribed manuscripts copied from rare ancient works, but arresting just the same—a map.

I peered closer. Encased in special glass, it appeared to be an original pen and ink map of Florence dated 1481, colored with a wash of tempura and carefully labeled. I stared at all the known landmarks and streets laid out exactly as they were today—the Ponte Vecchio spanning the Arno along with other ancient bridges, the roads leading up narrow streets where buildings huddled together, the Duomo appearing like a star from which radiated so many streets, and text that highlighted many other churches. Amazing how few changes there had been across the centuries. Unlike most of Europe, Hitler had not bombed Florence with his usual destructive gusto. The bones of the original city still existed and I could stare down at it as if I were a bird hovering over another century.

Lars poked his head around the corner. I must have been standing in his blindspot. "I'm working," I said. He stifled a yawn and nodded, quickly stepping back to his post.

I returned my attention to the map, keeping my back to Angelo. In seconds I had fished my phone from my bra, skimmed over the texts covering my screen, and opened up my camera app to take several quick photos of the map. I then brought up my brother's doodles in my photo library and stared hard. The telltale tremors started radiating through my body. I was on to something. I broke out into a sweat. Oh my God—brilliant! My brother was diabolically brilliant!

Quickly I tapped the crossed-out ear icon. This application would send a blocking signal within a radius of twenty-five feet where no listening device could send a signal in or out but mine and other Evan super phones. That done, I read my texts, focusing on Evan's first. Of course he knew my exact location.

Evan: *Phoebe, are you all right up there?*

I texted back: *Fine, so far. I'm finding interesting clues and have a dynamite hunch. What's the status of everyone?*

Evan: *Nicolina and Seraphina have escaped. I have no idea how. Baldi smashed their phones so we've lost contact. Baldi found both his guards upstairs dead. He's threatened everyone in the house but I understand that his men are unusually lethargic. One appears to be asleep, Rupert says. Rupert's phone is intact, BTW.*

Me: *Poison?*

Evan: *A drug. I assume Nicolina and Seraphina were never as sick as they appeared.*

I smiled. *Can you get me into Florence?*

Evan: *Your hunch is that good?*

Me: *I felt the tingle. I have a pretty good idea of the approximate vicinity where the Botticelli may be hidden but I just don't know why it was hidden there in the first place.*

Evan: *Let's focus on the where for now. Give me a few minutes and I'll get back to you.*

I texted Peaches next. Several irritable messages had come in from her ranging from *Are u okay????* to *I'm hiding out in this bloody knot garden*, and one final, *Rapunzel, let down your hair!*

Me: *Okay, okay. I have a guard watching me up here. Evan's going to arrange a ride into Florence for us.*

Peaches: *Us?*

Me: *I need your engineering and architectural knowledge. Need Zann and maybe Angelo, too. Can't go as long as the Corsis are in danger.*

Peaches: *Somebody dosed the guards' coffee, probably Nicolina. Zann sneaked a package of a drug to all three of our peeps. Don't know how many Baldinos drank it. Baldi didn't. Maybe seven or more guys still in the woods here. U need help getting out of the tower?*

Me: *I'll let you know.*

Switching the phone over to the stun app, I strolled into the middle of the room. Angelo was still at work, head down, but Zann now stood at the doorway with her arms crossed. Stepping aside, she pointed to Lars, slumped against the wall, snoring.

"You drugged him?" I asked.

"Yup. Same drug I dosed Peaches and Nicolina with days ago only stronger. Smuggled some upstairs for them to use, too. If they use it on Baldi's gang, perfecto."

I grinned. "Perfecto is right. Looks like they managed to dose at least some of the Baldinos."

"But Baldi doesn't do coffee."

"What is this!" Angelo scrambled to his feet, panic flaring in his eyes. His gaze swung from Lars to my phone. "Why you do this? Baldi will hear and shoot us all!"

"Baldi can't hear a thing at the moment, Angelo. I have my blocker on."

He raised both hands. "Don't zap me, please don't zap me!"

"I'm not going to zap you. I'm going to offer you a chance to stay alive. Work with me."

"I will not work for you! I must live!"

"I said work *with* me not *for* me."

"I have a family. Baldi will kill me and my wife if I do not do as he says. He has already...hurt me many times. I do not want to lose another toe!"

"Calm down," I said. "I have an idea where the painting may be hidden and you don't. Working with us may be the only way you can stay alive and keep the rest of your toes. Interested? If not, we'll leave you behind and then he'll probably do worse than slice off a toe. Did he do that to you already?"

The man nodded. "Twice—two middle toes." He began untying his shoes. It was then I noticed that his left shoe was stained red.

"Did he just do that?"

"On the way here," Angelo said miserably. "Here, I show you." He began untying his sneaker.

"No, no—not necessary. If it's swelling, you might not get the shoe back on. Shit—that bastard." I turned to Zann. "Can you vouch for this guy?"

Zann studied the trembling man. "Don't know him that well. Baldi only brought him on a few weeks ago, but if Baldi's chopping off his toes, he's probably okay."

"That's what I thought." I turned back to Angelo. "If you want to live, you'll come with us. Otherwise, I'll stun you and leave you to your fate. Several of Baldi's men are already out cold, thanks to Zann's drug punch. The ones that are left will have to deal with my colleagues who are out rounding them up now. The odds are in our favor—sort of. What's it going to be?"

"I come with you," he said. "I'll do whatever you say."

"Good choice. Zann, remove any devices he may have on his person. Wait, a text is coming in."

"Sure thing." While she went to work patting down Angelo, I read the message.

Rupert: *Phoebe, are you managing all right?*

Me: *Yes. Update, please.*

Rupert: *Two Baldinos dead, three drugged. Baldi tried to shoot the Corsis out of pique but I managed to knock the gun out of his hand. He ran from the building screaming into his phone for backup. I did not follow. I have alerted Interpol. It is time for higher intervention.*

Me: *Agreed.*

Then a text came in from Evan copied to all of us: *I've lined up a transportation system to get four of us into Florence. It's complicated but should work. I have an idea that will distract Baldi & Co. which will go off shortly. Phoebe, meet me at the base of the hill in twenty min. Cut through the woods. Don't take the road.*

Me: *We're bringing Angelo and Zann as well as Peaches—make that transporta-*

tion for five. If Baldi knows I'm heading for Florence, he'll grab all his functioning troops and follow, leaving the Corsis alone. Somebody has to stay behind to keep them and the library safe."

Rupert: *Nicolina, Seraphina, and I will protect the Corsis and library.*

Me: *Great! See you in twenty, Evan.*

I then proceeded to unblock the signal and spoke into Baldi's listening device. "We found the painting!" That should set him spinning. "Come on, gang!"

I paused by the window to gaze down on the illuminated knot garden. "See any interesting patterns there?" I whispered while taking a picture that I doubted would even come out.

"Nope. Too simplistic-looking," Zann remarked.

"This is not important!" Angelo insisted. "We must hurry!"

He had a point. Without further delay, we climbed over Lars's limp form, Zann pausing to take his rifle, and crammed into the stairs. We were about halfway down when the tower shook.

15

"What the hell was that?" Zann asked.

"Evan must have ignited Baldi's explosives."

"I cannot take this! Leave me and go." Angelo sat down on the steps and buried his head in his hands.

"Move!" Zann dragged him to his feet and down the stairs.

At the bottom, I ran the de-locking device over the tower door until it beeped open. Peaches was waiting on the other side. "Evan detonated the road," she said.

"I heard," I said. "How do we get down the hill without banging into Baldi's gang?"

"Follow me. There are now Baldinos all over the place. I've picked off a few myself but they keep on coming as if he breeds them somewhere."

"Baldi has many troops," Angelo said.

"Why's this guy even coming with us?" Peaches peered over my head at Angelo.

"He's going to help," I told her.

"But he's a snake," she said. "Remember the Laurentian Library incident with me spending hours in a police station?"

"I do as Baldi says," Angelo explained. "I have no interest in doing these things. I was working on my research when he made me work for him."

"I believe him," Zann said. "Would you have a guy like this working for you otherwise?"

"We're running out of time. Evan's expecting us in fifteen minutes. Peach, lead the way pronto," I urged.

And so she did, taking us on a circumventive route to the back of the garden wall and stopping by the far corner. "This is the best place to climb because there's a shorter drop on the other side. The wall abuts a little embankment," she whispered. "Who's going first?"

I looked up, noting the stones jutting out that would make perfect footholds. "I'll go." Thus I began to climb, congratulating myself for wearing leggings under my skirt.

"I will use the gate," I heard Angelo say below.

"Are you nuts?" Peaches said. "Do you want to traipse down the main lane and offer yourself as target practice to your fellow henchmen, really? That's fine by me, by the way."

"There is problem!" Angelo cried. "I cannot climb wall and jump down other side. Not possible with my feet." He broke into rapid Italian, which Zann countered with something like, *I'll help you. Don't be such a wimp.*

"Peach, will you give this guy a leg up before he drives us crazy?" That was Zann.

"Keep your voices down," I hissed.

There was the sound of scuffling below until finally I saw Angelo's balding head rise before me as I straddled the top of the wall. He clutched the uppermost stones before hoisting himself up to hang hinge-like over the top.

"Angelo," I said. "Back up so you can go down feetfirst instead of headfirst." I could just see a fire burning through the trees—the road, I figured.

In seconds, Zann had passed the rifle up to me before climbing up herself, followed by Peaches, who quickly leaped down the other side. Luckily, overhanging trees kept us deep in the shadows as I leaned over Angelo's back and said to Zann: "How are we going to get this guy over the wall?" I was seriously regretting bringing him along. By chance, I glimpsed what looked to be lights moving in the woods farther down the hill. "They're coming!"

It was like flipping a beached tuna but within seconds we had the reluctant scholar right side up and pushed off the wall into Peaches's waiting arms. Breaking branches and muffled curses followed after which Zann and I landed in the thicket. Soon we were on our feet and stumbling downward. I kept looking over my shoulder, thinking we were being chased before realizing that the real trouble lay ahead.

Multiple lights were bobbing in and out of the forest toward us.

"Are those all Baldinos?" I asked.

"Must be," Peaches whispered back. "As far as I know, there's just Evan and us down here at the moment. The others are back at the villa."

I stared hard. "So they've encircled us. The only way we're going to get past them now is if we zap them with our lasers and hope they don't rain us a shower of bullets."

"I could machine gun them down," Zann said.

"Not possible," Angelo said, hanging on to Peaches to keep from tumbling backward. "They form triple line. You will only kill first line but the others surround us and shoot."

"Roman tactics," Zann remarked.

"We will all die," Angelo whined.

Peaches was gazing down at her phone. "Looks like there are three levels of dots approaching us from the base of the hill. I'm counting maybe thirty. Where's he getting all these guys?"

"He called in backup from Florence and other places. Baldi has big network, some even work as police," Angelo said. "We will all die."

"Stop saying that," I said. "We'll have to use our lasers, Peach."

Peaches held her phone before my eyes. "Not going to happen. See this? Failing battery alert. I've zapped too many Baldinos full charge. I don't have time to use my recharger."

"Then we'll use my phone," I said. "Let's go!"

The longer we waited, the tighter that circle would become. Our only chance lay with somehow slipping through the advancing lines and making a dash for it. I couldn't focus on the likelihood of success—too grim. Evan must have expected that blowing up the road would slow them down but hadn't counted on the sheer numbers of the infantry. We needed an advantage but damn if I knew of one.

"Down there to the right," Peaches whispered. "There's a big pile of boulders with a narrow wedge between them. Found it earlier on one of my scouts. If we can squeeze in and wait until they file past us, we might stand a chance."

I doubted any of these backup guys even knew the terrain so it was worth a try. We followed Peaches, trying our best to be silent, though Angelo was forever tripping and stumbling. The first line of lights was still ahead when we located the stony outcrop and squeezed in through the crevice that narrowed into an even leaner opening on the other side

There was only room for the three of us to fit in one at a time and Peaches had to remain in a crouch but there we waited, staying silent while I tracked the advancing line on my phone. I counted thirty-two moving red dots and one green orb much farther down the hill—Evan, who was still five hundred yards away. Once we broke free and made a run for it, the Baldinos were bound to chase us.

I texted Evan: *Holed up in a pile of boulders.*

Evan: *I'm tracking you. Head for black car at very back. I'll flash you. Hurry. More troops coming.*

I brought up my map of the property. At the bottom of the hill lay the wine depot set in the valley. A narrow drive curved down from the main road to the winery parking lot and then around the depot to the lower service entrance parking area where the road led up to the hamlet. The flashing green dot showed at the back of the lower parking area.

Me: *Where are u—behind the wine depot?*

Evan: *Correct. You'll see plenty of cars parked every which way. Those are Baldi's.*

I waited only long enough for the last line of red dots to pass us and make it about a hundred yards uphill. One straggler lagged behind but we'd deal with him when the time came.

"Okay, gang," I whispered. "Move it! Head for the last black car."

We tumbled out of the crevice and began a headlong dash down to the bottom of the hill. A bullet fired over our heads. Angelo stumbled. Zann swung around and fired into the shadows. Ahead, I saw a jumble of cars of various makes and sizes with plenty of luxury sports cars among them—Baldi's troops traveled well. I focused only on the low black beauty at the farthest point, the one that flashed its headlights. "Hurry!" I cried.

We were running hard, Zann and I up front, Peaches and Angelo behind—or so we thought—but once we reached the Ferrari, we realized that Peaches and Angelo were not on our heels.

"Get in!" Evan called, flinging the back door open. "Where are the others?"

Good question.

Zann turned, dashing back the way we'd come, rifle raised. I followed with my phone's laser feature set. Peaches came stumbling from the shadows with Angelo on her back, piggyback style, an armed guy dressed in total black chasing after. Zann fired once and the Baldino fell to the ground. I waited only long enough to see the army turn back on the hill above at the sound, thirty lights now bobbing through the trees heading our way, someone shouting—maybe Dunbar—and knew all hell was about to break loose. Turning, we ran for the car.

Peaches and Zann crammed into the back, Angelo squeezed between them, while I took the front passenger seat beside Evan. The door whispered shut and the engine revved. In seconds we were peeling away, spitting up gravel as we sped toward the upper parking lot.

I barely looked at Evan as the seat belt automatically strapped me in. "They're going to follow us."

"They're going to try," he said. "I let down their tires. There are six other vehicles identified as belonging to the Baldi boys heading here from the surrounding countryside. My informants tell me that the Baldi network has been activated. Hello, Phoebe. It's great to see you again."

That wonderful voice. I laughed. "Even in these circumstances?"

"In any circumstances."

"Okay, you two—enough of the romantic interlude. Ev, are you seriously planning to drive a Ferrari all the way into Florence?"

It was a fair question. A scurry of lights and accompanying gunfire behind us, ahead nothing but narrow dark road cluttered with indistinguishable objects. I picked out what looked to be a car door in the middle of the lane with a smoldering pile of wreckage to the right. The remains of a white van lay on its side among upended olive trees and shattered pots. The Baldinos must have blown up every car or van they could find.

"Great to see you, too, Peaches, but no. I hot-wired this one but it's probably tracked. We need to ditch it ASAP. I have a relay of assistance lined up between here and Florence that will help get us there but I won't know what my contacts have planned until we reach each point. We'll be traveling blind."

"Do you have army, too?" Angelo asked from the back seat.

Evan glanced into the rearview mirror. "Not an army but a network of contacts. And you are?" He swerved to avoid a pile of smoking debris.

"This is Dr, Angelo Ficino," Zann said, "Baldi's temporary and very disposable-to-him Medici scholar, and I'm Zann Masters, one of his ex-archaeologists. Great to meet you, Evan. Heard so much about you."

"And I you," he said.

"Yeah, but don't believe all of it, okay?"

A bullet shattered the Ferrari's taillight.

"Ev, push down the window," Peaches called, and in seconds she was leaning out firing Zann's machine gun behind us. "Where'd they all come from? Some must be posted at the winery!"

"Yes," Evan said as he maneuvered around more smoking car parts. "I tried to get every one of them but clearly missed a few. Luckily, they're all on foot for now. We need to reach the main road. Phoebe, I've plugged my phone into the GPS. Bring up the screen, please."

I tapped on the dashboard screen. Up popped a map grid on a dark background with red dots scattered on various blue lines which I took to be roads. "I take it that every red dot is a Baldino?"

"Correct."

"Then there's a car heading towards us from every possible direction."

"Let's hope they don't know every direction possible," he replied.

"Pardon?"

But he was focused on the road, specifically on the Land Rover that had just appeared over the rise ahead, heading down toward us from the highway. We were on a narrow two-lane drive designed to lead traffic from the main road to the winery. The roofless Rover was driving dead center, barreling straight for us. I could just detect two guys in the front passenger seat.

"Hang on!" Evan yelled as he gunned the accelerator while swerving the Ferrari back and forth. He planned to play chicken in some last-ditch attempt to maintain the road. I would have tried a different approach considering that a sharp drop on either side could only lead to disaster for somebody, a high probability of that somebody being us. But then, I'm not fueled by testosterone.

The Rover guys started firing. Peaches fired back, peppering the road with bullets, trying to hit a tire. Suddenly the gun went silent. "Shit! Ran out of ammo!"

While the Ferrari sped up the hill and the Rover barreled down to meet us, Angelo began reciting the Lord's Prayer in Italian. I brought up my phone's laser app and aimed for the Rover's driver's side.

"Any final words?" I asked before pushing the button.

16

It was more dramatic than I expected—the Rover swerving off the road and tumbling over and over before bursting into flames in the vineyard below. I had to tear my gaze away from the mesmerizing orange glow.

"Ev, put your headlights on," Peaches called.

"We can't risk them," he said. "They already know where we are and what direction we're heading. Phoebe, where is the enemy on the map?"

I peered at the dashboard screen. "I see one red dot maybe ten kilometers ahead and another coming from the opposite direction." I pushed down on the road lines tracking across the screen. "We're on the SP125, by the way." Which was a two-lane road winding through the hills and valleys of mostly vineyard territory, I guessed.

"What's the name of the nearest town?"

I tapped the closest white circle. "Villore."

"How far away is Vicchio?"

"Maybe ten kilometers past Villore."

He began talking to somebody and I realized that he was wearing an earpiece. I heard him say in Italian that we needed transportation for five and that there were enemy cars approaching from both directions. He checked the screen and gave our coordinates. After listening for a few minutes, he said, *"Sì,"* and fell silent.

"So what's the plan?" I asked.

"Somewhere ahead just outside of Vicchio there's an unmarked lane on the right which we'll have to watch for. It's shortly before the sign saying Vicchio 1K. We pull over there and the next leg begins."

"Which is?"

"I have no idea."

My eyes fixed on the road. Nothing to break the darkness ahead but one set of headlights weaving toward us from the hills beyond, so far above it seemed as if they were descending from the sky. "I hope the object ahead is farther away than it appears."

"Either way, we need to disappear long before it reaches us."

"As in get to that exit before they do?"

"Exactly." The car hugged the road despite the speed as he navigated by the moonlight. Everyone in the car sat locked in a tense silence as we zoomed through the darkness. Evan was an expert driver with proverbial nerves of steel but all it took was one false move to send us to the same fate as the Rover. Angelo whimpered in the back seat. I stole a glance at Evan's chiseled profile. If one wanted to fall for the manly sort, he made an excellent candidate. I had fallen long ago, in fact.

After negotiating a switchback turn, Evan revved the car even faster. I glanced at the speedometer—eighty-five kilometers edging up to ninety, then one hundred in a fifty kilometer zone. We swerved to avoid an animal, something that looked to be a wild boar, before the car straightened out to a clear patch.

"I'm turning the headlights on to see the sign ahead. We must be close."

I caught the reflective flash immediately. "Sign ahead."

Evan slammed on the brake. "Get out and run toward that sign. I'll meet you there."

The car screeched to a halt, Evan activated the doors, and we all tumbled out.

"What are you doing?" Zann called to him, but the doors glided shut and the Ferrari slipped away.

"Watch and see." Peaches hoisted Angelo up piggyback style and we began jogging along the road, everyone's eyes fixed on the Ferrari's taillights. Several seconds later the car stopped for a moment, after which it suddenly accelerated and shot off again. We watched the Ferrari jolt off the road and plunge down an embankment to crash through the vineyard before smashing to a halt and bursting into flames.

"Decoy," I called. "Evan's fine." Which I seriously hoped was true since no silhouette appeared anywhere near the flaming mass. When we reached the sign, still no Evan, though a strange little three-wheeled truck awaited us on a narrow gravel track. A man stepped from the shadows and told us in Italian to get into the back, which consisted of a large open box-like container.

"This is a vehicle for tending the vines," Angelo explained as Peaches helped him up into the open back. "It is narrow to allow workers to go down the rows to tend the grapes."

"Thanks for that, Angelo. Could you just shove your butt back so we can all get in?" Peaches asked. Zann climbed in after her and the driver urged me to get in, too.

"Not without Evan," I said. "You go ahead and we'll catch up."

"Signore Barrows says you get in pronto!" the man said in English.

"You go," I said, "and we'll catch up." I had no idea where Evan was but had no intention of leaving without him. "Does he know where you're going?"

The man didn't grasp my mangled Italian so Zann translated, after which the guy spat out a tirade of what I presumed were curses before slamming the truck gate shut.

"He swore at you for being an obstinate woman, or at least I think that's what he was getting at."

"Children are obstinate; women have their own ideas," came my retort.

"Yeah, I hear you," Zann said, watching the guy climb into the driver's seat and start the engine. "I think we're going without you." The truck sputtered into action.

Peaches was standing now. "What the hell do you think you're doing, McCabe? Do you seriously think we're just going to leave you here?"

"Leave me here!" I called as the truck pulled away. "You need to take care of Angelo and I need to find Evan. I'll catch up!" Not that I knew exactly where I was catching up to.

I watched her hesitate, leaning on the truck gate with a snarl on her face as the truck trundled down the dark lane toward a vineyard. Once I was sure she'd stay with the others, I swung around and bolted for the main road.

The Ferrari was still burning, the flames licking the sky, illuminating a track of broken vines that led to up to the road. Away to the right, I could see headlights zipping down a hill, growing closer by the second. I scanned the area, looking for signs of life or anything human, dead or alive, but there was nothing but moonlit fields and that burning car.

"Evan?" I called.

"What the hell are you doing, Phoebe? Get off the road!"

What happened next was the equivalent of a football tackle that sent me spinning off the road to tumble down the opposite embankment, him rolling with me. When we stopped amid the grass, he was straddling me. "Damn it, woman, do you want to get yourself killed?"

Panting, I gazed up at his shadowy face. "Not particularly but I didn't want you to get killed, either."

"I can take care of myself," he said between his teeth.

"The way you took care of yourself in Spain when those bozos were beating you senseless?"

"I'm never senseless, Phoebe."

I shifted under him, trying to push him off, yet he remained immovable. "My point is, there's no time for heroics. We're part of a team out here."

"Right now I'd rather be part of a pair." And he kissed me, deeply and with his usual deliberate perfection as if we had all the time in the world, as if we weren't hiding in the grass with an army of criminals hunting us down. And I responded. Blame hormones, blame adrenaline, blame something.

Then the earth shook and fireworks lit up the sky. I mean that literally. He pulled away to gaze up. "Excellent—they tripped the explosives. Another Baldi clutch down. We'd better catch up with the others."

He stood and pulled me up by the hand. It's safe to say that recent events had left me breathless, possibly confused, and temporarily speechless. He led me by the hand through the thicket toward the lane like a child.

I forced myself from my stupor. "What just happened back there?"

"After I rigged the Ferrari to plunge into the field and combust, I set up an explosive trip wire that blew up the approaching car. The plan is to temporarily trick the rest of the gang into thinking there'd been an accident that destroyed us all."

A farm building appeared at the end of the track, gleaming ghostly in the moonlight. "I wasn't referring to the explosion and you know it. I was referring to that kiss and your questionable sense of timing."

His face remained immovable, his tone serious. "I thought my timing excellent. Consider all the special effects added to enhance the experience, not to mention the element of surprise. I trust you enjoyed it as much as I?"

"Be serious! I told you I wasn't ready for the next step."

"I *am* serious, Phoebe, as I keep reminding you, and that was not the next step but just a kiss. Carpe diem."

Of all the infuriating, machismo-fueled, self-satisfied things to say. It ignited all my triggers, all the things I both loved and hated about male-female dynamics—the powerful chemistry, the biological urges putting heart over head, heat over brain cells, and that total sense of powerlessness I always experienced in the presence of a man I cared about. "I'm too angry to speak. Let's just catch up to the others before I combust."

"We'd better hurry. These things don't go fast but they have the benefit of traveling where more powerful vehicles cannot go." He was indicating one of the parked vine scooters lined up in the barn's shadows, this one being a four-wheeler ATV-style unit with a tractor seat and a small metal tray perched on the back. "Are you angry at me?"

I made for the driver's seat. "Yes and no."

"Well, that's clear. Phoebe, unless you want me to ride in the back like a kid crammed into a shoebox, I suggest you permit me to drive while you sit on my lap. Why are you angry? It was just a kiss, I said. Were the special effects too much, is that it?"

I laughed. There was no time to argue. Besides, the corrugated aluminum tray in the back was for holding tools not tall men. He had a point.

"Let's not talk about this now. You drive. I'll sit on your lap." I stepped aside as he climbed into the tractor seat. In minutes, I had perched more or less between his thighs, gazing straight ahead while he gripped the handlebars with one arm and put the other around my waist. I kept my gaze fixed on the vine-rowed shadows ahead.

"When can we talk about this or should I just send you a text?"

"Keep your eyes on the proverbial ball, Evan. Where are we going?"

"The vineyard ends at the bottom of the hill beside a river, actually a tributary to the Arno."

"We're going to Florence by boat? Excellent idea. Baldi won't expect that, at least not right way."

"Traveling to Florence on the Arno isn't as brilliant as it sounds."

I had no idea what he meant but I was a bit distracted. It was a bumpy ride. I was seated between his legs. Because of how the seat was arranged, that meant I had to brace my feet on the foot bed while his legs straddled mine. Remember the bumpy bit. It was all I could do to focus on the narrow track ahead as we descended steadily downward.

Evan began speaking through his Bluetooth device. I gathered that the others were waiting. We had no idea whether the Baldinos had yet reached the smoldering remains behind us or how long it would take for them to realize they'd been tricked.

I pulled out my phone and checked in with the team back at the Corsis'. Rupert informed me that all the conscious Baldinos had been called away, leaving seven of their men in various states of unconsciousness who had to be bound up and locked in the wine cellar, including Lars. The two Corsi boys had been most helpful. Nicolina, Seraphina, and the Corsis were napping and the team were spelling one another in case any gang members returned. I updated him on our progress and then stored my phone. I stifled a yawn. It was 1:15 a.m.

Several minutes later, a curve of water appeared winding its way through the hills in a ribbon of moonlight. Our group waited on a rocky shoreline beside what looked to be a battered flat-bottomed speedboat designed for navigating shallow waterways.

Without a word, we waded to the craft and climbed in. Luckily, it was large enough to accommodate all of us comfortably and even came with a windshield. A brief scan with my phone light assured me that the craft was well maintained and wouldn't sink along the way.

"You think I didn't check already?" Peaches asked, catching me in the act.

"Sorry, Peach—habit. How are you doing, anyway?"

"I'm beat like everybody else. Just so you know, this thing doesn't come with life jackets so if we tip..."

I grinned at her. "Guess we'd better not tip."

Both of us had grown up on the water but I wasn't sure about Angelo or Zann.

"We're about thirty kilometers from Florence according to my phone," Peaches told me. "That's not far but I have a feeling it may as well be."

I didn't have a chance to ask what she meant because the driver was pushing the boat into deeper water and bellowing at Evan.

"That's Luigi," she said. "Zann found out that he's part of the agency's international help network that we never knew we had. Note to selves: grill Evan and Rupe on that point when we next get a chance."

"Noted."

"When he's not on standby, Luigi owns this vineyard."

"Great."

"Got to recharge my phone."

"Sure," I said, only half listening.

In minutes we were slipping downriver, Evan at the wheel, leaving Luigi far behind.

"How long until we reach Florence?" I asked Evan.

"I'm not sure exactly," he called over the putter-putter of the engine. "We have to change craft. The Arno is not an easy river to traverse. Pleasure boats are not viable until you're close to the city itself. There are places where the river is silted up or flood control measures have been constructed, which creates all manner of obstacles. I seriously questioned whether we should try this entry at all, especially at night, but going by road would be no better. Baldi will have all the roads watched."

"And it's summer so the river is at its lowest point but I read somewhere that there has been a fair amount of rain nonetheless," I remarked, gazing out at the moon-licked waterway. At the moment, the river was smooth, broad, and edged by willows, but I had a feeling that it would not remain that way.

"Exactly. Phoebe, I—"

I touched his arm. "We'll talk later." I indicated our companions with a nod of my head. Even though all three appeared to be settling in for a snooze, pitching our voices over the engine wasn't the best idea.

"Right. Why don't you get some sleep and I'll wake you when we arrive at the next point?"

I took him up on that suggestion, dropping into a deep sleep almost as soon as I leaned back on the seat boards. Peaches was already nodding off in the well of the boat with Angelo's head falling against Zann's shoulder as they both leaned against the stern. It seemed like only minutes before Evan roused us awake.

"Time to move, everyone," Evan called.

I blinked awake, totally disorientated. We were in the middle of a dark void with a light flashing off to the right. We were slipping toward the shore, the current so light that Evan switched off the engine to let us coast. Two guys waded up to pull the boat to shore, which was no more than a sliver of scrabbled beach. The moment my feet plunged into the chilly water, I became alert enough to notice the big yellow inflatable craft waiting there.

"A raft!" Peaches exclaimed. "Are you kidding me? We're going to Florence not Val di Sole."

Evan was in an intense exchange with one of the guys, both of whom were in their early twenties and eager to kit us out. I hadn't yet reached dry ground when one dropped a life jacket over my head and tossed me a helmet.

Zann was protesting. "We're going white water rafting—seriously?" She paused to listen to the men talking. "We're seriously going white water rafting," she said. "Damn if I expected that."

"Store your stuff!" Peaches cried.

I shoved my phone back deep into my bra.

Angelo was protesting vehemently as Peaches strapped him into his gear. One of the young guys, Petro, was going with us to help navigate and I could just see Florence's glow in the skyline ahead.

As the other guy held the raft, the rest of us climbed in, putting Angelo in the middle with Evan, Peaches, Zann, and I each taking an oar and Petro perching up front, Evan in the back.

"More rain than usual in July so we make it, yes?" Petro called. "If not this..." And he shrugged.

Angelo demanded a seat belt but soon even he fell silent as the raft slipped silently across the broad back of the Arno, everyone paddling. Without engine noise, all appeared still and calm under the moonlight with nothing to break the peace but the sound of our paddles. I could see occasional headlights moving along the roads on either side but hopefully nobody would look toward the dark impassible river. With the current, we soon picked up speed.

And so we went with the flow, rounding a bend where the lights of towns glowed in the dark and we could see villas and farms far in the hills above.

"First coming up!" Petro called.

First what? He urged us to steer to the left-hand side where we could hear rather than see the sound of angry water. On the right, a low barrier of stone; on the left, rapids where the stones had washed away. We slid over the edge and splashed through the churn before the river smoothed out again. That was easy. The next bit was another washed-away barricade where we needed to half hoist the raft off the rocks by our paddles. No problem there, either. We all began to relax: we could do this.

We sailed under a bridge as the houses on either side became more frequent and something that looked to be a modern housing development slid past.

"Hang on!" Petro shouted.

Hang on? I could see nothing ahead.

"What—" Peaches began, but she didn't finish her question before we went right over the edge.

17

It was like a water slide in a fun park only no damn fun. We spun down a slanted water-skimmed cement wall into a second level pool only to plunge over the side of that straight onto the rocks, the raft bumping and jostling all the way. Evan, Zann, and I tumbled out, luckily incurring nothing worse than scrapes and bruises. Everyone but Angelo helped to shove the raft off the barrier toward the ribbon of smooth water flowing beyond.

"Another flood break," Petro called once we were back in the raft. "The Arno has flooded many times. Smooth sailing now."

Smooth sailing was a relative state as we sat soaked and shivering in the warm night. Two more smaller flood breaks were yet to come, both more bearable than the last because by then we were getting the hang of it. Finally the river broadened and Florence crowded in all around as we sailed under one bridge, two bridges. Another loomed ahead.

"Ponte alle Grazie," Angelo said. "We are almost there, thank God."

"This would be a good time for you to tell us where we're going, Phoebe," Evan called.

"I don't know exactly," I replied. "I know the vicinity but our collective brains will need to help find the exact spot."

"Easy." He grinned. That's why I adored that man: he'd follow me anywhere.

"You don't even know?" Zann protested. "I thought you got one of your fabulous brain farts back in the tower."

"It didn't come with specifics or signposts. As soon as we stop, I'll tell you what I have to go on."

Still in the middle of the Arno now awash with city lights and possibly Baldino lookouts watching the river everywhere, I felt compelled to wait. A deep unease descended on us as we paddled the raft along, keeping close to shore.

"We stop before Ponte Vecchio," Petro told us. "Look for flashing light."

Florence took on a different perspective from the river—more remote and even more mysterious, the dark shoreline wrapping the city margins in shadows as thick as time itself.

The flicking on-off of a flashlight appeared to our right below the Vasari colonnade that linked to the Uffizi. Deep shadow clustered under the passage but street traffic would be easy to detect on the road. So far it remained empty.

We landed on a stretch of grass below a wall that separated the portico from the river. Another guy, this one older, waited. He stepped forward to help secure the raft. A rapid exchange of instructions with Evan followed. We were to take the keys he was providing—six for the six Vespas we would find parked down the street at the back of the museum. We were to look for six blue vehicles, all rentals, all side by side, he assured us, and not easily detected. I wasn't sure what he meant by that since six people zooming around Florence at two a.m. might be noticeable by anyone who happened to be looking, regardless of paint color.

The two men were eager to help further so Evan sent them up to the street to act as lookouts while everyone gathered around me. I stood against the wall and opened my phone.

"Look," I said, holding up the photo of my brother's geometric doodle. "I thought it was a maze at first until I found this in the Corsi collection. If you imagine Toby's doodle superimposed over this section of the Florentine map you can see how the rectangles and circles line up. They're actually buildings, domed churches, and streets."

Peaches whistled. "So Toby sent you a map of a neighborhood? Wow."

Angelo leaned in to study the images. "The entire Ognissanti? There's a piazza, a church, houses—how are we going to find anything there?"

"Botticelli lived on Via Nuova, now della Porcellana, and so did the Vespuccis," Zann pointed out. "It makes sense it would be somewhere there. That's the neighborhood where I found the sketch, too. The Vespuccis lived right down the street."

"As in Amerigo Vespucci after whom the Americas were named?" Peaches slipped my phone out of my hand to study the images more closely.

"Yeah, cousins. The family were close Medici allies and frequent patrons of Botticelli," Zann continued, "but I racked my brain to discover where Botticelli may have hidden that painting but came nowhere near there. I thought maybe at the Corsis', maybe even in that chapel with the frescos."

"The chapel plays a role but not the way you may think," I said.

"Phoebe, put us out of our misery." Evan gently removed the phone from Peaches's fingers. "Let us follow along with your thinking here. Where did Botticelli hide the painting?"

"And why not hide the painting the same place he hid the sketch?" Zann asked.

"Because he hadn't painted the portrait when the sketch was hidden and he didn't hide the sketch in the first place—Gabriela did, in the walls of her father's workroom. The painting was completed months, maybe years, later and was meant to be a wedding present, I'm guessing. Only Botticelli couldn't get it to the young couple in time. Savonarola had threatened damnation on all those who celebrated beauty for beauty's sake and Botticelli was stricken with the belief that his soul was in danger," I said. "By then he had returned to painting mostly ecclesiastical work and kept this portrait hidden until Gabriela could return and claim it. Savonarola drained the joy from Botticelli's art. This may have been his last testament to beauty for beauty's sake."

"*I am the hailstorm that shall break the heads of those who do not take shelter,*" Angelo said quoting the radical friar.

"And the hailstorm that was Savonarola was thickening so fast that the subject of the painting and sketch escaped Florence with her friend, possibly future husband, since she could no longer risk her art in the city following her father's death."

"Her art? She was an artist, too?" Evan was smiling at me. He loved it when I did this kind of gathering of diverse clues thing.

"Gabriela, the one who hid the sketch in the walls of her father's house, was also an artist, only of another medium."

"And she knew where Botticelli hid the painting, her gift?" Evan asked.

I was so excited I was nearly tripping over my words. "Botticelli must have believed she could figure it out. He would have expected her—or them—to understand whatever clues he planted. They were all in the same circle, all working as artists and artisans. He believed she would return some day to retrieve her portrait, only she never did."

"Gabriela who?" Zann asked.

"Yes, for God's sake tell us," Angelo said.

"A tailor's daughter, Gabriela di Domenico, who also happened to be a brilliant designer in her own right. I found an entry in a Lorenzo letter referencing her father's business but alluding to 'the goddess of the thread.' Lorenzo de' Medici was a great lover of art and wise enough to appreciate artistry in any guise. One of his tailors, Francisco di Domenico, had a daughter who worked with him in his studio until she disappeared sometime in the second quarter of the 1400s. I'm guessing that Gabriela's designs may be seen in many of Botticelli's paintings—the gorgeous gowns, the exquisite craftswomanship. She was a 'goddess of the thread' and Botticelli respected her as an artist in a way that was hardly common even in the great awakening that was the Renaissance."

"The great awakening that rarely included women, you mean?" Zann remarked.

"It's very possible that Lorenzo de' Medici may have used her designs for his family for years," I continued. "She designed for the Medici, the Vespucci, maybe even for him. The vision of Simonetta probably wore her creations as did most of the muses that populated Botticelli's art—the *Primavera* and the portraits. Gabriela just may have been Florence's best keep secret amid the ruling classes that circled the Medici-Vespucci orbit."

One of the guys leaned over the wall and called for us to hurry up. We scrambled toward the steps leading up the street.

"Where are we going?" Evan asked.

"The one place that all three knew well and had access to," I said as I dashed up the stairs. "The Chiesa di Ognissanti—the All Saints Church."

※

"NOT THE CHURCH!" ANGELO MUMBLED SOMETHING IN ITALIAN THAT sounded like *God preserve us*. "Say that you do not suggest we desecrate a tomb!"

We were scrambling down the deserted road toward the back of the Uffizi where, as the guy had said, six shiny Vespas waited for us in the shadows. Vespas! That was like riding a scooter. I eyed the two more powerful motorcycles nearby, presumably our helpers' rides.

"Of course not," I told him. "Why would Botticelli place a painting in a tomb when he expected Gabriela would need to retrieve it? Breaking into a crypt was hardly practical and would be performing a desecration."

"Because it is the safest place, these tombs. Follow me," Angelo said. "I know all back ways. The Ognissanti is on the other side of town."

"I'm taking one of the Basanti cycles and, Peaches, you take the other. Sorry, gentlemen," Evan announced, gazing at the two guys. "I presume those are supposed to be your rides." One shrugged.

I thought I should take one of the faster ones, too, but Evan went on to explain his rationale. "We'll be flanking the others, riding shotgun for the rest of you. If we get separated, we'll meet at the church," Evan said.

"How are we supposed to know where the church is?" Peaches asked.

"Facing the river," Angelo said. "Past the university."

"Oh, like I know where that is. Never mind, I'll figure it out."

"Angelo, Zann, and Phoebe, you two go first, and Peaches and I will be behind you," Evan called. "There won't be room to ride abreast in some of these lanes."

Peaches looked ready to argue but stopped when she saw a headlight approaching from far down the road. "That could be a Baldino."

"We play decoy," one of the two guys called. "You go!" The two men took off on Vespas toward the headlights while we took a hard right around a corner following Angelo.

It was nothing but a narrow lane behind the Uffizi so we had no choice but to ride single file. Since the city maintained much of its medieval footprint, I knew this would be the norm if Angelo planned on using diversion tactics.

Which he clearly did. We maneuvered in and around more narrow lanes, passing through a back parking area onto a little square where our headlights swept across empty market stalls. Angelo made a hard left onto another, broader street that stretched between the walls of buildings and here he opened up the Vespa's throttle, the engine's whine echoing against the stone.

Evan pulled up beside him, Peaches hanging back, both of them on the much faster vehicles. Now we were going full-speed down what felt like an urban canyon and it almost seemed that we could trasverse the whole of the city simply by staying on the same road.

"Not far!" Angelo called. "Straight ahead."

Or so he'd hoped, but when the buildings fell away to reveal another square overlooking the Arno, three black motorcycles were waiting near a small roundabout.

"Shit!" Peaches cried.

Evan veered away and barreled straight toward them, Peaches following. I heard gunshots but was too focused on keeping up with Angelo to look back. He was diving down another narrow road squeezed between the buildings.

Zann was shouting: "Angelo, courtyard to your right!"

Angelo zipped under an archway, Zann and I close behind. We entered a treed area that appeared to be a parking space for the surrounding flats. Zann moved ahead of Angelo, leading the way along a dirt path that wove around the cars.

We had to disembark long enough to wheel the Vespas through a gate toward an adjacent one-way street. We were far from the river now. Back on the Vespas, we sputtered down the road until we screeched to a halt.

Four headlights headed straight toward us until another swerved into their path from adjacent street. One fired at the others, causing spin-outs and return gunfire. It had to be either Peaches or Evan. Still, one cyclist managed to break away and jet toward us.

"Ditch the Vespas," I called. There was no way in hell we could outride them all, anyway, and how long Peaches and Evan could hold them off was anyone's guess. The bastards kept on coming. "We need to go on foot or we'll lead them right to the church."

"But it is still too far away," Angelo said.

"Nonsense," Zann countered. "The Ognissanti is just over those houses, not far as the crow flies."

"But we are not crows!" Angelo protested.

"I grew up not far from here. I know ways to get us over the roofs on foot. I used to do it all the time as a kid. Come on!"

She dropped her bike and tugged Angelo from his.

I glanced toward the bike buzzing toward us—still far enough away for the driver to miss three figures in the shadows. We slipped from doorway to doorway until we could duck down a side street. There we flattened ourselves against a wall when the cyclist zipped by seconds later. When we heard the Baldino pausing to inspect our fallen Vespas, revving its engine all the while, we took that moment to bolt down the sidewalk.

Zann did know this area. She was looking for gates that led into private courtyards and found one halfway along the next block.

"Open it!" she hissed.

I ran my phone over the wrought iron gate's mechanism until it beeped open. The three of us huddled around the corner inside what looked to be a cobbled parking area as the Baldino coasted by. He would hopefully comb all the nearby streets looking for us. Once it zoomed past, I turned to Zann. "Now what?"

"This is a communal area for maybe thirty or forty flats and offices," she whispered. "All the buildings link together so once we get up to the roof, we can go almost anywhere undetected. It's like flying!"

"By roof?" Angelo croaked.

I hushed him. We followed Zann as she crept through the courtyard, which turned out to be many courtyards linked by long winding back alleys leading to parking areas and private gardens. In the final opening, the tall buildings huddled together with only a patch of sky visible above.

Zann was looking for something. "A shed or a garage or anything we can climb. There—perfect."

She was pointing to a small modern addition built onto the side of one medieval building, perhaps a storage area. These were once villas, I suspected, now sectioned into flats or offices. At a glance I could see that once we reached the shed's terra-cotta-tiled roof, it would be an easy climb up the various extensions and conservatories that owners had built over the centuries. That is, if we made it that far.

We were halfway up and hoisting Angelo up from a glass conservatory toward the next extension when a security alarm began shrieking.

"Shit!" Zann hissed.

We had three more extensions to climb before reaching the top but now every occupant would likely be roused from sleep. The next leg consisted of a little glass add-on that led to a tiny balcony. By climbing onto a patio table, we could reach the glass roof and carry on up to the next level.

We were just tugging Angelo up by his belt when the light came on beneath us. I saw a flash of greenery below, saw a woman pointing up, before the three of us scuttled up and across the tiles to press back against the wall of the last extension.

"This will wake the whole neighborhood!" Zann whispered. Angelo leaned back and closed his eyes.

"And alert everyone on the street besides." I pulled out my phone to send the others a quick group message. *On roof*, I typed. *Heading for church.*

Evan responded immediately: *We'll lead the others away. Meet you there.*

No response from Peaches. I stowed my phone to assess the last leg of our upward journey but Zann beat me to it. She was peering over the next section of roof, beckoning us to follow.

I pried Angelo from his perch and nudged him toward Zann. This section was chin-height and, once we climbed on top of that, led straight to the sky. With the alarms still pealing, we had no time to waste so quickly hoisted ourselves up and scuttled across the terra-cotta terrain on our hands and knees until we reached a foot-deep drop leading to another roof. Now we had to stand and scamper across the tiles like rats, jumping down or climbing up various levels. Though dark, there was enough ambient light for navigation.

It was like traversing a shadowy domain, every connecting section a different height, some peaked, some flat, and most following a footprint unchanged for centuries. The occasional square protuberances had probably once been towers and all the buildings linked together as if a huge ancient organism had subdivided section upon section over the years.

"Look," Zann whispered. "The Ognissanti is over there."

I followed her finger past the large dark gulf to our left, a palazzo that opened before the church's stepped facade. Bizarrely, the church seemed so close and yet far away. Many roofs and at least one street lay between us and that cluster of white buildings.

We were now standing on a flat rectangular space filled with stacked tables and chairs, clearly a restaurant, far enough away from our entry building that we relaxed a bit. At least the alarms had finally stopped, though a police siren screamed down the street. That might even send the Baldinos scattering. I risked peeking over the railing.

Below, the square sat illuminated by the occasional streetlight. A single cyclist circled the piazza like a shark, keeping the engine to a low putter. Riveted, I watched as the rider slipped under a streetlight. Female shape, black leather jacket over camo pants. The black helmet gave away nothing, but the braid hanging down the back said it all. I shooed the other two back from the railing.

"It's her, Lani!" I whispered.

"Killer Lani? That's not good," Zann said.

"Call the police," Angelo urged. "Tell them to come here and protect us."

"Forget that, Angelo," I whispered. "The regular police would just throw us in jail for trespassing and who knows what else. We have a message out to Interpol. They're the only ones who can extract us from whatever crimes we're about to commit." Actually, calling Interpol meant contacting London, who then contacted the Italian division, who would then alert the Florence contingent. In the wee hours of the morning, I guaranteed that wouldn't be a speedy process even though Rupert initiated it hours ago. "All we have to do is cross these roofs without anyone seeing us and access that church unseen pronto. Any ideas?"

"The Ognissanti has many buildings attached—cloisters, rectory, courtyard. If you can climb roofs that way, maybe you enter unseen. I will wait here," Angelo said.

I laughed. "You're coming with us. Move it."

I led the way down to the adjoining roof, a two-foot drop leading to another flat rectangular area sporting an air-conditioning unit. At the end of that, I stopped and stared: a gap yawned between us and the next group of six-story buildings.

Visually I measured maybe a yard and a bit. Below, no more than a service alleyway for storing trash bins and a relatively easy jump—if one could jump. Angelo would never manage it with his dodgy feet. And assuming one made the crossing without faltering, the next challenge was to keep climbing up using momentum to reach the peak.

Zann and I looked at one another. "You go," she said. "I'll take Angelo the long way."

"The long way?" I asked.

She pointed. Far to our right, maybe a block away, as if Florence really did standard blocks, something that looked like a medieval pedway linked two buildings across a street.

"I remember it from when I was a kid. I'll take Angelo that way and meet you at the church."

I had a flash image of Zann as a curious little urchin climbing over the roofs of Florence. Maybe I actually liked her, after all. "Where at the church?"

"It's a big complex," Angelo said. "Many entrances."

"That's why I asked. We need a back entrance, Angelo, not visible from the street," I said.

"I don't know the whole place, only the interior church," he replied.

"We could just hope to find one, I suppose," Zann suggested.

Reaching down into my bra, I pulled out my phone and brought up Florence on Google Maps, tapping on the flyover version. Up popped a bird's-eye view of the city on a sunny day, every detail clear. By sweeping along the Arno, I found the Ognissanti so that we could look down on the ambling church complex from above. It was huge.

"There." Zann pointed to a back section that looked to be an enclosed garden. "That cloister should have a back entrance because that little square is a parking area. All you need to do is unlock the door at that point and let us in."

"Easy," I said because it wasn't. "Meet you there."

I watched as they climbed over the low railing to the right and onto the adjoining roof, hanging back until I could give Angelo a push up the small incline and Zann tugged him over the other side. Once they were out of sight, I returned to figure out how best to get a run-on when a two-foot edging barricaded the way. All I had to do was trip and that would be that.

Maybe the best way was to stand on the edge and spring for the other side. I didn't much like that idea, either, but doubted I could work up much of a trajectory otherwise.

I balanced on the balls of my feet. Theory whammed into reality. Below me, a chasm of darkness; ahead, the opposite roof barely visible in the shadows. What the hell was I thinking? I should have taken the long way around, too. I needed to pitch myself forward in order to keep from toppling backward, assuming I even made it to the other side. Damn, Phoebe! Stop overthinking.

Then I heard a mechanical buzzing deep in the alley's throat below. Fear twisted in my gut. When the shot fired, so did my adrenaline, and I jumped.

18

I had just enough time to sense someone waiting below before hitting the other side—literally. My chin slammed against the roof as I scrambled for a grip. Corrugated tiles, bumpy ridges. I was sliding down.

Another shot rang out, shattering a tile by my left foot. A second shot, then another. The sound of two motorcycles roared below. Finally, I managed to cup the raised tiles with my hands and gain a little friction beneath my feet. The downward slide eased and I clung there listening to the ruckus below.

Somebody, maybe Evan or Peaches, was drawing the dragon lady away. I squeezed my eyes shut and sent a silent thanks before spidering up the roof inch by inch. Once I reached the top, I slid down the other side on my bottom before leaping to my feet and scrambling across the terra-cotta terrain.

This long multileveled section appeared to connect to the church complex—great—but once I was two roofs over, I realized that the only way down was via a six-foot drop. No problem, I told myself, except I had a wonky ankle from an old injury and wasn't sure I could land exactly in the crouch that provided the most protection. It's not like I practiced these things. Somehow I managed to land perfectly, anyway, congratulated myself, and continued.

Here I was dashing across the top of Florence, so far removed from the modern world I could have been transported to another century. Just me, the stars high above, and a drug gang somewhere below, risking my neck over and over again. How perfect could life be?

I leaped to the next level, this one slightly slanted but abutting against the remains of a tower. Supporting myself against its brick sides, I reached the next three-foot drop, jumped, and kept on going. I was getting closer now. The silhouette of the church's medieval bell tower loomed ahead. Three small roofs more and I'd reach the first of the church buildings.

Again, I pulled out my phone and brought up the flyover map. I pinpointed my location and plotted my path up a couple of small peaked roofs, down to the long roof of a cloister—I couldn't quite tell from the angle—and then a quick jump to the courtyard. Then I'd enter through a door and unlock a back entrance, or so I hoped. If I wasn't so positive that I'd need Angelo and Zann before the night was done, I'd head directly for the main church, but as it was, I needed to find that back door.

As it happened, I made good time and, even better, found a little shuttered window tucked away behind an alcove on a third-story section. It looked to be some kind of secondary building judging by the lack of main windows. Guessing this one must lead to a storage room or something similar, I ran my phone across seeking an alarm and finding none. A simple jiggle of the shutter pushed the rotten wood open, a further nudge on the rusty latch and I was in, climbing onto a table into a dark stuffy room.

Silently I admonished the priests or whoever maintained this place for not realizing that God worked in mysterious ways. Why not install proper security? Still, here I was, inside the church—somewhere—and I didn't even need to make too convoluted an entrance. I turned on the flashlight and ran the light across the room, illuminating boxes, folded Christmas trees, wooden angels, a nativity scene. Now, if I could just find the back entrance.

When I entered into the hall seconds later, I found myself in a long dark corridor with stuccoed walls permeating the scent of floor polish. A row of closed doors lined the hall—offices, I thought, or more storage areas. I knew from the flyover that the cloisters and living areas were mostly on the other side of the main church, making this part uninhabited. Next, find a staircase down and a back door somewhere.

All was going so well. By the time I reached the lower hallway and followed along until I found an exit, I figured I was on a roll. On one side of the corridor, broad windows opened onto a treed garden, which meant that the parking lot must be on the right.

Deactivating the alarm, I opened the side door onto a cluster of cars—bingo! Now all I needed was to see Angelo and Zann waiting for me somewhere in the shadows. But the place was deserted.

Propping the door open, I crept out as a security light flicked on above. Another narrow back lane led to this little parking space with nothing around but cars, a jumble of mostly medieval buildings, and the occasional new addition squeezed between.

Pulling out my phone, I texted Peaches and Evan. No immediate response. Understandable if they were chasing bad guys. Then something like a yelp interrupted the dark. It came from somewhere down that narrow alley.

Diving into the shadows, I peeked around the corner. Two shadowy figures were struggling in the dark, a third bent over on the ground. Pulling up my phone, I stepped out, crying: "Stop or I'll zap you where you stand."

The taller figure turned around, dragging the other in what looked to be a headlock.

"Yes, you zap Zann. I want her dead also!" She shifted Zann in front to use like a shield.

Lani, shit! I tried to beam the phone light right into her eyes but she ducked behind Zann while keeping a grip on her throat. Zann's mouth was open. She was squeezing the life out of her while Angelo moaned on the ground. No rifle, either. Where was killer girl's rifle?

I stepped out. "Let her go, Lani. You won't win this one. Release her. It's me you want."

"I want both."

"Let her go and you can have me."

She gave me a feral smile. "Drop phone. Fight like warrior."

Yeah, like I was a warrior. My last martial arts training was prepandemic and my body felt one hundred times older than that. "Sure." I laid the phone on the ground. "Let her go."

Lani flung Zann away like a sack of potatoes. For a second, I was afraid she was dead as she rolled into a heap on the ground until a feeble gasp gave me hope. I took a step forward. "Okay, come and get me."

Lani lunged, flinging me back onto the pavers with such force the breath left my body. I kicked out and missed. She kicked back and I took a direct hit in the gut. Lani laughed. I tried to perform a rolling maneuver that theoretically should have brought me back onto my feet. Instead, I ended on my knees. Lani kicked me over again, my skull whamming against the cobbles. It was safe to say I was going to lose this one.

She intended to enjoy every minute of this. Slow kill was her thing. She circled me as if deciding which nasty move to inflict next. I rolled onto my belly in an effort to protect my vitals, wondering what command I could send that would prompt my phone to intervene. But it was facing the sky, not the enemy. I gazed at the mute square of light emanating from my screen knowing that it may as well be a million miles away. My eyes blurred. I was heaving breath into my lungs. I'd soon would be a goner.

Lani's biker boots crossed my line of vision. She crouched beside me, grabbed my hair, and twisted my face toward her. "Poor little Phoebe. Do you hurt? I hurt, too. I hurt because sister is dead. Now I hurt you; I hurt you bad."

And then I caught a shadow behind her and suddenly Lani was toppling over. Choking in outrage, she tried to rise but something slammed her down again. I flipped onto my back to see Angelo standing over her holding a cast iron planter in both hands.

"Is she knocked out?" he asked.

Propping myself on my elbows, I stared at the unmoving form, at the trickle of blood at her temple. "Knocked out, yes, but still breathing." I was gasping. "Thanks, Angelo. How's Zann?"

Zann came stumbling over to us, rubbing her throat. "Bitch!" She kicked Lani in the ribs. "Why didn't you just zap her?" she rasped. Turning, she moved toward my phone.

"Don't touch it!" I warned as Angelo helped me to my feet. "It will think you're an intruder and burn your hands."

"Really?" Zann paused, watching me hobble over to retrieve my phone. "Can you make it know me?"

I tapped the screen, entered the settings, and activated the "friendly" feature. "Here, place your thumb here and here." Zann followed my directions. "Now it knows you." Remember, I was a befuddled at the time.

"Cool." She was studying the screen. "And those are all the famous features I've heard so much about? Pretty intuitive." Her breath was raspy but she appeared fine otherwise.

"Forget the tech session. Damn, my stomach hurts." Really, I wasn't paying much attention. Just happy to be alive, feeling grateful and all that, not to mention woozy.

I was bending over taking deep breaths planning to force myself back into operation when I heard the familiar sound of my phone electrocuting flesh. I straightened to see Zann tasering Lani over the heart.

"That's for that family you burned alive in Logar and those kids you shot in Herat. You'll never harm anyone again, bitch!"

To tell you the truth, I didn't care. I was just glad Lani was gone and that I didn't have to be the one responsible. I whipped my phone out of Zann's hand and made for the door. "Let's go."

19

The compound was huge. By the time we reached the doors to the main church and deactivated the alarm, another fifteen minutes had passed. We stood inside the darkened nave lit only by the streetlamps beaming in from the tall windows above. Even in the half-light, the shadowy frescos, marble surfaces, sculptures, and ornate niches left me totally overwhelmed. Where would we begin?

"You think he buried painting in a tomb?" Angelo was genuflecting.

"Absolutely not. I keep saying that. Can you imagine someone sneaking in here after hours to rob a crypt?"

"We do not know that it was Botticelli that hid it. We do not know there even is a painting that still survived," he pointed out.

"Such a pessimist." I frowned at him.

"Still, a tomb might be a place to start. I always find tombs rich in artifacts and full of secrets," Zann offered.

"Because you're an archaeologist, not a painter fearing for his soul," I pointed out.

"Guess I should fear for my soul, shouldn't I?" Zann asked.

I let that one drop. Hardly my area of expertise.

"I show you something." Angelo took off down the aisle and we followed as he cut through a row of pews. We didn't stop until we were gazing down at a round marble plaque embedded into the tiled floor. I beamed my light full on the inscription.

"Alessandro di Mariano di Vanni Filipepi," he read.

"Nicknamed 'Botticelli' or 'little barrel,' presumably for his portly girth," I said.

"It is in memory only," Angelo said. "His real tomb is in a side chapel and possibly his remains do not lie there, either."

"Even Simonetta's remains are supposedly no longer here—lost." Zann pointed to another round marker to our right.

"How do you lose a grave in a church?" It seemed like a reasonable question.

"By flood," she said. "When the Arno breeched its banks in 1966, the church experienced so much damage that many tombs were destroyed or, in Simonetta's case, disappeared. They think she may have floated downstream, or that's one story. No one's been given permission to search for her remains here yet."

"Oh, yes," I said. "I remember now. The world lost thousands of paintings, hundreds of sculptures, and at least 1,500 books, if I recall. All of Florence was under water. I didn't realize it destroyed tombs, too. That makes it even more important to find Botticelli's painting, but he would never have placed it in a tomb. He'd find a place he'd think would be more accessible."

"But where?" Angelo asked.

I stepped back and gazed up at the ceiling. Even without light, I could see that it was richly frescoed like the ceilings of so many other Italian churches but in a manner too late to be from the Renaissance period. "Some place Botticelli would think might be permanent and safe. Why does this church look more baroque than Renaissance classical or even medieval? Wasn't it built in the 1300s?"

"Originally, yes, but it's been altered many times," Zann remarked. "It went from simple to this."

"And passed hands to different Franciscan orders," Angelo added.

"Okay, so think: where would a Renaissance man hide a painting inside a church?"

"Behind another?" Angelo pointed to the church's side altars, which were richly decorated by frescos, statues, and even paintings.

"Too late. Those are mostly sixteenth and seventeenth century," I said.

"And as family memorials," Zann added, "they might change over the centuries."

"I have not been to this church for many years." Angelo shrugged. "I do not know it well."

I was just about to protest when the lights came on. We swung around to see three priests standing at the main doorway, each dressed in identical brown robes with bare feet clad in white slippers.

One demanded an explanation in Italian. The little man, probably in his early sixties, took a cautious step toward us saying that the church was not open. If we were in need of solace, they would be happy to help but breaking into a church of God was not acceptable. One of his brethren, a tall lean younger man, held a cell phone and looked ready to call either the police or God at the first sign of trouble. The third, a totally bald guy, simply looked worried.

Angelo stepped forward, removing his wallet and taking out his identification as he went. He proceeded to introduce himself, I realized, catching snippets here and there. He was a scholar of the Medici and his colleagues were his assistants. There was a great urgency to find the secret hiding place of a presumably lost painting by Botticelli rumored to be hidden here —not to steal, he assured them, but to preserve. Criminals were attempting to take the painting to sell on the underground market for drugs. We must secure the painting for the Uffizi or lose another great work of art forever.

The little priest looked dumbfounded and said in Italian, "What, you are like Robert Langdon?"

Zann snickered. "Straight out of a Dan Brown novel, right?"

I shushed her.

"I am Father Agosti and my Franciscan brethren are Fathers Fontana and Leoni." The two nodding priests looked bewildered. While Father Agosti studied Angelo's credentials, I stepped forward and introduced myself in beginner Italian. The friar lifted his hand after my first few words and winced. "Please continue in English."

I thanked him and introduced myself, bringing in a few of my recent exploits, assuring him that I was affiliated with Interpol. I was only halfway through when I realized how the man's eyes twinkled with excitement.

"It is possible," he said, nodding. "I have thought of hidden art many times. This was Botticelli's church. If he were to hide one of his works, why not here? But the church was completely renovated in 1627. Many pieces of art were moved, even the frescos taken from the walls, and then God brought the flood to remind us that such grandeur is not needed for the soul to reach heaven. The Ognissanti has suffered much over the centuries, much like humanity itself, but still we live on in spirit and faith, yes? God has left what remains in our hands and now we must protect it. How can we assist you?"

I smiled at my new ally, but before I could get a word in, he was leading us up toward the nave, describing his church as he went, his slippered feet shuffling on the tiles. "During the Renaissance, Botticelli and Ghirlandaio painted here, it is true, and many others. Our church still holds many great treasures but many more were lost. God be praised for preserving Giotto's cross and Ghirlandaio's *Last Supper* in the refectory. And of course Botticelli's only fresco in Florence remains here. Do you know of them?"

I did, I assured him, though I had yet to see them in person. For some reason, this gem of a church had never been on my mental map.

The little friar was animated and clearly passionate about art and the history of his church. "The *Last Supper* was contemporary with Botticelli and remains in its original location. Let us start there. The two artists were possibly rivals. Both were given commissions to paint the choir screen. Botticelli was commissioned by the Vespucci to paint a fresco of Saint Augustine and Ghirlandaio painted another of Saint Jerome but both were moved. New altars, paintings, and sculptures were installed in the seventeenth and eighteenth centuries by my Franciscan brethren, and then in 1923 one of our convents served as a barracks for the Carabinieri. You see, in such a long contorted history, where would we begin to find the remnants of our lost Botticelli?"

It was *our* Botticelli now. The man was a kindred spirit. "By reading any remaining images from the artist's time," I suggested.

"Then let us begin in the refectory."

"Thank you, but would you mind turning out the lights first? I'm afraid to alert the criminals of our location."

"But of course." The priest gave instructions to one of the brothers, who scampered off to switch off the lights.

The refectory was located between the first and second cloisters in the old convent section. We were halfway there, carrying on an animated conversation about Renaissance ecclesiastical art, all of us chatting away, when a thought struck me with so much force that I slammed on my brakes.

Father Agosti turned in surprise as Zann bumped into me.

"What?" she asked.

"Lani must wear a tracker," I said.

"Of course, all Baldi's—" And she stared at me, equally stricken. She swore, slapped a hand to her mouth, and apologized to our companions.

"What is wrong?" Father Agosti asked.

I explained about the assassin and our struggle in the church parking lot, how it forced us to kill in self-defense, but that the killer probably wore a tracker which will lead her criminal colleagues straight to us. The priest's eyes widened. "You left her body there?"

"We didn't have time to do anything else," I explained.

"She should be properly buried and her soul restored to God," he said, lifting his hands.

"You'd never be able to save that one's soul, Father," Zann told him. "The devil got her long ago."

Even in the dim light, I could see he was prepared to disagree.

"Please, we must hurry," I urged. "I'm afraid that the gang are already on their way." I did a quick check on my phone. Still no messages from either Evan or Peaches. My anxiety spiked.

"I did not realize until now the seriousness of this matter," Father Agosti said. "Alarming." I thought I heard Father Fontana mutter, "Indiana Jones," and had I time, I might even have been annoyed by all these references to popular fiction.

A couple more turns and we scrambled down darkened hallways until we arrived at double doors which the priest unlocked with a security code. In seconds we were inside a long sparsely furnished space. Father Leoni flicked on a flashlight toward the large fresco at one end.

"This would have existed in Botticelli's time," Father Agosti said as we scurried toward the other end. Of course the fresco was magnificent, a work of incredible complexity with dynamic figures engaging with the figure of Christ at the Last Supper, but I was now single-minded.

"Regard the symbols," Angelo intoned, "the evergreens, quails, doves and fruit…"

"…which were not duplicated on Gabriela's sleeve. These are are references to the Passion and the Redemption. I can't see how this masterpiece would feature in Botticelli's clues." I ran my light over the surface, shaking my head. "I know that Domenico Ghirlandaio's work spurned Botticelli on and that they collaborated on many pieces but they were said to be more rivals than friends. One was known for portraying beautiful figures, the other a master at capturing human character, but whether Botticelli would embed a clue based on his rival's work, that is the question. I doubt that he would. We need to look elsewhere. Besides, neither Gabriela nor her friend would have access to a refectory in an active monastery."

"Who is Gabriela?" Father Agosti asked. I filled him on my detective work.

"But wouldn't a refectory be perfect? The friars would only be using it during mealtimes," Zann asked.

"Our early church did not segregate men from women," Father Agosti explained. "This brought accusations of licentious behavior and eventually the order was replaced by more observant Franciscans."

"Wow, friars and sex—got to love what goes on under the hood," Zann remarked.

I was dashing back down the room, everyone scurrying to catch up. "It's not here. Father Agosti, please take us to Botticelli's fresco."

"But it has been moved," he said as he ran up to me, puffing and panting.

"I must see it." Down through the halls we went, the night-lights dimly illuminating our path as we retraced our steps back to the church. "The fresco was painted in 1480, I know, many years before he painted our missing portrait, but if I were an artist wishing to hide something, I would start there, something I had a little control over," I said.

Father Agosti led us back to the nave. "It has been restored quite recently. Originally it would have been on the screen in the choir, which was demolished in 1564. Here you see it in its new home."

We clustered around a side altar as I shone my light up on to the painting framed by curlicues of baroque trompe-l'oeil plaster made to look like marble. The fresco, damaged along the edges, the colors newly brilliant after the recent restoration, portrayed Saint Augustine sitting in his study, one hand crossing his chest to touch his shoulder, the other holding a book, his face suffused in startled wonder as if he had just received a shock.

"According to the tale, Saint Augustine is reacting to a vision of the death of Saint Jerome, but since Ghirlandaio's Saint Jerome is in the fresco opposite, maybe he was just having a premonition," Zann suggested. She was looking across the nave at the companion piece but I remained firmly fixed on Botticelli's fresco.

A clock portrayed behind the scholar was showing the hour at sunrise when Saint Jerome supposedly died. An open book propped on the shelf behind the saint bore clearly visible writing as if it were a notebook of some kind. "What does the writing say?" I asked no one in particular.

"It reads," Angelo began, "'Where is Fra' Martino? He fled. And where did he go? He is outside Porto al Prato.' No one knows what it means. It has baffled scholars for decades."

"But it means something. There are geometric drawings visible there, too," I whispered.

"Nonsensical," Angelo said. "We do not know who Fra Martino was or why he fled to the tower by the bridge known as Porto al Prato. A joke, possibly. Botticelli did enjoy jokes."

"But in a church? That seems a rather odd time to make fun of something or someone. Though it's impossible to tell after restoration, what if that message was placed in the book many years after the fresco was painted? Would anyone even notice?" I asked.

"Probably not," Angelo conceded.

"As a known artist in his neighborhood church, no one would protest if he wanted to make 'repairs.'" I put the word in air quotes. "What if Botticelli placed that message later, specifically to alert someone else, perhaps the only one who might understand its meaning?"

Angelo turned to me. "Filippino Lippi came from Prato."

"He did," I said, barely daring to breathe.

"And 'martino' means 'warrior of Mars,'" Angelo said

"And Mars features prominently in the fresco in the Corsi chapel, plus

Filippino was at war with the swell of anticlassical beliefs rising in Florence at the time."

"And Filippino's father, Fra Lippi, was a friar, not of this order but a man of cloth, yes?" Father Agosti said excitedly. "We—"

But he didn't finish his sentence before a huge crash reverberated through the church.

20

"What the hell was that?" Zann asked.

"*Il porta!*" cried Father Fontana.

Father Agosti spoke to him in rapid Italian and soon both of the other friars were on their cell phones. "We must rouse the others if they are not already awake," he explained.

"Someone's trying to break in through the front door—seriously?" Zann said. "Surely the Carabinieri would have noticed something like that? Aren't they just down the street?"

We rushed up to the huge double wooden doors—thick standard-issue old-church variety, maybe made of cedar. "They will need some kind of battering device to break down those," I said. "Just a guess." Another thump shook the timbers.

My phone beeped and up popped a message from Peaches: *We're in the church somewhere. The Baldinos have surrounded us and the police are swarming the streets. Like a war zone out here. Following your signal now to find you.*

"We may as well turn the lights back on. Our location's no longer a secret", I said, barely containing my relief. "My friends are inside the complex."

When Peaches and Evan came around the corner of a side hall seconds later, I wanted to hug them both but instead managed to blurt out introductions before leading them into the nave. "Quick, where would Botticelli have hidden a painting?"

"Oh, like that's a simple answer. Did you Google it?" Peaches said. Despite the jokiness, I could see she was in rough shape—a cut on her forehead, her stretchy black outfit ripped and muddy, blood. Evan didn't look much better but he cracked a smile. Both emanated strength and determination, though, and the gaze that Evan fixed on me caused a strange internal buoyancy all its own.

"What happened?" I asked.

"The short answer: we tried to keep the bastards away but they found your location somehow," she said.

"At which point, we decided to join you before we were arrested or shot by the police," Evan added. "It appears as though the authorities are under the assumption that these fine brothers are being held hostage while you attempt to heist the church's treasures."

"But that's ludicrous!" I cried.

"Yet very Baldi-like," Zann assured me. "He has a connection with someone high up in the local police around here. Don't know who. All he has to do is string them a story and presto! fake news."

Father Agosti nodded. "Perhaps I should open the door to assure them we are not captives?"

"No!" we all said at once. "But thank you for the offer. Let's just find this painting. Have you heard from Interpol?" I asked Evan.

"Nothing yet. How far have you come with your deductive puzzling?" Evan quirked just a hint of a smile. I had the overwhelming urge to touch his face.

"We are slowly—too slowly, I admit—unpicking the knot that wraps this mystery." I turned to our companions, now staring at us expectantly. "All right, everyone, group think time: where would a Renaissance painter hide a painting in his neighborhood church? Back to the fresco and let's work this out!"

As we dashed back down the aisle, I realized that the banging had stopped but the sudden silence brought little comfort. "What were they doing out there?" I asked.

"They've surrounded the complex. My guess is that Baldi's gang will attempt to break in while the police fiddle around deciding next steps and sort out protocols," Evan replied. "A church is still considered a sanctuary, a point I doubt Baldi will let stop him. Expect an unpleasant interruption soon. My welcome maneuvers have been exhausted."

I didn't have time to ask what that meant.

"Here," Father Agosti said as we arrived before Saint Augustine. "As we were saying, this is not the original location. In the fifteenth century, it decorated the screen of the choir." He pointed to the front of the church.

"He's looking up," Peaches exclaimed, indicating Saint Augustine. "Come on, you guys. We're in a church. Look up!"

Which we did, far up to the frescoed ceiling where saints, angels, and a friar I suspected might be Saint Francis of Assisi in his brown robe cavorted on puffy clouds while Jesus looked on. With the church lights blazing, its colorful glory was fully illuminated and had the added effect of inducing vertigo.

"But Giuseppe Romei's fresco didn't exist in Botticelli's day," Evan said. "It was painted sometime around 1770."

"It doesn't matter," Peaches insisted. "Botticelli was a Renaissance dude, right? He would have known about Brunelleschi's dome and know enough architecture to understand how these places were built. The Renaissance artists were the ultimate cross-disciplinarians. They grasped architecture, right?"

"They did," Evan agreed.

I grinned at her. "You're brilliant!"

"What do I keep telling you?" she said.

"Then perhaps we should be looking at the ceiling over the altar where the choir must have been originally," Evan suggested while heading toward the front of the church.

"But the cappella maggiore was not built until 1574," Father Agosti explained, hurrying after him.

"Let's take a look, regardless," Evan said.

We stood together beside a gilded altar so ornate that the eye barely knew where to land, and gazed up past the golden candlesticks, past Jesus on the cross, past the four angels spreading their wings against a gilded background, and finally to a dome graced by a circle of saints and angels gazing down.

"Not a true structural dome," Peaches decided.

"Half trompe l'oeil," I remarked.

"This is another late addition," Father Agosti said, resting for a moment on the marble steps. "It was not here when our Ognissanti was but a simple church."

"So only the nave is structurally original?" Evan said.

"Yes, that is so," said the friar. "In Botticelli's day, it was plain."

Back toward the center of the nave we went. By now we could see flashing lights pulsing through the upper windows.

"Botticelli painted clues in his fresco that he expected his once apprentice, Filippino Lippi, or his friend and Filippino's love, Gabriela, would understand," I said.

"Filippino and Gabriela were lovers?" Zann asked.

"I believe so. Gabriela was a designer and the brilliance behind many of the glorious clothes painted and worn during Lorenzo de' Medici's time. She dressed many of Botticelli's subjects, both real and imagined. Remember the painting of Venus and Mars—two lovers after lovemaking? That, too, is a clue and Venus's gown a Gabriela design. When Botticelli hints at 'Fra Martino' he is alluding to Mars and to that painting. Either Filippino or Gabriela would have grasped the reference if they had ever returned to this church again. This was Gabriela's parish church, too."

"All church records have been lost," Father Agosti said.

"And the reference to Prato is also a clue for Filippino, who was born there," Angelo added. "The Renaissance communicated in symbols and classical references."

"And Fra Martino, referring to Filippino, did flee," I said. "'Where is Fra' Martino? He fled.' He fled because Florence was not safe for artists and designers anymore. Lorenzo de' Medici was dead. There'd be no more protection from Florence's once powerful champions of artistic license and beauty. If you explored subjects beyond the Bible, you were a heretic, and your art became a crime against God. Too much of a show of wealth was also an insult to Christ's poverty but for an artist, 'poor' translated to a lack of color, texture, and vibrancy. Certainly for those who loved beautiful clothes. Gabriela and Filippino fled Florence the night beauty burned in the streets or maybe even before."

"I do not agree with Fra Savonarola, though I understand, of course," said Father Agosti. "Beauty is God's work no matter what the guise."

Evan touched my shoulder. "Inspired brilliance again, Phoebe, but we still don't know where the painting was hidden."

I turned toward the windows, the faint blush of dawn just visible despite the flashing lights. The sound of sirens drove me to distraction. "He wouldn't have hidden it at ground level as Peaches says. Saint Augustine is looking up."

Which Peaches never stopped doing. "Original pitched timber roof, right?" she asked Father Agosti.

"*Sì*," Father Leoni offered.

"We've got to get up there," Peaches said.

"How?" I asked.

Father Agosti smiled. "Our brethren wash our windows and repair the roof with a system as old as time. We use harnesses, pulleys, and slings like our ancestors. These were also used for fixing leaks. Perhaps this could bring you close to the ceiling, yes?"

I turned to him. "You don't hire professional window cleaners or roofers?"

"We prefer to do our work in-house, as you say, and the old ways bring us much closer to God, yes?" He pointed up and smiled. I returned his smile. "I will rouse my brethren to bring the harnesses," he said as he pulled out his cell phone.

"That could help us to cross the ceiling," Evan pointed out, "but if I'm not mistaken, those lights installed around the top edge of the rafters required a more recent alteration."

"But of course," Father Agosti said, turning. "There are stairways leading there, many stairways. Father Fontana will show the way while we locate the harnesses."

"You may also ask your brothers to post a watch throughout the building to alert us to the first Baldi break and entry. If I'm not mistaken, they'll try to enter from the back," Evan suggested.

"*Sì*, but remember that we are not warriors but servants of God."

Father Agosti proceeded down the aisle, speaking hurriedly into his phone as he went.

Father Fontana indicated for us to follow him, which all but Angelo did. "I will sit here and assist with my broader view." He took a seat in a pew, stretched out his legs, and leaned back. I thought he might have planned to snooze but the sound of gunfire abruptly ended that idea.

21

"They come!" Angelo cried, diving under one of the side altars.

"Sounds like it's coming from the cloisters!!" Evan called as he followed Father Agosti. "The rest of you go ahead. We'll try to hold them off."

Father Fontana had led us down the left side of the church to where a stairway rose in an arched opening to reveal Giotto's cross shining in brilliance under a canopy of painted stars. For a moment, I was stunned by its beauty.

I was just about to take the first step, Zann and Father Fontana having gone ahead, when Peaches touched my arm. "Maybe I should go with Evan."

"Yes. Zann and I will try to find the painting," I said.

"Only you don't know architecture and engineering and I do. I'm staying. Besides, I can't see you swinging from a sling from the ceiling," she protested.

"Have a little faith. I can swing with the best of them. Besides, he needs you more."

Evan, the man with the finely tuned hearing, stopped at the side door and called, "Stay with Phoebe, Peaches. Find that painting. The brothers and I have this."

Peaches shot me a quick look. "You'd think he had God on his side. Come on, Phoeb, let's go."

Zann called down from the top of the stairs to hurry. Together we scrambled up to a landing beside the glowing cross, through a side door, down a long hallway, and through another door to dash up a narrow set of stairs until the four of us were standing in single file along a narrow ledge overlooking the nave. The only thing between us and the thirty-foot drop was an iron railing. Overhead, the trompe-l'oeil ceiling seemed much farther away but it still had to be at least fifteen feet overhead. More painted baroque plasterwork lined the walls where the windows now washed with red dawn light while the spotlights at our feet beamed up at the fresco.

I squeezed past the others to the far end of the ledge where I leaned over to inspect the gilded organ that commandeered at least half of the remaining wall to the left. Behind me, the friar said something I didn't grasp.

"He says the organ is a later addition, too," Zann told me.

This church was layered with visual tricks and optical sleight of hand, none of which existed during Botticelli's time. Baroque had had its way here.

More crashing and the sound of broken glass came from somewhere deep in the complex. I looked over to see four friars slipping onto the balcony opposite ours equipped with a variety of ropes. A younger one burst through the stairway to our ledge calling to Father Fontana, who urged us to back up against the wall, which we did.

Now the friars on both sides were tossing cables up to the ceiling as if fishing among the saints and angels. Whatever they were aiming for must have been expertly hidden among the clouds because I couldn't see a thing. Then a clink of metal against metal caused one friar to praise God. I gazed up. Miraculously, a rope now hung suspended from the painted sky. Within minutes, others followed until the ceiling was strung by a network of ropes and pulleys designed to transport individuals in a kind of grid formation.

Zann whistled through her teeth. "Amazing. This contraption is so ingenious it looks as if it could have come straight out of a Da Vinci notebook."

"Maybe it did," Peaches said. "They used a system like this along with scaffolding back in the day to repair and build their roofs. And we think we have all the answers. Good thing the hardware is modern."

I gazed at the carabiners the brothers had fixed onto the railing's edge, sharing her relief. Now two friars were joining us on the ledge holding slings, a toolbox, and bags.

Explaining their use in Italian, Zann translated: "You climb into the sling and then drop over the edge. The ropes support you and by pulling on them, you can crisscross the ceiling almost any place you want using the pulleys. Return to the ledge and move over to another line each time you want to move farther across more quickly. The friars ask that you to please not destroy the fresco, by the way."

Peaches held up her phone. "Tell him that we're using an X-ray app and that nothing will be smashed indiscriminately.'"

"How do you want me to translate 'indiscriminately'?" Zann asked.

But the gunshot heard from somewhere inside the building nixed the answer.

"Hurry," I urged.

Peaches and I stepped into the slings, wide canvas straps that crossed between our legs and fastened under our chests. There were only two sets.

"Damn. I wanted to fly, too," Zann muttered. "Any guesses where in that expanse of sky you're going to look?"

Peaches was already sitting on the railing, her feet dangling over the edge. "I'm going to search for a cavity within the beams. The hooks must be embedded in the support timbers so that's where I'll start."

"I'll visually scan the surface for any anomalies since my phone is out of juice," I said. "I might see something by eye, anyway. This ceiling would have been nothing but timber beams in his day."

Botticelli may have used a system something very much like this to hide the painting initially. Maybe one of the friars had even helped him. Or maybe he didn't hide it at all and I was on the wrong track. Or maybe it was discovered long ago by my bastard ex and was now in someone's private collection, possibly lost to the world forever. But then, why would Toby have sent me the clue?

I was still sitting on the railing waffling while watching Peaches slip away across the ceiling when a loudspeaker blared from the street outside.

Zann translated. "'Come out with your hands raised and you will not be harmed' but somebody doesn't know the word for *harmed* and used *slaughtered*. Then he finished with 'Release the friars at once!' Not big on original scripts obviously."

"You've got to be kidding," I said. As if our surrender wouldn't result in all of us being thrown in jail and Baldi ending up with the painting somehow. No way. And with that, I pushed myself off the ledge and flew across the church.

Yes, it was very much like flying—very much like falling, too, until the ropes caught my weight. I dangled for a moment gazing far down at the illuminated splendor below before I snapped to and began to hoist myself across the space by pulling on the ropes. It was a bit like zip-lining across a roped grid and an absolutely exhilarating way to traverse this noble landscape while bringing me closer to the magnificent fresco. Below, the church glowed in the soft light, every gilded surface shining, while above I flew with the saints and angels.

"Find anything?" I called to Peaches, who was running her phone across the surface.

"Nothing so far," she called back.

Now we heard a roll of machine-gun fire—against one man and a brethren of friars, seriously? Sudden despair hit me. We'd never scan every inch of this ceiling in time. We were doomed. How could I feel so much despair while flying so close to the angels?

Zann called from the ledge. "The friars say that the Baldinos have entered through the back cloisters. They have barricaded the doors. See anything?"

"Not yet," I called. And maybe never would. Maybe I was wild-goose-chasing a notion that could get people killed, innocent people, good people. Even me.

Another loudspeaker message, this time in English in case anything was lost in translation. "Come out with your hands up! Do not force us to break down door! We will shoot!"

Sure, shoot the wrong people, bozos. Baldi was pulling strings, all right. I was studying the surface, hoping against hope to see something that Peaches's super app might miss, something telling, something that hinted at a secret receptacle behind the plaster. I spun around, ready to hoist myself back toward the ledge in order to cross in another direction, when the sun broke through the window.

I stared, twisting slightly in my sling. The golden light poured in through the opposite window and landed on a spot just above where we had been standing. I grabbed the rope to still myself and stared. "Zann, where would Saint Augustine be looking if the fresco was still in the choir again?"

"Maybe right there!" She pointed at the sun bolt at her knees. "But the sun may have been at a different angle when the fresco was painted and we don't even know the month it was created!"

Below Angelo scuttled out from under the altar. "Saint Jerome died at dawn!" he called. "It is dawn!"

Peaches was swinging toward the sun's landing place, me following. I arrived beside her, both of us bracing our feet against the wall. The friars helped us back on the ledge and we watched expectantly as Peaches held her phone over the sunspot. Nothing registered at first but several inches to the right and she finally got a hit.

"There's a cavity behind there," she said, waving the app across the surface. "Anyone got a hammer?"

There was a flurry of activity among the friars until one removed a hammer from a toolbox.

Peaches flashed him a brilliant smile before whacking the wall below the window. Great slabs of painted plaster fell to the floor as the friars cried out. I watched as the destroyed pseudo curlicues shattered to reveal a deep rectangular cavity.

For a moment Peaches, Zann, the two friars, and I gazed in wonder before I reached into the opening to remove a twelve-by-twenty-inch leather container no deeper than an inch dusted white with plaster and a skim of mold. Holding it up in both hands so the friars on the opposite ledge could see, I cried: "Behold, Botticelli awaits!"

And then a shot fired on the ceiling overhead.

"Behold and watch your new buddy die!" someone cried below.

I looked down. There stood Baldi surrounded by six of his men and Peter Dunbar, who gripped Angelo in a neck hold with a pistol pressed against his skull. Five brothers were also held at either gun- or knifepoint with neither Evan nor Father Agosti anywhere in sight

"Toss down the container and I let them live. Disobey me and they all die," Baldi bellowed. "All of them!"

22

My brain went into overdrive. Baldi couldn't shoot the brethren without facing consequences. There were witnesses and the police were just beyond that door. I wrestled with my conscience, my determination, my anger...

But I underestimated the depth of Zann's own rage. She began flinging tools and insults over the railing at the Baldinos below—hammers, screwdrivers, an ax. "You're not getting this painting, you scourge of the Western world! Eat dirt, you scum!" And much worse.

Dunbar ducked to avoid a flying ax as Angelo broke free and scuttled back under a side altar. Baldi fired toward the ledge at the same time as the lights went out all over the church. Somebody called out in Italian, another screamed in the shadows as I secured the container under my chest strap—awkwardly, I admit—and leaped over the side. It was all that I could do to pull the ropes and hold on to the box at the same time.

Peaches was somewhere behind me as I swept across the ceiling. The nave had plunged into shadows, illuminated only by an occasional bolt of streaming sun. I caught fleeting glimpses of what was happening below—a chaotic flurry of noise and fluster, friars flowing in from every quarter, shouts and commands, gunfire, and cries.

"Baldi's left the nave on the right-hand side holding a brother at gunpoint. I think he's heading to the ledge to get a better shot at you. Head for the back balcony!" Peaches called out to me. "Over there!"

There where? I could just see a pair of small balconies on either side of the high altar, each as wide as the window above. Closed curtains bled a red rectangle of light over each. Where there were balconies, there'd be doorways, I reasoned. Destination found.

I crossed the ceiling until I was within feet of that window. There'd be another stairway up there, maybe even an escape route.

Suddenly I jerked to a halt. Shaking the rope made no difference: I couldn't budge. I looked up toward the shadowy ceiling. The rope had snagged in the hook embedded at the edge of the fresco. Way too far up for me to untangle or even see clearly. Returning the way I had come was out of the question, too, since no matter how hard I tugged and pulled, I wasn't going anywhere.

"Peaches!" I called.

But she was already halfway across the ceiling and couldn't hear. Somebody had arrived on our ledge and was slicing a flashlight beam across the ceiling until it struck me. The curtains of the window where he stood were open so I could see them bathed in sunrise—Baldi still holding the friar hostage, Dunbar by his side. Zann and the other friars had disappeared. Peaches was approaching from the left, shrouded in shadows.

"Drop the painting, Phoebe McCabe, and I will let the good brother go and all these people will live!" Baldi called.

I shielded my eyes against the light. "You have no intention of letting anyone go, bastard," I called. Then I began to rock back and forth as if on a swing hoping to either get unstuck or gain the momentum necessary to reach the balcony. Baldi fired and missed. I began praying—seemed like the right time and place. My rocking was bringing me closer and closer. Another few heaves and my feet might touch the stone. A few more shots and I might die.

Something exploded below. I turned around and looked down long enough to see the police swarming into the church. At that moment, Peaches reached the ledge and was tackling Dunbar while Baldi and the friar disappeared through the door. He had to be coming for me using that poor man as his navigational aid.

I heaved and heaved until the forward swing brought me so close to the balcony that I could almost touch it. Suddenly the rope released and sent me flying toward the balcony. I braced for impact, hit knees first, grasped the railing, and pulled myself up and over until I lay on my stomach, landing full on the container. I gave myself only seconds to thank the angels, check for damages, and spring to my feet. Then I unbuckled the ropes and dashed through a side door, still wearing the sling. No time to detach that thing when on a headlong run down the stairs.

Holding a flat box in front of you isn't easy if you need at least one hand free to hold on to a wall. The stairway was narrow and dark. I didn't see the door until I whammed into it. Seconds later, I opened up the low hatch and peered into a short corridor lined with barrels, buckets, and cleaning supplies. The minute I stepped out, footsteps and voices sounded somewhere down the hall. I hesitated. Behind me voices, ahead nothing but a blank wall.

Then Baldi appeared steering the friar. Seeing me, he flung the man aside and fired. The bullet grazed my leg while I dashed back inside the stairwell. No inside lock. Nothing to do but scramble back up the way I'd come.

A cold realization hit halfway up that stairs: by now the police must know the truth about Baldi—the friars would have set them straight. That meant that the bastard's one chance to escape was to disappear with the painting. He'd kill me and take the portrait. I'd served my purpose. He probably had it all planned, with many soldiers waiting outside and many more lined up to cover his tracks. What did he have to lose? I was as good as dead in his eyes.

But my adrenaline was pumping like a fuel injector. Back on the balcony, I shoved open the curtains, unlatched the window, and climbed through, holding the painting under one arm. I remembered from the flyover that a short roof abutted just below each of these two back windows, with the roof of the nave and altar between. All I had to do was scamper away to safety, which sounded so simple. Baldi was right behind me shooting at every opportunity and by now my scampering had turned into more of a wobble. One leg was searing with pain, both knees badly bruised.

The roof was tiny and wedged between two stone and stucco walls. I skidded onto another short slanted roof and from there scrambled up onto a long narrow tiled construction that probably topped the cloisters—didn't know, didn't care. I was running blind by then, thinking only of escape, trying to balance while holding the painting.

The sun rose over the city, the air fresh and warm, and it set me to wondering whether this would be my last sunrise on earth. I leaped up to another level, risking a quick check behind where I spied Baldi pausing long enough to aim a clean shot at me. I turned to spring away, then realized that there was no place to go, unless straight to my death. Below lay nothing but a drop to a cobbled courtyard maybe three stories below. I hesitated before slowly turning to face the monster.

He was perspiring heavily, not in such great shape, then. "There, McCabe, it is over, see?" Panting, he straightened, holding the gun in both hands with his legs bracing him on the slanted surface. Not comfortable with heights, either. "You lay down the painting and I don't shoot."

That was almost funny. He must have thought me stupid. I considered dropping the container to the courtyard below but the risk of damaging it was too great and the chance of a Baldino lurking down there even greater. Though the police must be all over this place by now, so must they.

I caught a movement on the roof behind him, just a silhouette crawling toward the edge. Impossible to tell whether it was friend or foe. Friend, I thought, or the newcomer would alert Baldi.

"Okay, Baldi. You win. I'll pass over the painting if you let me live," I said.

"Good girl, good girl." He paused to wipe his forehead on a sleeve. "Do not lay it down. You must pass it to me so it doesn't slide off."

I took a tentative step forward, suddenly aware of how much my leg hurt. I made to reach the painting forward. Baldi didn't move—afraid to lose his footing, I guessed.

"You come to me," he said.

"You'll have to meet me halfway," I said. "I've been wounded, see?" A quick glance down proved that I was bleeding, my leggings soaked in blood. It was a surface wound but he didn't know that.

He hesitated. To stress my point, I sat on my bottom. "Sorry," I said. "Guess I'm more hurt than I thought." I tried to cry. "Help me."

He took another tentative step, afraid to shoot me outright in case I rolled over the edge taking the Botticelli with me, afraid to move too quickly in case he toppled over himself. Holding up his hand, he said. "You stay. I come to you. Do not worry."

Yeah, right.

At that moment the stalker jumped. I watched stunned as the body landed on top of Baldi, both rolling toward the edge. It was Zann, enraged Zann, reckless Zann. I scrambled forward to grab the gun still clutched in Baldi's flailing hand. Several shots fired wild. He turned on his stomach trying to grasp for a handhold when I slammed my foot down on his fingers, hearing a satisfying crunch. Zann was still punching him in the head as I retrieved the gun.

"It's okay, Zann," I cried. "We've got him. Stop!"

But she wasn't stopping. "That's for enslaving me, you miserable bastard! That's for all the pain and grief you've inflicted on people worldwide! That's for every piece of history you stole and deprived us of our heritage! That's for—"

Baldi's limp body rolled to the edge and finally Zann climbed off him but seconds too late. He shot out his good hand on the way down and dragged her over the edge with him.

Zann scrabbled for a hold, clutching the eavestrough, while Baldi dangled over the edge, wrapping his arms around both legs.

"Hang on," I cried. "Don't let go!" I lay the painting on the roof and grasped her wrist.

She gazed up at me. "It's okay. Did what I set out to do. Got the painting, got Baldi. They'll lock me up, anyway. Let me go, Phoebe."

"What are you talking about? This is where you celebrate, not give up."

"Not giving up—I won, right?" She gasped for a moment, struggling for breath before continuing. "I was with Baldi for years, remember? Hardly innocent." Tears in her eyes, tears in mine.

"What about your dad? Is this how you want him to hear about your redemption? You don't even have the photo op yet! I said hold on!"

Several people appeared beside me, including Evan and Peaches. Someone rescued the painting. Someone grabbed the gun. Evan reached down to grab Zann's other wrist while Peaches leaned over and fired at

Baldi. It took two shots before the bastard released her and finally fell to the pavers below. A crowd had gathered to watch his arrival.

"You're not going anywhere," I told Zann. "We still have business to do and a story to tell, which you need to hear."

23

We gathered around the long table in the church's current refectory with a light breakfast served with plentiful coffee laid before us. Evan, Peaches, Zann, Angelo, plus the Interpol agent and Father Agosti all sat together as the sunlight streamed through the windows from the courtyard garden beyond. Our phones were charging and so were we, or at least that was the idea.

We were exhausted, in some cases wounded, filthy, and trying to remain upright using nothing but jolts of caffeine and crusty bread with cheese as props. I swear, I thought I'd topple over onto my plate at any moment. A physician and nurse had entered long enough to bandage our bleeding bits and administer salve where needed. My leg was bathed and bandaged after the doctor had braced Peaches's sprained wrist, obtained from slugging one Baldino too many.

"Look what the good folks here use for ointment," Peaches announced, though most weren't listening. "Naturally derived creams from the Farmaceutica di Santa Maria Novella. None of this cheap sleazy chemical stuff."

Evan, who had more bullet scars than any human should have, escaped this time with nothing worse than a broken arm. The sling looked good on him, by the way. Zann seemed more internally than externally battered and refused all care, but it was Angelo who required the most attention. The medical team spent a great deal of time bathing the man's feet while muttering something about "barbarians." I tried not to look too hard at his injuries but could see that an infection had taken hold at the remains of one toe. He was provided with a dose of antibiotics before the medical team left. At least none of us were on the verge of any permanent collapse apparently.

Though still in the process of answering questions from the police represented by Interpol plus an officer who came in and out of the room, we were in a kind of holding pattern. The container would only be in our keeping for a short time before officially handed over to the authorities. These moments would be all we'd likely get before the painting was eventually whisked away into official care and pounced upon by conservationists and art historians worldwide. It may take years before the portrait actually appeared on the gallery walls for the public's appreciation.

Still, we had to wait before opening the receptacle. Giovanni and an Uffizi official were on their way over and, with great difficulty, we agreed to hold on until he arrived. After all, we needed to consider the possible condition of the painting since time was not usually kind to art. It was best that the museum's official art historian participate in the big reveal.

Meanwhile, there were other matters to consider. Both Baldi and Dunbar were dead, a point that could be cause for celebration had not two friars lost their lives, one shot by Dunbar and the other by Baldi. They were good men caught in the crossfire and we mourned them even though we had never met them personally.

"They died protecting our church and our legacy," Father Agosti had said with tears in his eyes. "Heaven will welcome them both." At his request, we had prayed together, regardless of our faith or beliefs.

The police had rounded up the remaining Baldinos inside the church but many more had escaped, scattering like rats in the sunlight, and now a full manhunt was in progress across Tuscany.

"There will be more, many more," Angelo said as stared down morosely at his bandaged feet. "Killing Baldi will not end this gang. Like Hydra, when the head is removed, two more grow in its place."

"Interesting analogy," I remarked, staring into space. "My brother said something similar."

Evan hadn't heard that particular exchange because he was busy providing details to the Italian Interpol agent, a one Rudi Donati, who insisted we call him by his first name. Rudi knew Evan from prior cases and listened rapt to his recounting of the Botticelli mission. Gratifyingly, the man seemed to hold our agency in great esteem despite the fact that we had torn through his city without issuing the appropriate alert. Think of it this way: they now had a known arms dealer off the map, at least temporarily, and a possible lost masterpiece returned to the city. That granted us a certain leniency.

As for how Zann would fare legally, nobody knew. So far Donati had accepted our insistence that both she and Angelo had worked counter to the Baldi operation in cooperation with our agency but further questioning was bound to follow.

I was trying to figure out how to ensure that Zann received her press release complete with a photo of her holding the portrait, at the very least. Now I realized how unlikely that was given the circumstances. The press were outside the church now and nobody but the police were permitted to make an official statement. Add to that the authorities' reluctance to make any announcements until the portrait had been thoroughly examined, which, in official terms, could take months.

I eyed the wide shallow box sitting at the end of the table with anticipation. In my heart, I knew that the portrait was inside but my head warred another battle. What if it had been ruined by leaky roofs or seeping plaster? What if Botticelli had played a joke on his young friends or somebody else had found the portrait long ago, leaving the empty receptacle?

In the midst of this musing, the refectory door flew open and in came another policeman accompanied by a silver-haired woman. I may have gasped at the sight of Dr. Silvestri diving straight toward Angelo and definitely gaped when they embraced.

"My wife," Angelo said as he wiped tears from his eyes and hugged his exquisitely dressed spouse, who was now murmuring endearments in Italian, French, and, I swear, Latin.

"You two are married?" I exclaimed, rising. Across the table, Peaches looked ready to choke.

"She is a modern woman," Angelo said with a proud smile. "She keeps her own name but to me she gives her heart."

Silvestri released her husband and swooped on me like an elegant bird of prey. In seconds I was being hugged—not bussed, not like one of Nicolina's air-infused embraces, but a full-on squeeze. "To you I owe everything. Thank you, thank you many times over for saving my Angelo. Baldi would have killed him or removed his toes or some part of his anatomy equally useful."

When she released me all I could say was: "So that's how Angelo knew what I was searching for in the Laurentian?"

"Yes, yes," Silvestri said in perfect English. "I was to intercept you and discover what you sought or Angelo would be further harmed. Baldi expected that you might arrive at the Laurentian but had also posted others to watch for you in many other places across the city."

"And then Baldi tracked Zann as we headed for the Corsis and pulled the pieces together from there. You were a real pain in the neck that day," I added, still bristling.

She nodded while beaming away, her red lipstick a brilliant foil for her silver hair and severe black suit. "Thank you. I wished once to be on the stage."

"Hey," Peaches interrupted while stepping up to the group. "I was the one who got held up at the police station for hours being interrogated like a petty thief. Who's going to hug me to make it all better?" She looked down at the police officer standing near. "You, maybe?"

The officer caught enough of the gist to shake his head and step back.

"I will embrace you, Peaches," Angelo offered, holding his arms wide. "I am the one who called you a pickpocket. Come to Angelo and he will make it all better."

But before Peaches could take up the offer, as if she ever would, another pair of officers arrived, this time accompanying Giovanni and a man I didn't recognize.

"Giovanni!" I exclaimed, rushing forward. "At last! This is the moment we've all been waiting for."

"I could not believe when I heard that you had found it! Oh, blessed day! The news claims that a notorious gang has attempted to steal the Ognissanti's treasures."

"Half true," I said as he grasped both of my hands in his and held my gaze in an instant of shared professional camaraderie.

"Phoebe McCabe, it pleases me to introduce my supervisor, Dr. Alice Alessandro." We shook hands briefly.

"How did you know where to search?" Dr. Alice asked.

"It's complicated, but besides the sketch there was a letter—a clue from my brother," I replied, "plus I used intuition, deduction, and just plain luck."

"Brain bolt is more like it," Zann muttered from somewhere behind me.

Smiling, I made a round of introductions as Evan and Rudi stepped forward.

"Let us not wait a moment longer," Father Agosti urged. "Let us see what our blessed Father has kept hidden for all these centuries."

Everyone agreed and together we walked to the end of the long refractory trestle table where the leather container lay on a white linen towel.

Donning a pair of equally white gloves, Giovanni gently lifted the container from the table. "It does not appear in good condition," he said, anxiety leaking into his voice as he turned it around, studying the mold spots, the time-chewed effect of very old leather.

"But the basic structure has not yet been corrupted," said Angelo. "The box is firm. Feel it."

"Though Italy is basically a dry climate, when the rains come, they come with fervor. Let's hope the leather gave it some measure of protection. In any case, it has endured a long enough imprisonment," Evan remarked.

"And it's time for us to release its contents at last," Peaches said. "What are we waiting for, Giovanni?"

A hush descended over our gathering as Giovanni released the little brass catch at the end of the box and gently slid the contents into one hand while passing the empty container to the first helping hand. Evan did the honors there. Giovanni then gently placed a mottled reddish-brown rectangle on the linen fabric. For a moment all we could do was stare.

"What is it?" someone asked.

"It appears to be wrapped in cloth," Giovanni said.

"Velvet," I said, peering closer. "Possibly soaked in some kind of oil or resin. It will required careful removal since it appears to have hardened to some degree but it should come away without too much trouble." I gently poked it with my finger before donning the gloves Giovanni offered. "Does anyone have tweezers?"

Peaches stepped up with her roll of lockpicks and passed me a little tool that would work perfectly. While the others watched, I leaned forward and carefully plucked a clump of fabric away. It peeled back all in one piece.

"I'm guessing it must have been painted on wood with a layer of gesso and egg tempura mixed with oil," Giovanni said as I picked up another clump, which also lifted away from the surface.

"Botticelli must have wrapped it in this fabric to protect the painting against scratches or damp," I said.

Giovanni leaned over to pluck away the last solidified folds with his fingers.

As the fabric peeled back, the painting lay revealed as if glowing from some inner light. Our breaths caught. The sunlight streaming through the windows landed on the profile of a young woman who gazed away into the future against a cloudless sky. Her cheeks weren't pale as in the beauty standard of the time but ruddy as if she had been hard at work just moments before she donned that dress.

That dress. The golden-hued sleeve exposed in all its glory was a work of art in itself, a symphony of color and pattern depicting flowers, insects, and emblems all frolicking in their tiny satin embroidered frames as if any disturbance might set them free. Touch that quilted triangle holding the wasp and hear it buzz, brush that bright little bee worked in gold and pearls and see it fly. Each detail was so finely depicted that you could almost see the stitches, almost feel the silken gloss and texture beneath your fingers. Taken together, the images told a story of great importance to both subject and artist and maybe others, as well. They were beautiful, they were powerful, the piece both exquisitely wrought and masterfully painted. Overwhelmed by beauty, I broke into tears.

I wasn't the only one. Many of us were overcome with emotion that morning. To stand before a masterpiece, to be the first ones to lay eyes on something that beautiful after it had withstood five hundred years of captivity, and to know that you may have somehow helped set it free...

"Gabriela, I'm so sorry that you never got to see your gift," I whispered while I pulled myself from my state of wonder long enough to take photos. Time was running out.

"Gabriela who?" Giovanni asked.

"I will tell you at another time," I said, leaning closer to the painting with my phone.

Seconds later, the magic moment disintegrated all around me. Giovanni's phone rang; a knock came at the door sending Father Agosti scurrying away; both Rudi and Evan were suddenly on their phones. I knew that at any moment Gabriela's painting would be enclosed in darkness once again as it became the ownership—possibly contested—of the state and then ultimately the Uffizi. Theoretically it belonged to the church, which might have the option to keep it, but since all treasures technically belonged to Italy, nothing was ever straightforward where art was concerned.

Despite the legalities of ownership, it was the story behind the painting that I most wanted to liberate, a story built on filaments of proof entangled with the glory of art and the tenacity of the human spirit.

I had just finished photographing when Evan touched my arm. "It's Rupert and Nicolina at the Corsis' on the phone." Smiling, he passed me his cell. "They need us back in Tuscany."

Pressing the phone to my ear, Rupert spoke first. "Phoebe, congratulations! Another incredible coup on behalf of art preserved for all humanity, a momentous occasion worthy of accolades! Bravo, my friend! Soon the Agency of the Ancient Lost and Found will be on everyone's lips as though we are rescuers of time itself. I—"

"Thank you, Rupert, but we'll have to keep this short. They're packing up the painting now." I knew Rupert to be loquacious to a fault and, right then, I craved only to be alone with my thoughts.

But Nicolina came on next. "Brava, dear Phoebe! This is so exciting and a big coup for Italy, yes? Please make arrangements to return to the Corsis' by tomorrow morning and do bring my luggage so I will have something suitable to wear."

"Of course, but I—"

Rupert again. "Yes, indeed, Phoebe. Had you permitted me to finish I would have added that Piero has a significant announcement to make and has arranged a press conference tomorrow afternoon for all the relevant dignitaries. You must be in attendance, of course, but of equal importance,

Nicolina, Seraphina, and I have no respectable transport to Florence that evening since all of our vehicles have been destroyed. Do hire us a proper ride, something suitably large and luxurious. A stretch limo will do nicely."

It was hard to get a word in edgewise. "Rupert, forgive me but I'm going to hand you back to Evan now," I said quickly. "I'm sure he'll know exactly what kind of vehicle will suit. See you tomorrow." Returning the phone to Evan, who caught my eye and smiled, I stepped away to watch the painting exit in the care of Giovanni and the police. As inevitable as that moment was, it left me feeling bereft.

Moments later, I tracked down Zann sitting in a deflated hunch against the far wall. Part of me wondered if I looked as physically spent as she did, but of course after the last few days, we must all look a wreck.

"Tomorrow we're all going back to the Corsi estate for a press conference," I told her. "I'm not exactly certain what that's all about but I see a prime opportunity for us to steal a moment to get that photo op for your dad. Have you been in touch with him?"

She gazed up at me. "Not yet. Afraid that any announcement will soon be followed with 'By the way, Dad, going to be extradited back home to stand trial for crimes against art. Might get to see you then.'"

"Oh, stop. You know we'll put in a good word for you. I really can't imagine you going to jail at the end of this, anyway. Remember you nailed Baldi. You're as much a hero here as anybody."

Her gaze dropped. "You know, I thought that if I succeeded, I'd feel such euphoria that it would keep me going for years but it's not like that. I just feel done in. It's like now that it's over, what's left?"

I swallowed hard and touched her shoulder. "Come. We all need a good rest. Let's return to the hotel. Tomorrow everything will seem much better." That sounded exactly like something my mother would have said, which gave it a note of truth.

As I turned away, I nearly walked into Peaches. We strolled together toward the door. "I heard that we're going to the Corsis' for some big announcement tomorrow," she said, adding in a whisper, "and you just invited Zann?"

"She played a role in this, too. She deserves to be there."

"But she's such a wild card," she pointed out.

"Look at it this way: wild cards can take a game into a whole new direction; they can turn into a trump card at the last minute and even have the potential to play the winning hand."

"Yeah, and make on like a joker sometimes, too. Since when did you become a card shark?"

I laughed. "Since I started swimming in the deep end of the pool."

24

I must have slept for fourteen hours straight, awaking to a day as fresh and filled with possibilities as a blank canvas. I bounded out of bed and took my leg for a test drive around the room while sipping room-service coffee until I was satisfied that my body was in working order.

A shower resulted in wrestling my curls into line without the benefit of my usual smoothers, which were stuffed in my bag back at the Corsis'. I stared at my image in the mirror, grudgingly admitting that I did have something Medusa-like going on. To up the elegance factor, I donned my hyacinth silk blouse and dress black pants. There, ready for a press conference.

I'm telling you all this because it's so ordinary and sometimes a dose of ordinary can be just what's needed. Those few stolen minutes sitting in a chair by the window knitting also fit in that category—the bliss of simple pleasures.

Propping my phone open with a picture of Gabriela's painting applied balm to my spirit as I knit in shades of butter captive in silk. Long ago this artist loved the same things I did, maybe many of the same colors, but expressed her passions in design, fabric, thread, lace, and thousands of embroidered stitches. Sometimes the distance that separates us can be measured in the length of colored threads, and though I didn't know her story, I felt it in my heart. For me, that was enough.

My calm interlude soon ended. Time for the day—the rest of my life, in fact—to truly begin. I snatched a light breakfast at the buffet in the lobby before heading for the garden to await our ride. By 9:30 that morning, I knew a stretch limo would be waiting in the hotel driveway with a professional driver hired to take us to the countryside. Our luggage, the hotel assured us, would be duly stowed.

I was halfway across the garden when I saw him standing by the pergola lost in thought—Evan. There was no one else around. He turned and caught my eye and, as corny as it sounds, I felt a tremor through to my core. As he stepped toward me, he held out his one good arm.

Dropping my knitting bag in the grass, I strode up to him and took that hand, my attention fixed on those warm green-gray eyes while our fingers interlaced. I sensed that he wanted badly to take me into his arms but having only one available at the moment...

"I have to tell you something that I should have said sooner but just couldn't," I said.

The expression in that beautiful face shifted as if bracing himself for something painful.

"It's not that." I reached up and touched his cheek, something I'd been longing to do for days. Tracing the rise of his cheekbones with one finger, I continued. "I'm not going to tell you to leave me alone or to stop ambushing me with kisses and pyrotechnics, though that exploding Ferrari was a bit much."

He quirked a smile. "I wanted our first kiss to be spectacular."

"It was, believe me." I laughed. "But seriously, Evan, I need to explain myself."

"You don't need to explain yourself to me ever, Phoebe. I know that Noel—"

"No, please." My finger moved to his lips. "Let me finish. Yes, Noel kicked the stuffing out of me but in the end I realized he wasn't worth the anguish. What shocked me most was how much I was once willing to let my fixation with the man cloud my judgment, even bury my moral compass. It's like I permitted my brain cells to be sucked away."

He began kissing my fingers one by one. "I would never let your brain cells be sucked away. I love your brain cells, every single one of them. In fact, I adore your brain cells at least as much as I do the rest of you."

I tugged my hand away and laid my palm on his chest. "Listen to me, please."

"Sorry." Dropping his arm to his side, he stood still as if forcing himself not to touch me.

"I need to take things slow, really slow. I need to feel totally confident that I've restored my bearings enough to enter a relationship fully. I'm asking for patience. You must know how I feel about you. Of course I realize that you're nothing like Noel—no need to convince me there. It's not trust in you that's holding me back but trust in myself."

"Ask anything of me and it's yours. If it's time you need, then time it is. You've always been the one for me, Phoebe. I knew it from the day we first met but the divide between us in the early days was far too deep for me to cross. Now, just knowing that we're standing together on the same side at last is enough. I also have to tell you something while I have the chance. And it's important."

"Hey, you two." I turned to see Peaches waving from the gate. "The car's here."

Evan grasped my hand. "It's about Noel."

I turned back to face him. "What about Noel?"

"He's still alive. I wanted to tell you sooner but didn't have the opportunity. Our contacts inform us that he's holed up somewhere still recuperating."

"I know," I said. "Toby told me but I don't care where he is or what he's up to as long as he stays out of my way. Let him limp along with his weakened heart for all I care. I'm done."

He squeezed my hand. "If only it was that simple. Brace yourself, Phoebe. That bastard's been acting as Baldi's praefectus praetorio for the past two years. Remember how we couldn't figure out how he could amass the resources for his escape in Morocco?"

I gaped. "You mean he's been working for Baldi the whole time?"

"For the last two years, at least. After you destroyed his depot in Jamaica, Baldi must have made him an offer he couldn't refuse. It had probably been his plan to oust Baldi from the beginning, knowing how the bastard works. Now he must be emperor or whatever Roman war games they operate under."

"Shit! You mean I just played into his hands again?"

He gripped my fingers tighter. "Killing Baldi was probably just a lucky byproduct from his perspective."

"That's how Baldi knew about my 'lost-art sniffer dog' moniker—Noel told him! And that's how the bastard found out about Toby sending me those clues and maybe even why Zann was poached for the organization in the first place. Noel couldn't have known exactly where the painting was hidden. He needed me for that! I'll kill him, I swear I will!"

I was spinning out, I admit. Evan pulled me close with his one arm. "I'll finish him, Phoebe. That will be my gift to you, I promise."

"What's the holdup, you two?" Peaches had arrived. "Oh, this is looking passionate and it's about bloody time but the gang awaits."

I snatched back my hand and turned to her while blurting out all the relevant news and watching her grin evaporate.

Peaches always could swear much better than I ever could.

THE DRIVE THROUGH TUSCANY WAS A GLORIOUS MOVING POSTCARD overlaid by my seething anger. I knew I had to shove my emotions to a back burner to get through the day, maybe even through the year, but learning that Noel had clawed his way back into my life had left me shaken.

Though Peaches boiled along with me, the rest of our group seemed jolly enough. Angelo sat with his wife, Sylvie, in the back seat and Zann, Peaches, and I occupied the other seats with so much room between us that talking was difficult. Evan kept the driver company in the front, no doubt uncomfortable with having to relinquish automotive control. Actually, I was surprised when Angelo and Sylvie appeared at the hotel but apparently arrangements had been made without my knowing. Another car followed behind with Giovanni, Alice, and other Uffizi officials. It was as if we were off to a summer picnic in the countryside.

When at last the winery appeared on our right, the full impact of the Baldi occupation became clear—scarred earth where the Rover had crashed through the vineyard, scorch marks along the road and in the parking lot where the centurion minions had burned every car they could find.

We navigated around the debris still being cleaned by troops of guys in coveralls. A uniformed policewoman flagged us down to ask what we were up to. Apparently ingoing traffic was still being carefully screened while the investigation was in progress and entry was by invitation only. Once Evan explained our identities, the officer beamed and broke into an animated monologue commending us on our efforts. It was all Evan could do to politely extricate us so that we could continue up the hill toward the hamlet.

Halfway up the drive, Zann pointed out the stage being set up on the winery patio below. Gazing behind us, it became apparent that whatever press event the Corsis had planned, they had no intention of scrimping on the details. A platform had been constructed with festoons of ribbons and banners across the front of the dais, too far away to read clearly.

"What do you think they're planning?" Peaches asked.

"I have a pretty good idea but would hate to spoil their surprise," I said.

Peaches laughed. She'd already guessed, too, of course.

There was no room for the limo to enter the hamlet's arched gate so we climbed out. Behind us the car of Uffizi officials came to a halt also. My only thought was to head for the chapel before anyone else.

While Evan left instructions with the driver and Angelo recounted his adventures at the hamlet to his wife, Zann, Peaches, and I bolted up the drive toward the chapel. My only thought was to arrive without the need for explanations or long tedious greetings and salutations along the way. Those would come soon enough. I sensed that the villa was humming with activity behind the doors and windows as we scuttled past.

"Why are we going to the chapel first?" Zann asked.

"Because part of Gabriela's story lies here and I need to let it all seep onto me before the crowd arrives."

"Is this one of your brain bolts?" she asked.

"More like a brain whisper, if you must call it anything." And of course she had to call it something—Zann was a namer—but I could never quite explain what flowed through my mind in these moments.

The chapel seemed to welcome us. The door had been propped open by the same potted olive tree that had held me captive the day before only this time it was adorned with a big blue satin bow. For a moment I was afraid there'd be people inside but luckily the tiny chapel was empty.

I stepped into the nave and gazed around, my heart thumping in my chest. Now lights beamed down on the fresco and for a moment the three of us could stand agape. Everything appeared so much more vibrant under the lights despite the signs of damage and fading.

"Wow," Zann whispered. "What happened here?" She stepped closer to study the painted procession as I watched her follow the remains of the well-garbed citizens toward the altar. "Why would somebody deliberately chip away at what must have been a magnificent fresco?"

She was pointing at the two figures at the front, a man and a woman, both of whom were missing their head and torsos. Here, the plaster revealed deep gouges as if the painting had been vandalized with a sharp object. "This wasn't an accident of time or neglect but because somebody took a chisel to them all." She swung around and studied the rest of the procession. "All of their faces have been erased and some of their clothing, too. Why?"

"I don't know," I said, strolling down the aisle. "Somebody wanted to eradicate their identities, is my guess. The procession must have portrayed real people, citizens whose involvement here would be seen as dangerous."

"Either that or somebody came along later and wanted to erase all evidence of whatever this fresco commemorates," Peaches added.

"A wedding," I whispered.

"A wedding?" Zann marveled. "Why would a wedding be dangerous?"

"Perhaps because the bride and groom and many of the wedding party were involved in some kind of dangerous intrigue and needed to conceal their identities or maybe the fresco had been embedded with a code of some kind," I said, "like embedded in the clothing, for example."

Peaches turned to me. "You think this is Gabriela's wedding, don't you?"

"I do," I said, "but I don't know the details and can't prove a thing. I'm only working from instinct."

Stepping up to the wall behind the altar, I touched the scabs of white plaster above the remains of a beautifully portrayed gold-hued gown with a trailing vine motif along the hem. "Supposing this was Gabriela wearing her own gown at her own wedding—extraordinary given the constraints of the time. On the surface she was a tailor's daughter who would not be permitted to design these clothes let alone wear them, in Florence especially. Sumptuary laws forbade even the noble citizens of the day to wear such riches unless under certain circumstances. But for some reason, Gabriela escapes Florence with a piece of her own creation and arrives here in the spirit of celebration."

"How, why?" Zann asked.

I shook my head. "I don't know but I swear that this gown is the same one as in the Botticelli portrait. Not only are the colors that same lemon gold—at least as much as I can tell after all this time—but the scroll on the hem echoes the band edging the bodice."

I took out my phone and opened it to the portrait. "I thought Botticelli may have hidden the painting to preserve it against the purist fervor that Savonarola unleashed but maybe that was only part of the story. I'm thinking now that something else was afoot here, too."

"The references to the Medici are a clue," said Angelo, limping through the door arm in arm with his wife accompanied by Evan, Giovanni, Dr. Alice, and a man and woman I didn't recognize.

"Yes," I said, turning to face them. "Maybe there was a message embedded in that sleeve symbology designed to be understood by a select few, a message sent by Lorenzo de' Medici himself by way of Gabriela's gown."

"And perhaps that message was multifaceted and contained not only the symbology but something else—a letter or key, for instance," Evan said, catching and holding my gaze.

"Yes, perhaps," I said, smiling at him. "Botticelli knew that the portrait, which was to be a wedding gift to his two young friends, also hid a dangerous secret and made certain that it did not fall into the wrong hands, which explains the effort he took to keep it hidden. This was a period of intense political intrigue among warring families and I believe that this dress, and in fact it's wearer, played a role in some perilous intrigue that involved the Medici. That it made it this far implies that the conspiracy, if that's what it was, saw some measure of success and that Gabriela may have had reason to celebrate, if only briefly."

"That is a bold statement to make without substantiation," said a woman in the Uffizi group. Her eyes sparkled and her expression was neither unkind nor confrontational, just bristling with scholarly challenge.

"It is," I agreed, "but I can't prove a thing. Bear with me for a moment further," I said, passing my phone open to the Botticelli portrait through the gathering. "Let me read what I can untangle from the clues in the sleeve. There are the crest and the ring, both recognizable Medici symbols, which indicate the family's involvement. There is the Vespucci wasp—another great family and Medici allies as well as a symbol that simultaneously means trouble—plus the plum for fidelity, the goose for vigilance, and the bee for work."

"And the sparrow, lemon, and peach denoting humility, marital fidelity, and silence in that order," Angelo added.

I smiled. "Taken together, I read that someone hardworking and lowly of birth promises her loyalty to the Medici and the Vespucci families while acknowledging the need for vigilance and silence. That the lemon indicates marriage brings us to this chapel. This is where the designer and tailor's daughter, Gabriela di Domenico, was secretly wed to the artist Filippino Lippi with a gathering of Florentine citizens in attendance either in reality or by imaginative proxy. Hard to say who really attended since obviously Mars and Venus also received an invitation and are racing through the clouds to arrive in time." Everyone turned toward the mythological figures flying to attend the ceremony.

"And of course Jesus and the saints are already here waiting over the altar. This was a Christian ceremony, after all, but not one that excluded the classical deities, which was completely in the spirit of Lorenzo de' Medici's Renaissance Florence," Evan added.

An outcry of wonder and disbelief erupted from the Uffizi audience. Somebody clapped—Giovanni, I think. "But that is quite extraordinary," said a gentleman nattily dressed in a light linen suit, "and though there is little to substantiate your theories I commend your imaginative telling, Signorina McCabe!"

"On the other hand, Signore Luffi, do gaze about you," said Giovanni. "What remains of this fresco does look very much in the style of Filippino Lippi, in particular the manner in which the forest and books are rendered throughout the scene. I've only seen such a style in the extraordinary *Apparition of the Virgin to St. Bernard*."

"And what we see of the clothing appears very much like Botticelli or at least influenced by him," I said. "Botticelli loved fashion, which is how his friendship with this talented designer began. Gabriela emerged as an artist in her own right and joined this esteemed circle in secret. I believe she even designed the fanciful clothing which robed Botticelli's goddesses and muses."

"But Filippino did not share Botticelli's affinity for flowing gowns and windblown hair," the Uffizi woman pointed out,

"No," I agreed, "but he did have an affinity for those who did love them and, after all, this fresco was his celebration, too. Later, Filippino's work became very mysterious and animated. It could be jarring, almost electric," I said. "If he were alive today, he'd probably be painting fantasy since so much of what we see in his more mature works unleashes a kind of energy implied in the conflict between the Christian religion and the Greek and Roman philosophy and polytheism rife at the time. I'm guessing that Filippino had little patience for the restrictions Savonarola imposed and we know that he left Florence to work elsewhere for years. Along the way, he briefly ended up here."

"In my family exists the rumor that Filippino Lippi painted this fresco under extraordinary circumstances." We turned as Piero Corsi arrived along with Rupert.

"Can you provide more detail, signore?" the Uffizi gentleman asked.

Piero smiled sadly. "That is not possible. Whatever occurred here was deliberately hidden and all evidence destroyed. My father researched the Florence archives extensively but found nothing. We know only that the Medici and the Corsi were allies and it is possible that they were involved in some kind of conspiracy, but how Filippino came to paint in our humble chapel is unknown."

"Phoebe's theory," Evan said, "one worth considering since I can testify to her incredible talent for unpicking stories silenced by time, is that the artist may have commemorated his own wedding right here in this chapel."

"But we need proof, signore," the Uffizi gentleman said.

"Indeed you do," Rupert agreed. "Nevertheless, there is proof and then there is truth and the two are not necessarily conjoined. I say that Phoebe speaks the truth, not all of which can be nailed to the wall of documented substantiation."

"What happened to Gabriela, Phoebe?" Peaches asked.

"I don't know," I said, staring at the wearer of the glorious golden gown standing at the altar with both her head and torso damaged with such deliberate finality. "I wish I did. I desperately wish I knew the end of her story. There is no indication that she traveled with Filippino to Rome or Prato or even returned to Florence ever again."

Piero clapped his hands to divert our attention. "I regret to interrupt this fascinating discussion but my other guests gather below the hill in readiness for my announcement. Come, my friends. Let us leave this for now and proceed to the winery."

Summer air alight with warmth and promise blew across the hills as we descended the drive toward the winery that afternoon. A tangle of birds flitted across the cloudless sky and the roses climbing the low stone walls along the driveway leading down to the winery punched rich fragrance straight to our senses.

This glory almost erased the scorched earth and the faint scent of petrol now covered by fresh gravel. All signs of violence and explosives had been hastily buried, and had I not known what had taken place only a few nights prior, I might have believed it had never happened.

The knots in my neck began to loosen and I began to consider the possibility of taking a vacation. Someplace remote. Maybe a beach with diving possibilities. I pictured a sailboat afloat on an azure sea. Perhaps I'd even invite somebody to join me but first I needed to tidy up loose ends.

On our way down the hill, I stepped beside a solitary Zann and laid a hand on her arm. "I agreed to get you that press release and that's exactly what I'll do before this day is over."

She nodded. "Thanks, Phoebe. After all I put you through I wouldn't blame you if you just turfed me."

"Yes, you would," I laughed, drawing her toward the wall as the others passed by.

"Yeah, I would," she agreed.

"But I have to tell you something first and it won't be any easier for you to hear than it was for me: Noel is still alive."

She stopped and stared. "What?"

"My taser damaged his heart but didn't kill him. Apparently he's hanging out somewhere recuperating."

Her face blanched whiter than a bleached ghost. "Shit, no," she gasped.

"Shit, yes, and he's been Baldi's top dog or whatever Roman playacting they named their second-in-command. Evan's Interpol rumor mill suggests he might replace Baldi as emperor."

Zann gaped. "We have to kill him!"

"Why does everyone keep saying that? We don't have to kill anybody," I pointed out. "As long as he stays off my radar and out of my life, we'll just leave him alone."

"How can he be off our radar when he had to have been behind this whole Botticelli thing? He must have informed Baldi that the agency had the sketch long ago and that's why Baldi hired me. He's been pulling our strings in hope of hanging us both!"

I took her by the shoulders. "Calm down. Listen carefully: I am not going after Noel Halloren. I work for the Agency of the Ancient Lost and Found and our mission is to locate lost or stolen art, not to chase down the head of arms cartels." I gave her a little shake. "I reacted the same way you have but I've put it into perspective and now you must, too. Look, we beat him, okay? This is our triumph, *your* triumph. Enjoy the moment. Come on, let's set up your press release."

Linking Zann's arm in mine, I race-walked her down the hill until we had sidled up to Piero. "Signore Corsi, as you've probably heard, we found what in all probability is a Botticelli painting by following the clues found among your Laurentian papers and elsewhere. I realize that the entire Baldi occupation must have been traumatic for your family and I'm very sorry about that but luckily no one was hurt. We're very sorry for the whole debacle, aren't we, Zann?"

"Very sorry, yes," Zann said as if shaking herself into the present.

"Right," I said. "Still, I trust you agree that finding a lost Botticelli is worth celebrating, even if it didn't unfold the way we had planned. Hopefully we are now forgiven?"

Ignoring Zann, he turned to me. "You are forgiven, yes. Besides, not all of my family found the occupation so traumatic—my wife and I, certainly, but my boys they found it thrilling. Like a television show, yes? Bad guys and gunfire. Gunfire does not thrill me but we adults see these things differently."

"We do," I acknowledged.

"So, I have heard the news about the Botticelli from your friends," he continued. "All has been explained. My father would be so excited to know this. Perhaps he does." His gaze briefly swerved upward. "Sir Rupert tells me that the discovery must be kept secret for now."

"Yes, apparently," I said, relieved that there appeared to be no hard feelings. "It will be tied up in red tape and officiousness for a while longer. Meanwhile, I want you to know that Zann played a huge role in our discovery. If it wasn't for her, all might remain shrouded in mystery, lost to us for decades, maybe forever. That initial sketch she found helped lead us there in the end and she assisted every step of the way. Everything she said was true."

Zann unlinked our arms and stepped over to Piero's other side. "So am I forgiven, Petro?" she asked.

He flashed a tense smile. "Stop calling me that, Suzanna. I am Piero to you now, nothing else."

"Sorry. So, Piero, will you see now how this fool of a girl that was me was tricked? I swore I would make things right again and hopefully now I have."

Piero turned to the woman who had regained some measure of her old self—quick, confident step, eyes twinkling with energy. "I forgive you, Suzanna. Even the letter you removed from our collection is back where it belongs so all is in the past."

She grinned. "Fabulous! Thanks a bunch."

"But Suzanna and I have one more request," I added quickly. "We'd like to make a statement about Zann finding the sketch at the end of your press conference. Just a couple of brief statements about her locating a canister long ago that was then stolen on the spot by—"

"A cutthroat, devious bastard of a boyfriend who we will publicly name and shame," Zann interjected.

"Or not," I said quickly. "We may not be able to mention the Botticelli painting but we can make a statement about that sketch. I won't mention your library, if you'd rather I not."

"Mention it, please!" Piero exclaimed, lifting his hands upward. "By then the Corsis' Medici holdings will be public knowledge for I am donating the entire collection to the Laurentian Library in my family's name."

"You are? How wonderful and thank you!" I clapped my hands together as if in delighted surprise. "Isn't that wonderful, Zann?"

"Fantastic and long overdue," she said.

This was becoming harder than I expected. "By the way, my announcement is for the sole purpose of sending to Zann's father to let him see that his daughter has been instrumental in preserving art," I added.

"To set the matter straight," Zann added.

"Very well. I am certain Signore Masters will be relieved to see such evidence. Now please excuse me for I must assist my wife with the arrangements below."

I had the sense that he couldn't wait to escape. Soon he was dashing ahead down the hill only pausing long enough to call back: "I will invite you to the podium when the time is right."

I waved at him while saying under my breath: "I knew it. My bet was on the Corsi collection being the center of this press release all along. I wonder what changed his mind?"

"We can thank Nicolina in part for that," Rupert remarked as he and Peaches arrived beside me, arm in arm. Evan, I noted, was still behind us entertaining the Uffizi contingent. "She launched a concerted effort to convince the Corsis to donate the collection immediately, saying that it belonged to Florence and not to a single family hidden from the public eye, regardless of how they came upon it." He paused to catch his breath while Peaches patted his arm and told him to take his time. "At first, Piero stated he wished only to bequeath it upon his passing should his sons agree...but the boys were vehement that the collection be shared at once. Do you know that Enrico is already fluent in Latin and Spanish, a prodigy, much like myself at his age?"

"Were you a really a prodigy, Rupe?" Peaches asked.

"Most definitely. My mother hardly knew what to do with me I was so advanced for my years."

"I can just imagine," she said mildly. "I just had a mental flash of a younger you spouting on and on about something."

"I certainly do not 'spout.' I—" he protested.

Time to intercept. "Did Nicolina also help to pull together this press release in what can only be considered record time?" I asked before Rupert launched into a description of his youthful proclivities and the two began squabbling.

Rupert adjusted the ascot and sighed in satisfaction. "She did, indeed. Oh, to be a countess in Italy! All that was required was to place a few requests in the correct quarters, and before Piero even knew what was happening, the media were nigh on tripping over themselves to receive an invitation. I understand that all the major networks will be represented."

"Everybody?" Zann asked. "Like CNN and BBC?"

"Both and all, I understand," Rupert said. "They are all syndicated apparently."

Zann grinned. "Well, we'd better get down there, then."

Good, I thought. The Noel bomb had been forgotten and we were moving on.

As we approached the steps leading to the Corsis' extravagant patio, Evan disengaged himself from the Uffizi party and joined us while Peaches steered Zann and Rupert away.

"Did you hear the nature of the Corsi press release?" he asked, stepping beside me.

"I did," I said, smiling up at him. For a moment all we did was smile at one another, a little inanely, I admit. Temporarily all my worries evaporated in the light of his gaze.

But the sound of Piero's voice over the loudspeaker prompted us to pick up our pace and soon we were joining the others while accepting glasses of wine from the circulating servers. On a dais overlooking the vineyard, Corsi, Alexandra, and their two sons stood flanked by a radiant Nicolina and a slightly less grumpy looking Seraphina, everyone smiling and nodding.

"Hello, my friends, I welcome you to the Corsi wine estates on this auspicious occasion," Piero began, and went on to introduce the Uffizi officials, representatives from the Laurentian Library, local dignitaries, and Nicolina and Sir Rupert Fox representing the Agency of the Ancient Lost and Found. Smartphones recorded clips for later news releases with each syndicate eagerly catching every word.

When Piero described his ancient family's connection to the famed

Medici family and announced his extraordinary donation, a collective gasp was heard throughout the gathering. A buzz of hushed comments followed. Piero raised his hand and went on to tell the tale of the possible Filippino Lippi connection, inviting people to tour the chapel following the ceremony, and even held aloft a Medici Book of Hours to tease the audience with the riches they might view in the future.

I stood rapt, admiring Piero's flare for dramatics as he bowed to each of the dignitaries in turn. When his family left the stage and joined the guests, Piero opened the microphone for questions. Following that, Dr. Sylvie Silvestri took the stage accompanied by the head of the Laurentian Library to formally accept the largess. More speeches, more applause.

When I sensed that the presentation might finally be winding down, Zann tapped my arm. "I need your phone to film my moment of fame to send to my dad," she said. Beside her stood the Corsis' eldest son. "Enrico here is going to film the moment while we go onstage."

"All right," I said, taking out my phone, "but stick to my script, okay? I'm going to claim your assistance in the discovery of a probable Botticelli sketch now in the care of the Uffizi. I will state that it was stolen decades ago but that you helped us relocate it with considerable risk. I will imply that the rest of the story will be released later. In the meantime, just nod and look pleased. No public commentary. No answering of questions. It's not like you're accepting an Academy Award or something."

"That's all you're going to say—no mention of scumbag Noel, Baldi, or the painting found in the Ognissanti?" she asked.

"Zann, you can't possibly have missed the police decree insisting that those events remain off-camera while under investigation. The retrieval of the sketch is enough. Your dad knows the backstory, anyway. Oh, look, Piero's giving us the signal." I passed my phone to Enrico. "Let's go."

Minutes later, Zann and I were invited to the stage. After introductions and applause, I leaned into the microphone, assuming my most official tone, and said: "And I'd like to acknowledge the important role Suzanna Masters played in the return of a probable Botticelli sketch of considerable importance which is now in the care of the Uffizi. I will post photos of this sketch on the Agency of the Lost and Found's website later today but in the meantime please join me in commending the archaeologist Suzanna Masters."

A chorus of exclamations and questions mingled with applause burst from the crowd. Zann stepped in front of me and grabbed the microphone from my hand. "Thank you, thank you. I dedicate this moment to my dad, Dr. David Masters, who always said I could be anything I wanted, go anywhere I wanted as long as I never lost sight of my goals. I haven't, Dad! I made it! And here I am a member of the illustrious Agency of the Ancient Lost and Found!"

I tried to wrest the mic away but she held tight.

"It's been a long time coming," Zann continued, "and began when I was just a young archaeologist hoodwinked by a ruthless bastard who has since become head of a powerful arms cartel. Noel Halloren, listen up: you have the Agency of the Ancient Lost and Found to contend with now, do you hear? There'll be no place you can hide your miserable face with us on your heels!"

Piero slipped in front of Zann while I snatched back the mic. In seconds, he was stating that the official part of the program was over and to enjoy the wine and stroll the property as his guests. Seraphina and I were leading Zann offstage when I glimpsed Peaches's stricken face, saw Rupert appearing to be on the verge of a cardiac arrest, and caught Evan retrieving my phone from Enrico's hands.

I knew without being told that the clip would soon go viral, that our collective lives had just become a whole lot more complicated.

The Agency of the Ancient Lost & Found
Book Four

THE ARTEMIS KEY

JANE THORNLEY

AFTERWORD

History is packed with untold stories and millions of muted voices tucked between layers of apparently ridged facts. I love nothing better than to unpack these stories while embedding them within the historical context. Fact is not always about truth. Sometimes we have to color the details in fiction in order to get at the essence of the story.

Did Gabriela di Domenico exist? No, but there are records of Lorenzo de' Medici using a tailor by the name of Domenico for many of his considerable wardrobe needs. Women were not allowed to openly design and create full clothing ensembles under any circumstances. They labored behind closed doors, piecemeal style, permitted to work their craft of embroidery or sewing as cottage work while remaining hidden behind the powerful men who ran the guilds. But how could a talented woman not bristle under such restrictions? What if she had ideas for exquisite designs but could only exercise them hidden behind a sympathetic male family member?

Florence, which had grown wealthy on the trade of rich textiles and beautiful apparel, had strict sumptuary laws that tried to curb any display of wealth and extravagance. One only has to gaze at Renaissance portraits to understand the irony there. Wealthy women who wore these exquisite designs—and there were many as the middle-class coffers grew with the textile trade—were forced to travel the streets shrouded in cloaks that hid their bodies head to toe. One eyewitness remarked that it was like watching a large moving tent cross the street. Should the fashion police catch sight of anyone, male or female, nobility or middle class, wearing excess fabric or too much of this or that, they could be fined on the spot.

Part of this curbing of luxury was based on the Christian values of poverty and simplicity. The devout Florentines worried about their souls while they grew rich on the trade of luxury items. The very same society (which included a bishop) who assassinated Lorenzo de' Medici's younger brother inside a church during the Pazzi Conspiracy, no doubt attended mass every Sunday with the rest of the devout. More irony.

The stage was thus set for Fra Girolamo Savonarola to arrive preaching the end of corrupt clergymen and the return to Jesus's teaching of simplicity and humility. He called for the end of secular art and culture that cut to the quick of the Florentine's creative soul. We will never know what beauty was burned during the Bonfire of the Vanities but there are accounts that Botticelli, himself a convert, threw his own paintings onto the flames.

Did Botticelli preserve at least one portrait for a young friend and his once apprentice, Filippino Lippi, her betrothed, as a wedding present? Here's where fiction takes over. Though the painting does not exist, the history of the Ognissanti church in Florence is true. That it was Botticelli's neighborhood church is fact and logically it could make an excellent hiding place for an artist who also painted a fresco in its nave. Which brings up the matter of that strange message written onto his fresco *Saint Augustine in his Study*. That text really does exist and was believed to read as I described until very recently when a new interpretation surfaced. Naturally, I prefer the original, as nonsensical as it first appears!

As for the friars helping Phoebe locate the painting, that, too, is pure fiction. The church is now the property of the state, though the Franciscans act as caretakers. The Corsi family is also fictive, though the location of their estate exists as half fiction, half reality, since it is based on the marvelous Tuscan hamlet B and B, the Castello di Gargonza, in Tuscany where I brought several knitting tours long ago. There exists both a chapel and a tower, though neither resemble those found in *The Florentine's Secret*.

One more thing, my reading friends: Gabriela. Sometimes a character strides through an author's head demanding to tell her story, and the more I researched Renaissance Florence, the more demanding she became. Gabriela will thus become the focus of another novel tentatively named *Spirit in the Fold*, part of the dual timeline *Time Shadows* series where the questions regarding Gabriela's secret assignation for the Medici will become revealed. I hope you will enjoy even more historical detail from the perspective of a creative woman trapped inside Renaissance Florence. I anticipate this novel's completion in 2022.

However, let's not forget that Phoebe has her hands full, too. Please join me for *The Artemis Key*, book 4 of the Agency of the Ancient Lost and Found, coming in December 2021, and if you'd like to see my research details and learn some interesting bits I discovered along the way, please join my newsletter here: The Agency f the Ancient Lost & Found newsletter .

Jane

ABOUT THE AUTHOR

JANE THORNLEY is an author of historical mystery thrillers with a humorous twist. She has been writing for as long as she can remember and when not traveling and writing, lives a very dull life—at least on the outside. Her inner world is something else again.

With over twelve novels published and more on the way, she keeps up a lively dialogue with her characters and invites you to eavesdrop by reading all of her works.

To follow Jane and share her books' interesting background details, special offers, and more, please join her newsletter here:

NEWSLETTER SIGN-UP

ALSO BY JANE THORNLEY

SERIES: CRIME BY DESIGN

Crime by Design Boxed Set Books 1-3

Crime by Design Prequel: Rogue Wave e-book available free to newsletter subscribers.

Crime by Design Book 1: Warp in the Weave

Crime by Design Book 2: Beautiful Survivor

Crime by Design Book 3: The Greater of Two Evils

Crime by Design Book 4: The Plunge

Also featuring Phoebe McCabe:

SERIES: THE AGENCY OF THE ANCIENT LOST & FOUND

The Carpet Cipher Book 1

The Crown that Lost its Head Book 2

The Florentine's Secret (Published Sept 12) Book 3

The Artemis Key (pre-order) Book 4

SERIES: NONE OF THE ABOVE MYSTERY

None of the Above Series Book 1: Downside Up

None of the Above Series Book 2: DownPlay

Printed in Great Britain
by Amazon